WarVerse

Forged by Battle

by Patrick J Loller

ISBN-13: 978-0692346990
ISBN-10: 0692346996

For those who stood with me in the trenches,

And those who helped me leave them.

and

Donavan Danger Donovan

You probably wouldn't have read it anyway.

During 2009-2010 I had the honor of serving with Delta Company 1/102ⁿᵈ Infantry. During our deployment I was privileged to operate as the medic for fifteen of the bravest men to wear the uniform. Not all of them made it into the first book, but the Condemned will be back, and WarVerse wouldn't exist without them.

SSG Walden, Derek – Killswitch

SGT Johnson, James – Rehab

SGT Elderkin, Ken – Beast

SPC Church, Christopher – Cowboy

SPC Clark, Jesse – Blackout

SPC Picard, Vance – Snowball

SPC Siwanowicz, Robert – Daredevil

SPC Dodd, Christopher – Longhorn

SPC Long, Robert – Trigger

SPC Turrell, Kevin – Tectonic

SPC Purves, Jesse – Locksmith

SPC Croce, Anthony – Klepto

SPC Ramirez-Mojica, Rafael – Ramrod

PFC Cole, Ronald – Widget

2LT Paksi, Charles Arthur Jr

I couldn't write you as anything but my lieutenant. Don't worry, I'll find a place in the series for your cries of "Take the hill"

Chapter 1

Vincent

War is hell.

Soldiers become monsters, fighting to survive, but my brother was always the exception...

Vincent crumpled up the letter and swept his arm across the desk. The eulogy, his father's knife, and a stack of dog-eared books went with it.

"How the hell am I supposed to write this?" He glared down at the balled-up melodrama. *He was the writer. All I do is fight.*

After years in training, submerged in the propaganda of valor and heroism, Vincent Barkhorn had finally been exposed to the ugly reality of combat. Nothing could have prepared him.

He had joined wanting it. Longing for it, even. Afraid the war would end before he had a chance to make his mark. His fears were unfounded.

Months of steady fighting on the front lines caused unseen scars,

1

which wore down the edges of his mind, and as he sat in the quiet of his cabin, he found the peace unbearable.

He had tried to start the letter at least fifty times since he received the news. First his father, now Derek. His mother needed to know.

At least I won't be writing the next one, he thought with a twinge of discomfort. How would his mother cope without any of them? How did countless grieving mothers?

"I should be asleep." He spoke aloud to break up the quiet, his voice echoing in the dark room.

A whimper came in response. He glanced over his shoulder at Rover, his German Shepard, who was sitting at the end of his bed.

"Off the bed," he ordered, but without force.

As Rover slinked down to the floor, Vincent stared around the rough log walls, trying to stop his circuitous thoughts. It had barely been a month, but it was tearing him apart. The front lines he could handle, the fighting he could handle—when the violence and fear were lost in the thrill. It was the silence he couldn't stomach. The aftermath.

Sighing, he stood and kicked the chair back beneath the desk. He moved over the bed and fell back in a heap. Any sleep would come accompanied by the same vaping nightmare. It was always the same, and probably would be, as long as the war continued.

"Damn you both." Vincent felt a tingle at his elbow, and looked down at Rover's muzzle pressed into him. Ears pressed flat, fur bristled, the dog whined low. Vincent sighed again. "Fine."

The dog wasted no time climbing back up beside him. A breeze rolled in from the open window, and Vincent closed his eyes. Maybe tonight he would break the cycle.

Thunder boomed in the distance. Vincent twitched in the haze of half sleep. The crack and rumble came again, close enough to shake through the room. Lighting flashed on its heels, late to accompany its brethren, except the flash was red, and it did not come from beyond the window.

Vincent gave a weary groan as the warning lights illuminated the room. His eyes snapped open as klaxons blared from unseen speakers. He sat up, kicking the sheets away from him as he did.

"Computer, disengage holographic model 'Dad's cabin,'" he ordered, springing to his feet. He stumbled as he struggled to pull his wits about him.

A chime sounded and the scenery around him began to fade away. The log walls became flat steel bulkheads, the dresser a metal footlocker. The thunder outside still shook the walls, but it was no act of nature; his ship was taking fire. The window shimmered and the curtains disappeared entirely, with only ventilation slits where the view had been. The serenity of the spacious cabin he had spent so many summers at with his father faded too. The war had found them.

"AMI status report." He stripped off his sweat-stained shirt and kicked off his shorts. The only door into his closet-sized cabin slid open.

His "artificial military intelligence," the organic computer nestled in his brain, sounded off: <Lieutenant, our ship and escorts are under direct assault by a Russian heavy starfighter-carrying cruiser with Separatist escorts. Pertinent orders as follows; All hands to battle stations, pilots scramble fighters.> Vincent ran a hand through his regulation length hair, confusion creeping into his thoughts.

As AMI reported, status updates flashed through Vincent's mind, his mental chip changing incoming data into memories. The Separatist carrier group had jumped in system, and without even an attempt at hailing, had opened fire.

What in the void are they thinking? Vincent thought. *We have a ceasefire.* His ship was only this far out in fringe space to scout a colony planet distress beacon, not to provoke the Separatist Fleet. There hadn't even been open conflict between the Joint Fleet and the Separatists since the Multi-Verse War had started. Even the tsars recognized the need for an alliance after what happened to Earth.

The *Inferno* and her escorts had been in orbit for a scant twelve hours, attempting to assist the colonists planet side with the raging fires and their evacuation. *How did they even know we were here?*

Vincent shook his head as he stepped into his ready room. He wasn't military intelligence, and it didn't matter why; he just needed to get to his fighter. He held his hands out away from his sides and keyed a mental command. Rover stopped short as a translucent shield closed around Vincent. The flashing light shifted from red to amber and a screen of blue beams slid over his skin.

The cobwebs that stubbornly lingered in his head broke apart as the details downloaded into his thoughts. Fear, guilt, and unbridled excitement tore through him with the wave of adrenaline. His hands shook, though he didn't know from which emotion.

As the laser sensors danced over him, he checked the AMI reports of his squadron's progress. Ten others were standing in tubes identical to his. One was missing, and Vincent made a mental note to reprimand Tanker when they returned. It was the third time that week he'd been late, and this time wasn't a drill. Vincent had no room for sloth in his squadron.

He broke off his mental checklist as a panel in the wall opened to show a read-out of his biorhythms. The feeds checked out: His vitals were stable and his brain waves optimal, His AMI confirmed he was all green across the board: <*Leader green.*> He broadcast out across the biometric network connecting him to the other pilots' AMIs, and his thoughts appeared in their minds, as well as the minds of the medics who monitored his squadron. The rest of his pilots chimed off in sequence after him.

The laser grid clicked off, and small ports around the room irised open. Vincent squeezed his eyes shut with a grimace and a deep breath.

A thick, purplish-black slime sprayed from the ports, sticking to him and congealing on his flesh. As the material coated him he became unrecognizable, a human-sized mass of goo. The deck beneath him crackled as an electrical current discharged, and the suit snapped taught across his body. Vincent made sure his fingers were spread to prevent them from sticking together.

When it squeezed to a skin-tight layer, a metal arm with a shield-shaped plate descended to cover his face. It pushed into the suit, then retracted, leaving a gap in the material where his eyes, nose, and mouth remained exposed.

Vincent looked the nano-suit over, searching for any tears or blemishes. He ran his fingers over the edges of his face to ensure a tight seal. Finding nothing wrong, he reached behind himself and pulled the chest rig and helmet from the now open compartment. Drawing the chest rig over his shoulders, he pressed it into the pliable material, and lights blinked on as wires spread out from the rig and down his arms and legs.

The nano-suit tightened around him in an upward cascade from his feet as it ran through diagnostics. Vincent stood as still as possible until it finished. Then the room's lights flashed green, and the shield to his cabin slid down. His dog entered the tube, Vincent's knife stuck to the tip of its snout. Vincent reached over and grabbed it, slipped it in into a special pocket he had added to the chest rig, then released a long-held breath.

The whole process took only two minutes, but reaching his fighter always felt like an eternity. His stomach flipped as the lift flew down its track to the hangar.

As the tube descended, the dog shuddered and distorted just as the cabin hologram had done. Beneath the animal disguise was a battered droid. Its general shape was that of a tortoise; six triple-jointed legs extended from a bulbous shell frame. A tail arched over the body like a scorpion, though in place of a stinger was a rotating assortment of tools. The two forward-most limbs extended slightly farther from the front, and were currently supporting two clamps. There was a series of sensor probes and lenses between the arms. The entire machine was covered in various scorch marks, scratches, dings, and dents, but its movements were quick and precise.

"Robotic Omni-Environmental Vehicular Emergency Repair Unit operational and awaiting commands," a robotic voice intoned from a speaker on its chassis. Vincent rolled his eyes. Eventually he would find and delete that obnoxious start-up program.

"I prefer your other look better," Vincent said. The robot didn't respond. Vincent had managed that much.

The lift slowed and then stopped, its doors opening with another clang. Before Vincent, the hangar stretched out to the left and right as far as he could see, the floor curving up and away. The entire hanger was a giant wheel, and he was standing at the 'bottom'. The wheel's rotation created almost earth like gravity.

With the looming battle, the hangar was all controlled chaos. Orange-suited personnel scrambled between the berthed fighters as they finished last-minute checks, pulled fuel lines, and prepared for emergency launches. The mechanics on Vincent's ship were finishing their work as he stepped out of the lift.

His Chimera class fighter sat in her launcher, refractive armor gleaming in the artificial lights. Similar in shape to pre-contact atmospheric jets, it had a thin body tapering down to a blunt nose. The cockpit sat in the center where the two bulky rotating wings jutted from the frame. Between each wing and the chassis thrummed a massive engine, which sent vibrations through the deck. Behind the cockpit, three smaller engines sat in standby.

The mechanics had installed the heavy payload package onto the fighter, the bulky frame adding armor and shields to the normally agile craft. On each wing was the insignia of the Grim Reaper Squadron: a shadowed figure wrapped in a star field cloak..

Sprinting up to his fighter, Vincent glanced left and right, and his other pilots paced him to their respective ships. To him it was like looking through a fun house, as each pilot was further along the ring, and looked as though they were running on the gently curving walls.

Vincent grabbed a ladder hooked onto the side of his cockpit and scrambled up it and into the seat. As he sat, the consoles around him fired up in response, sending a myriad of data flashing across his vision and through his mental chip as they powered on. He settled into the adaptive cushions and took a deep breath of the sharp metallic air tinged with musky fuel.

Vincent disregarded the traditional mental commands, choosing to let his hands do the work punching in the start-up sequence. While he worked, Rover skittered up the side of the ship. The bot made a full round over the fighter as it fired through a list of inspection points, then came to a meter-wide divot behind the cockpit, where it seated itself. Once sealed in, Rover lay flush with the hull.

"Reaper Actual. By the numbers, dial it in," Vincent called over his com, again favoring speech over mental communication. His pilots were quick to respond.

<Reaper Two, the Duchess, standing by.> His wingmate responded using the bionet as Vincent's cockpit closed with a hiss around him.

<Reaper Three, Zombie, standing by.>

The life support system clicked on, filling the cabin with chilled air.

<Reaper Four, Starburst, standing by.>

Lights dimmed, the consoles illuminating Vincent's face.

<Reaper Five, Forge, standing by.>

Joysticks extended from beneath the console into Vincent's waiting hands.

<Reaper Six, Tesla, standing by.>

Vincent tapped his foot against the rudders and checked the maneuvering thrusters rotating along the ship's hull.

<Reaper Seven, Animal, standing by.>

The ship rotated nose down, lifted by its docking clamps, as the floor beneath irised open.

<Reaper Eight, Preacher, standing by.>

Lights flashed across the hangar, warning the techs to move away.

There was a pause.

<Reaper Nine, Tanker, standing by.>

Vincent shook his head, pushing the distraction from his mind.

<Reaper One-Zero, Steel, standing by.>

Vincent keyed in the code for takeoff.

<Reaper One-One, Havoc, standing by.>

The ship shuddered as the launcher primed.

<Reaper One-Two, Fledgling, standing by.> The newest and final Reaper's voice cracked.

"All pilots green and go. Move for the tubes," Vincent ordered.

Another touch of a button and his ship was lowered down, nose first, between the doors set in the floor. The clamps moved with him, rotating along at a ninety-degree angle, clearing the doors behind and allowing them to close. Vincent sat in darkness as the atmosphere was cycled from the room, then the doors beyond opened and the interior of the armored shell of the hangar became visible. Like a gyroscope sized for titans, five concentric rings spun round, all encased within the safety of the spherical outer hull. Each ring was spaced like the slices of an orange, so that the outgoing ships could launch simultaneously.

The clamp disengaged and Vincent's ship dropped away from the rotating ring. Once free, Vincent was left in microgravity, with only his restraints and inertia keeping him in his seat. His ship pulsed its maneuvering thrusters on its own as AMI took control and maneuvered toward the launch tubes. With so many ships exiting the docking rings, allowing the pilots control in the nest could be disastrous. Still, Vincent sneered as the computer moved his ship. The two launch cannons were at the relative top of the sphere, and Vincent's squadron moved in line. He admired the swarm of fighters that rolled and flew through the enormous docks. He could see the muted flashes of tightly controlled engines and maneuvering thrusters bringing the different ships in line.

Vincent's fighter reached the docking cannon and flew inside, and lights flashed down the length of the cannon as he entered into the bore. Inside, a light flashed green on his console.

"Let's punch it," he called, then reached out and flipped open the safety. A smile touched his lips as he depressed the button beneath.

Chapter 2

The Exile

The Exile snapped awake, reached down for her concealed knife, and caught herself just as her fingers brushed against the worn leather hilt. It was only turbulence. She admonished herself for letting her guard down on the busy shuttle, but the last few days had been difficult, and she needed the rest. She was coiled like a spring, but Exile forced herself to relax. Unbidden, a mantra sprang to mind. *Tension causes panic; panic breaks control.* She scowled.

Despite catching herself before drawing her blade, Exile had still grabbed the attention of the other passengers. Her sudden jerk of movement had drawn them in, and her appearance made them leer. She had endured those looks from humans since her infiltration began years ago, but after everything that happened, she found it intolerable.

The older female across from her was trying the hardest not to stare, but her thoughts betrayed her. She was unshielded and undisciplined in the use of her AMI; it was the psychic equivalent of screaming. *Oh, what lovely blue skin, and those silver spots,* she was thinking. Exile instinctively pulled away from her open connection.

10

A more obtrusive thought intruded upon her own, and Exile looked up. It was a male three rows down. His thoughts were lustful as his eyes roamed her body without shame.

Exile checked her fury; it would do her no good to slam him against the bulkhead walls. It would only hinder her ability to blend in. The male's gaze infuriated her, though. Among her own people she was untouchable, so tainted that no male would have her, but the humans judged not on the merits of the mind. Only pleasures of the flesh mattered to them. An anger born from deep regret flared beneath his gaze.

To the human men, her obviously alien features were overlooked for the smooth lines of her chest and rear, and the tight muscles between forged from a life of service. Her body looked human enough, while her blue skin made her exotic, and her almond-shaped green eyes only furthered their interest. The bony protrusion that extended from above her eyes and swept back along her skull was often ignored; in fact, her face was oftentimes overlooked entirely. The humans referred to her as a nymph, some nonsense creature of beauty. It was a generalization she found particularly loathsome.

While contemplating smashing the gaping male like the pest he was, she rotated her body just enough to allow him to glimpse the metal cap that ended below the shoulder of where her right arm had once been. Her disfigurement—something even humans detested—was enough to stunt his gaze.

The man looked elsewhere, disgust coloring his thoughts. At least they agreed on something.

Her brief, uncomfortable sleep aboard the cramped vessel had clouded the Exile's focus, and so she sat back into the seat and concentrated. Stripping away her exhaustion and discomfort, she delved deep within her mind to find the calm center. She was never truly calm, not really; an undercurrent of anger was her constant companion. It had been that way since she had lost her arm, and it wasn't likely to change, so she found the closest thing to peace and settled in.

She cast out her Web, invisible tendrils of her thoughts that touched upon each of the AMI units around her. The Exile, like all other members of her race, could read the thoughts of others. Her mind received and interpreted the bioelectric field created by active brainwaves. The conclave called it "The Sight" and proclaimed it a gift from their gods. Exile thought that asinine. Whimsical powers and abilities were the taint that came from beyond the portals, what she could do could be quantified, could be explained.

Creating a link with each of the AMI units around her, she strengthened her Web, which gave her snapshots of each person's sensory inputs, thoughts, and feelings. It allowed her to be far more aware of her surroundings, which was a major advantage. That same advantage could be just as swiftly negated, however, when the Web was too large, or if emotions ran too strong.

Emotions were always closest to the surface. Determination from the pilots controlling the ship leaving the planet behind. Annoyance from the mother of two wrestling with her brood to keep them secured in their seats. Anger from a young couple at the back of the compartment in the heat of argument. The children had no units, and their thoughts were secure. Exile thought it strange that so many civilians had military-grade hardware installed. This backwater planet they were fleeing had more secrets to tell.

Focusing, she listened to the pulses, the spikes in mental activity, and as she did, she could "hear" the humans' passing thoughts. The words they mulled over in their minds to pass the time were turned to airborne flotsam by their chips. One man wondered about arrival times, while another puzzled over a stain on his shirt. Trivial matters rolled over and over to keep the claustrophobia, the danger of spaceflight, and the always-looming threat of war from overwhelming their senses. These people were fleeing from their colony world, escaping the fires that ravaged the surface, and tension rang out through each of their minds.

Exile cast her unseen wanderings back to the pilots, and as she did, pulled back from the others. She drove a concentrated spike of effort into their AMI and was met with little resistance; the men were too concentrated on their flight to even notice that she had connected to their thoughts. In a moment, she was looking through their eyes as the fleet garrison grew in the viewport ahead of them. A twinge of excitement passed through the pilot into her upon seeing the warships.

They floated in a wedge, with representatives from several of the Joint Fleet's races present. Thin, elegant grelkin frigates beside the rough, durable human destroyers. Repurposed asteroids that housed the shogoths beside the miniscule tannimite scout craft. In the center however was a ship she had never seen before. From where they sat, the ship resembled an impossibly large split sword. The bottom "blade" jutted out from the split top, which curved down in two prongs like fangs around a tongue. The long midsection met and extended back over a crossguard of two down-swept wings. At the end, eight massive engines blazed, a diamond of four diamonds upon each. The hilt extended back between and behind the engines. The pommel at the end was a sphere with two forward-facing cannons running parallel and forward. The ship looked deadly. The Exile approved.

With her mind firmly within the pilot's, she was blasted with the same wave of fear and uncertainty he felt when the Separatists arrived. Without the shuttle's sensors, they would never have seen them—space was simply to large. The red warning lights and magnified screen images were more than enough to terrify the pilots, though. Exile snapped back into her own head, working to separate their emotions from her own. She was already balancing on a blade's edge, and she could not risk anyone else's panic taking root within her.

Mentally, she erected barriers against any further spikes in emotion, and with those walls so built, she reached back for the pilot's mind. She needed to know what was happening. Plasma blasts and laser fire filled the forward screens as the Separatists opened fire, and Exile forced down the fear that rose within her.

Through the pilot's eyes, Exile watched the battle expand before them, Joint Fleet and distant enemy ships disgorging swarms of fighters. From so far out, the blossoms of light and flashes from explosions seemed no more real than if she were watching a video. The pilots did not seem to agree with that sentiment, and their fear was so strong that her mental bulwarks could barely withstand it. The Exile used her Web to soothe them as best she could; she pressed her will into their minds to keep them from panicking, but they were too far gone to feel the effects.

Thankfully, they were closer to a moon than they were to the planet behind them, and the pilots had enough sense to maneuver behind it to wait out the battle. Their thoughts were so unshielded that Exile knew they were ensigns, that they had never seen combat, and that they were very close to losing composure.

With something to focus on, they maneuvered the ship on a trajectory to orbit the small moon, planning to cut their speed once they were hidden behind it. But before they could even start their turn, the warning lights flashed again and several smaller enemy craft appeared from around the moon. Ambush.

Red warning lights flashed over the cabin and let all the civilians know they were in danger. Chaos took hold, and Exile was thrown violently from the pilots' minds as the fear of those around her overpowered the Web.

With so many emotions and thoughts pressing down on her, the Exile could not erect the necessary barriers to protect herself. Her Web twisted and thrummed with the acrid fear of every passenger, mixed with anger and denial. Exile twisted in her seat and fell to the floor in a ball, trying to shut out the voices that assaulted her.

It was no use — there was too much raw emotion too quickly for her to overcome. She was overtired, stripped of her resources, and she could not find her center. The wall of the ship pressed in against her, threatening to break and allow in the void beyond. Accepting defeat, Exile pulled her dagger from its sheath.

Despite the raging emotions, she could feel the sudden spike of ancient hunger the dagger released. She fought against the urge to strike out at the passengers beside her and instead turned the blade around in her palm to press the cool metal into her forearm. The dagger bit into her flesh, the blood pooling around the metal and traveling down the blade's fuller toward the obsidian stone set in the base. When the blood struck stone, the chaos that assaulted the Exile's mind ceased, and black shadows twisted around her arm toward her core. Raw power exploded from wherever the shadow touched her, and Exile returned the dagger to its leather sheath.

She wouldn't have long, so she stood and turned to face the majority of the passengers, and lashed out with her Web. Were someone to review the security footage, they would see only a blue-skinned alien standing alone, wreathed in shadow. To the passengers, she was a monster. Exile projected a ferocious image into their minds, enhanced with the power from the blade, and they saw her flesh twist and distort as muscles forced their way out of her skin. She expanded the image until she nearly filled the cabin, and was hunched forward to rest on bony knuckles. Then she opened a maw filled with mismatched fangs and roared.

Several of the passengers passed out from fear alone; with the others, the Exile would need to be more direct. Two fleet personnel stood

15

as if to fight her, and she used her increased reach to slam them backward. Though her size and strength were an illusion, to them it was as real as the shuttle around them, and their bodies reacted as their minds did: They crumpled back into their seats.

Another man pulled a weapon, and Exile lashed out at him as well. Her imaginary claws caught him full across the face, and his skin was forced apart by the violent muscle contraction of his mind anticipating the blow. Within moments, all of the passengers were silent, and Exile allowed the illusion to fall away. She would need to scrub the security tapes of this encounter, lest the Joint Fleet see what the conclave was truly capable of, especially armed as she was. Then she remembered.

Standing alone within the ship, chest heaving as the power drained from her, it finally hit her. She had been so focused on running, so intent on surviving, that the reality never sank in. They destroyed more than her arm. The misguided fools took everything from her. Everything she had sacrificed, had done for the greater good — meaningless.

Anger flared, consuming her doubt like kindling. *No,* she thought, *I will finish what I began.* The mission that had brought her to the dagger, cost her an arm, and erased her name.

She moved closer to the front of the shuttle and prepared to possess the minds of the pilots once more. She needed them to fly the ship, but more importantly, she needed to use them to survive.

Chapter 3

Johnston

Rear Admiral William H. Johnston stepped onto his bridge, and chaos became order. Men and women leapt to their feet; the shouts of "Captain on Deck," sounded louder than the alarms that had woken him.

He nodded, and then in a voice that drowned them all out, asked, "What is our status?"

The eye of the hurricane moved on, and the flurry of movement resumed. The bridge officers scrambled back into flight chairs and to their duties. Even in combat, he required they come to attention. Not for his ego, or because it was written into the fleet policy, but because that moment of stillness brought a clarity and calm to an otherwise unwieldy bridge. He could see the confidence growing in his crew as they went about their duties.

"Separatist battle group has jumped in system, sir. Supercarrier group with four battlecruiser class and two battleship escorts," his executive officer, Captain Christopher McKinley answered.

"Commander Belford has ordered fighter launch, and our battle group is maneuvering to defend the planet."

"Thank you, Commander," Johnston answered. On the bridge, only he held the honorific of "Captain." He stepped past McKinley to his command console. It lit up beneath his palm as it connected with his AMI. The information for the battle was already downloading into his thoughts, arranging itself like memories so he could focus on the present. It was as though he were rediscovering an old skill—the information sprang to mind as he needed it. The data confirmed everything his XO had told him.

"How is she holding up?"

"Shields holding strong at ninety-eight percent, ship AIs are in tandem, and the guns report no problems."

"Then the shakedown cruise is over. Bring us about, and let's see if we can't reason out this breach of the ceasefire." Johnston distanced the dataflow in his mind and looked around his bridge. From his command dais he had a good view of every bridge officer without needing to turn. The deck fell away from him in tiers, and each officer had their own depression surrounded by monitors and controls. Ahead and above them all was a bank of massive screens that displayed the battlefield and the blue-and-green backdrop of the planet below. The view gave the illusion that they were looking through an enormous window from the prow of the ship, but the ship's designers were not so naive. The bridge was nestled into the deepest part of the ship, and would be protected even if every other corridor and chamber were vented and destroyed.

The viewscreen showed him the Separatist Fleet, their carrier to the rear, the battlecruiser flanking on either side like an umlaut, and the battleships leading the charge. Already, the space between them was filling with the smaller blips of fighters, though enemy bombers were suspiciously absent.

The ship's AI worked with two petty officers as they compiled the details visible on the hulls of each ship, taking into account their drive signatures, classifications, battle damage and repair jobs against all known Separatist ships. The information they winkled out displayed on Johnston's dais. The battleships and carrier were Russian-made, the battlecruisers a mixture of Chinese and Korean. The crews aboard would be human, the Separatists misguided notion of Terran superiority persisting despite the grelkin technology they needed to fight.

"Open a transmission with Admiral Kolchak," Johnston ordered once the information appeared on his screen. The communication tech bent to his request. While he waited for the connection, he submersed himself in the data feed of his AMI. He could see virtually everything about his ship, and if he wasn't careful, he would lose himself trying to look at it all. That was why his bridge crew was so essential: Their delineation allowed him to see only the pertinent data.

"Connection made, sir," the com officer announced.

"Patch me in directly. Security screens active for any infiltration attempts."

"Aye, sir."

The security screen activated around the admiral and the sounds of the bridge crew faded to a low buzz. The head and shoulders of the Russian admiral displayed at eye level. Johnston gave the man a level stare, remaining silent to see if the Russian would make the first move. It would be far easier to intimidate him in person, as Johnston dwarfed most men.

"This space is a restricted zone. The Grand Union of Terran Planets holds jurisdiction over this colony." The admiral spoke in English, another concession on his part.

"Admiral," Johnston spoke slowly, deliberately, "this colony requested assistance with evacuation and fire suppression. Our fleet is well within the bounds of the treaty to provide assistance."

"Svoloch! You are here for the research facility. You Americans are slaves to your orders, and are taking advantage of our people."

Johnston bristled but pressed on. "I am an officer of His Majesty's navy, and this fleet is comprised of sailors from every signed colony in the Joint Fleet accords."

"Did you expect that we would not respond? That we would leave our people to die as you so often do? As you did at Sol?" the admiral spat. Johnston's expression became dangerous.

"Cease your hostilities and allow us to assist the colonists. Fighting here will do nothing to stop the fires."

"Suka poshel nakhuy uyebok."

Johnson did not need a translator to understand the admiral's words. It was clear their conversation was over, so Johnson ceased with the pleasantries.

"You have fired on a Joint Fleet battle group, broken the conditions set forth in the Treaty of Lexington, and are interfering with a rescue operation." Johnston let some of his anger vent as he continued, "You will stand down your fleet, dock your fighters, and surrender yourself to my custody. If you do not, this will be a declaration of war, and we will respond in kind."

"You have trespassed into our space, captured our colonists, and stolen our research. You will leave this system in chains." And with that, Kolchak cut the connection.

Johnston keyed for the privacy shield to drop. "The Separatists have reignited the conflict between us. Message to all ships: Fire at will."

Chapter 4

Vincent

Vincent's head snapped back in the seat as his fighter rocketed forward, propelled by the cannon's magnetic rails. The running lights blurred as he picked up speed, momentum pushing him further and further into the seat, the starlight erupting all around him as he blasted into space. He hugged the larger ship's hull and tapped his rudder to avoid the cannons that jutted along the spine. Their shots illuminated his cockpit with each blast.

Vincent winced as plasma blasts splashed harmlessly against the *Inferno*'s forward-projecting shields. Vincent could see the *Inferno*'s escort ships, their guns bellowing silently in the black as they added their own long-range bombardment to the fray.

The other squadrons launched and blasted further afield. The Vapefalcons, the quick response force of the ship, launched first. The lightning-fast crafts were dedicated to intercepting the enemy before bombers closed the distance. The Reapers slower Chimera fighters followed in their wake.

<What the hell are they thinking?> Havoc asked over the squadron's bionet.

<They are Russian, they do not think,> Forge replied.

<How do you manage to broadcast an accent.> Tesla wasted no time in antagonizing his wingman.

"Reapers, cut the chatter," Vincent snapped, only to hear a series of groans in his mind.

<Preacher has to give the sermon, it's tradition.>

"Make it fast, preacher."

An uncomfortable jolt rolled over Vincent as he passed through the *Inferno*'s shield at its weakest point, but once free from the larger ship's protection, he dialed up his engines and flipped on his gravity propeller. The whole craft shook as it came online, and the propeller generated split-second singularities that dragged his fighter along.

<Today's sermon is of Johnathan, who climbed barefoot up the tower.>

As the engines roared, the sense of weightlessness faded and Vincent was pressed back into his seat. He reached up to dial down the inertial dampeners; one of the mechanics had taken it upon on himself to change Vincent's settings.

<Sick from his recent travel through the heavens, Johnathan was forced to combat deadly adversaries and the jeers of those below as he climbed ever higher.>

The Russian ship seemed, to the naked eye, to be just a metallic glint in the corner of Vincent's screen, though his enhanced imagery and computer readouts showed her true fangs.

<His greatest adversary was cunning, and tried to trick Johnathan. But his evil could not stand against the righteous.>

Vincent's sensors began picking up friend and foe markers as the enemy fighters flared their own grav props. Commander Belford, aboard the *Inferno*'s bridge, issued out assignments, and the "heads-up" display in Vincent's cockpit flashed his squadron's assignments.

"Wrap it up, preacher."

<Johnathan reached the peak of the tower, and cast his enemy down. His immortal words echoed in the villain's ear. Yippee-ki-yay, motherfucker.>

Ten other voices repeated the line. Vincent sighed. Damn gnomes watched too many movies.

Before the rest of the pilots could build up steam, Vincent cut back in. "Alright, Reapers, you know the drill. We're on screening detail. Fledgling, keep close to Havoc. Let's touch down twelve fighters when it's over. Stay light on the stick, those long-range guns are still pounding." A series of groans issued across the bionet. Vincent agreed with them, but not for want of glory.

The Falcons' grav signatures flared on screen as they took the lead. The Reapers hung back to shield their mother ship from enemy bombers. Vincent released one of the joysticks briefly to twist open his multitool, a habit his father had passed on, before he reconfigured his fighter.

Once he slipped the memento away Vincent reached above his head to a series of levers with large stylized symbols beside them. One of them portrayed a medieval shield. With a twist and pull of the lever, Vincent activated defense mode.

The shudder caused by the grav prop's microscopic singularities was nothing compared to the violence the shifting combat roles inflicted on the fighter. The wings along the side of the fighter split apart and flared open, as did the nose, and as the armor sheet reconfigured, the craft went from sleek to bulky. Vincent's view of the battlefield went from unobstructed to blind, and only the senor nodes outside the armor provided him with what he needed to fly.

Around him, his squadron's ships shifted modes in tandem as they prepared themselves for contact, and on the sensors, eleven other asteroid-shaped lumps of armor fell into formation around the *Inferno*.

<When is that bastard ever going to deploy us in anything other than turd mode?> Zombie asked, his bitter feelings seeping into the net.

"Vape it, zombie. They record the AMI chats." Vincent growled. Whatever leniency fighter pilots might enjoy would not cover insubordination.

<Sorry, boss.>

In the corner of his HUD, he could see the other pilots' vitals scrolling across the display. Fledgling's heart rate had spiked with his orders. Vincent's newest pilot had gone through the extensive training all the Reapers endured, but nothing could compare to the thrill, and terror, of your first dogfight. Vincent considered opening a private channel to give Fledgling some words of encouragement. Somewhere on the *Inferno*, a group of corpsmen were watching the vitals with an unblinking eye, and would be quick to pull Fledgling back if he went above their unnegotiable limits.

Vincent didn't want to see Fledgling grounded because the numbers didn't add up, flying was about more than that. Before he could tell AMI to contact the new pilot, however, he saw that Havoc was already taking care of it, and the decrease in heart rate made it clear that it was working.

With all his pilots in the green and ready, Vincent dialed up the gain of his HUD to see the fighting laid out before them. As the Vapefalcons connected with the enemy, the scene turned from organized squadrons to indecipherable chaos. The fight seemed like a swarm of bugs laced with fireworks. Vincent checked and double-checked his weapons. *Not long now*, he thought. Vincent took stock of his thoughts;

24

despite his growing excitement for the battle, this was not a fight he relished flying into. The last several years had been a fight he could get behind, against an enemy not even from his own universe. Fighting his own kind, no matter the reason, was not something he took lightly.

Vincent twisted his multitool open and closed again, and with each snick-snack of the metal he was reminded of the nightmare he had stayed awake to avoid. He stared at his unchanged readouts as his ship orbited the *Inferno* and waited. *Snick, snack, snick, snack.* He was waiting for anything to move close enough to distract him, and wondered why the bombers hadn't been launched against them yet. He dialed out his sensors, looking for their telltale signature on the HUD.

Vincent rolled his ship into a lazy turn to take in more of the battlefield. Why would the enemy disgorge its fighters without bombers to make any real impact? As he finished his roll, he saw the planet's moon, and on the HUD, the friend tag that was blinking between it and the planet.

He tapped onto the console to zoom and saw a shuttle that had been traveling towards the *Inferno* when the fighting started. They were just outside the moon's orbit, and would have to turn back. Vincent was surprised to see they were still accelerating towards the fleet, and doubly so when an SOS signal broadcast. The surprise faded when the red blips started filling the sector from behind the moon. The enemy bombers had made their appearance.

"Flight Control, Reaper One, I had positive ID on multiple bogies coming in from behind the moon. COBs in danger of attack. Permission to engage?" Vincent commed back to the ship. No response.

"Flight Control, Reaper One, I say again I have civilians on the battlefield. Permission to engage." More silence.

Vincent didn't ask a third time.

"Reapers, follow me," he commed, and rolled out of the defensive orbit to blast towards the closest planetary moon.

His squadron followed in his wake.

A transmission came through from his wingmate. *<Sir? Were we diverted?>* Duchess asked.

Vincent reached to the com unit to key in a private channel. "No, bombers just appeared from around the moon. Linking coordinates now. We have COBs between us and them."

The Duchess commed back a sense of approval, a transmission without words.

The *Inferno* had been locked in tidal orbit around the colony planet before it maneuvered for the attack, so the moon was only a few hundred thousand kilometers away. Vincent had his AMI pull up a holographic display to type in a brief calculation, then grunted in frustration when AMI crunched the numbers and set them on the screen.

"Thanks," he muttered.

<Lieutenant Vincent, why have you left your grid?> said an irritated voice across his private net. *Commander Belford,* Vincent thought with a sneer. *This should go well.*

The enemy decided that Vincent would not need to respond. Another squadron of bombers dropped into view from behind the moon. There was no way the *Inferno* could ignore the threat now.

Vincent keyed a wide beam transmission. "Multiple hostiles approaching carrier group." He glanced at his readouts. "Heading fower, tree, six, niner, by eight, niner, five, tree. Reapers set to intercept. Permission to engage?" Vincent knew he needn't bother giving heading or even calling the targets. His computer had already sent a beam back to the ship with far more detail. He certainly wasn't ensuring everyone saw Belford's blunder. That would be petty.

<*Engage all hostiles.*> Belford did not sound pleased.

Vincent's lip twitched upward.

Chapter 5

Johnston

"Damn flyboy," Belford snarled, causing Johnston to look up from his dais toward the CAG. "Commander of the Air Group" was a term the wet navy used for their atmospheric fighter commander. Belford was in charge of all the *Inferno*'s squadrons, and though they operated in a vacuum and not air, the moniker stuck. After all, Johnston had started his career twenty-five years ago on one of those water-dwelling ships.

"Problem?" he asked.

"Chimera squadron left their post to chase after some bombers," Belford said. "They were our fighter screen."

Johnston sank into the data stream the squadron in question had been beaming back to the ship. Two bomber squadrons and escorts from the far side of the moon. As the details filled in, Johnston had to restrain his mounting annoyance. The squadron was the closest and most appropriate deterrent, Belford should know that. Johnston had an entire battle group to manage, he didn't have time to coordinate the fighter squadrons because his CAG's personal feelings got in the way.

Chimera squadron... Lieutenant Vincent Barkhorn, son of the legendary Chase Barkhorn. Kid's face was posted on every recruiting station the colonies had. Old animosity between Belford and Barkhorn, and Johnston had the worse of that pairing. What he wouldn't give for Chase to still be alive, now there was a fighter pilot.

"Multiple hostiles approaching carrier group," Chase's son said over the intercom. "Heading fower, tree, six, niner, by eight, niner, five, tree. Reapers set to intercept. Permission to engage?"

Johnston turned his head so Belford would miss the smile. "Acknowledged. Divert the *Independence* to support them. CAG ensure the civilians are protected. They are our priority here." The kid was rubbing it in Belford's face. He would have to deal with the two of them before long.

Belford scowled, but he had no leg to stand on. The Reapers were in a prime position to intercept and protect the civilians.

Johnston turned his attention back to the battle. His fleet was closing the distance, and the real battle would commence. The plasma blasts they traded were powerful, but easily negated at range. The computers could anticipate point of impact and engage defensive split-second singularities. When they closed the distance, and could bring their mass drivers to bear, then the real slug match would begin. Even the most sophisticated AIs couldn't predict and defend against every projectile in a point-blank broadside. At those ranges, raw fire power and hull strength were the deciding factors.

Even with all the technology the gnomes had given them, and all subsequent advances since then, it was still human minds that brought the fight. AIs were powerful and necessary tools, but they were predictable. Humanity lacked technology, but on a galactic scale, they made up for it with ingenuity and adaptability.

"Shields singularities are at seventy percent and holding."

"Failure in gun battery eighteen, two casualties taken to medical."

"Engineering reports reactor core stable."

Johnston couldn't help but feel pride in his crew — well, most of them — as they worked seamlessly together. The Warstar Class ship wasn't just the newest in the fleet, it was the first to incorporate all the races that comprised the Joint Fleet. Giants, gnomes, nymphs, and even shogoths were aboard, and Johnston was the one they'd chosen to lead them.

Up until that point in the war, the races had been segregated. He still had race specific crafts in his battle group, but for all humanity brought to the table, the technology that had been thrust into their laps was barely two decades old, and they needed to work together to keep up in their war against what lurked on the far side of the portals.

With his officers working to compile and sort all relevant information from their respective ship systems, Johnston was able to see the battle as a whole. Until they closed, he had little that required his full attention, so he planned ahead. He called up a hologram from his command dais and reached out to manipulate the field. His own ship was armed to the teeth, and had enough singularity generators to hold its own against anything the Separatists fielded. He would lead the charge. His escort ships, however, were far smaller, though what they lacked in firepower and defenses, they made up for with maneuverability. He used the hologram to plan out their attack routes, allowing the computer to power through the precise calculations while he worked out the general idea.

He had four ships go "up" in relation to him, and another four "down." They would accelerate away from the carrier, and once far enough away, turn to catch the enemy between them. With the *Inferno* charging up the center, the enemy would be forced to stay within the trap, or more likely, execute their own plan.

It was a simple maneuver, one every officer learned at the Naval Academy, but there was no sense opening an engagement with your trump card. It was a game of rock-paper-scissors, and the plays would change a dozen more times throughout the course of the battle. Once the enemy reacted, Johnston could react, and then again and again until he emerged victorious. He rested his hands on the console and looked up. On the view port, the formation was already breaking up as the ships went on their proposed paths.

A pair of eyes turned on him in his periphery and he looked over. One of the nymphs was staring at him from her command console. Her purple skin and the two dark gray horns growing from her forehead made her hard to ignore. A tingle in his mind alerted him that she was trying to speak.

<Sir, something is wrong with that civilian shuttle.>

Johnston did not have to ask how, with no monitors in her workstation, she came by that information. She was connected with several others of her race around the ship, as well as the two that piloted the Chimera ships. Nymphs had a knack for picking up anomalies the sensors could not. The kinds of anomalies that came from portals.

"Classification?" he asked.

<Unknown, sir, but it's powerful. I can feel it from here. Some kind of weapon.>

"Tell the fighters to be on high alert. It seems the Separatists are covering up something far worse than a wildfire."

Chapter 6

Vincent

Vincent wasted no time putting the attack order into action. "Reapers on me, switch back to attack mode," he commanded.

His fighter shifted the armored plates away, giving him an unobstructed view of the field again. In reality, the only change was from total darkness to some pinpricks of light—the enemy bombers were still too far to make out with the naked eye. His sensor's magnification was a different story.

"Reapers, key in maneuver tango fower." Using the phonetic radio code for T-4, he keyed for his ship to slave its first salvo of missiles to the targets he designated. Faster than he could blink, AMI laid out a set of variables across his HUD, having powered through the calculations. Vincent grunted in acknowledgment, swallowing his distaste.

He glanced at his weapons and set his blasters to rotating fire, then his Gatling cannon to standby. He lined up a bomber in his sights to paint its hull with a sensor, and when reticule changed from red to green, he flipped up a plastic shield and depressed the trigger beneath. Two missiles streaked ahead of him into the oncoming bombers, while simultaneously, twenty-two other missiles filled the shortening space between ships. Each missile was tipped with a nuclear warhead with enough destructive power to wipe out a city, and just enough to be effective in the void.

The enemy bombers were arranged in cube formations so their gunners could overlap. As the missiles streaked in, the sandcaster round leapt out to meet them. The simple clouds of sand hit the missiles like a thousand bullets, and destroyed any they touched. They couldn't hit them all, however, and as seven of the bombers were struck and destroyed, an eighth took a grazing hit in the port engine and went spinning out of control. The oxygen mix within the ships blossomed into short-lived fireballs in the vacuum, and sent a spray of debris to litter the battle space. A sour taste welled up in Vincent's mouth, but years of experience overrode the feeling — this wasn't the first human he had shot down.

An immediate spike in the vitals monitor flashed below Vincent's peripheral — no surprise there. His excitement level was just as high as the rest of them. But despite his numerous engagements, and the horror of every death, he still reveled in every twist and turn.

The bombers continued in their formations, blasting sandcaster clouds out around them like a wall. The more sand around them the harder it was to maneuver, but it forced any attacking fighters to fly straight in. The grav prop would pull in and defend against the particulates, but any sharp maneuvers would leave them wrecked. With the speeds they were flying at, even the smallest grain of sand could cut right through their ships, and in attack mode, Vincent's cockpit was exposed. It was strafing runs against the bombers' gunners.

The bombers numbered three dozen, with a squadron of fighters for support. The Reapers would be hard-pressed to keep them all from letting their payloads loose, even with the extra time Vincent's maneuver had bought them. Several of the ships dropped torpedoes that blasted into the Reapers' midst, the more maneuverable Chimeras were able to dodge the incoming projectiles. As the Reapers jinked and weaved among the incoming fire, the lead bombers grew desperate enough to launch their payloads at the *Inferno*.

Vincent cringed as the missiles streaked towards his home. He turned away without looking to see if they connected, and concentrated on stopping the remaining bombers from loosing their own missiles. Let the *Inferno*'s own point defense systems worry about the strays. With a quick kick to the left rudder, he popped into a tight turn. His maneuvering thrusters turned his tail and his grav prop pulled his craft onward, taking him out of the path of the bombers, and their sand clouds.

The fighter escort broke out to engage the Reapers, and Vincent locked onto one. As he painted the target, it juked left then followed with a sharp turn to the right. Vincent followed a moment later, stealing himself to the spin as the toned-down inertial compensator allowed him to feel a small percent of the g-forces his ship was pulling. As the fighter leveled out, he attempted to paint it with another missile lock. The enemy pilot responded with a tight roll up and around.

A less experienced pilot might have attempted to repeat the maneuver, but Vincent only rolled his wrists forward on the joysticks so the ship snapped upside-down, and with his grav prop turned down low to reduce drag, he continued backwards with the inertia and painted the target. It was a dangerous maneuver to have his unprotected flank traveling forward, but he was rewarded with a flash: The enemy ship flared bright as a star in its destruction. Vincent flipped back around, keeping his grav prop forward to catch any debris in his path.

The other Reapers had broken down into four groups of three, Vincent flying with the Duchess and Zombie. Not feeling the need to oversee his well-qualified pilots, Vincent let his squadron's position fade into the back of his mind, concentrating instead on his own path.

<I've got a fighter on my tail,> Zombie called.

"Break off, I'll take him," Vicnent said as he swung up and around.

<I can't shake him.>

"Zombie, cut hard," Vincent commed.

<Roger that.>

Vincent dialed down the power on his grav prop while the Duchess and Zombie spun in a helix around him. As he lost momentum, one fighter shot past him to chase his wingmates. Vincent squeezed out a shot with his blasters, scoring a glancing blow against the oncoming fighter's shields. As the blast connected, the refracted light fed into his sensors, the data showing negligible damage in the strike. Both fighters banked away.

Knowing he would not trick them again, Vincent directed power back to the engines. His speed peaking, he took his wingmen into a turn up and around to strafe a group of bombers. As his HUD keyed onto the new opponent, he rotated the frequency of his blasters. He sent out a call to Duchess and Zombie, who rotated their own frequencies to different wavelengths from his own. Hoping to overload the bombers' shields together, they triggered a trio of blasts. The beams slammed home, though when the light faded, Vincent cursed as the shield shrugged off the combined blow.

"Some kind of new armor, it's absorbing the shots," Vincent said. "Switch to cannons. We'll shoot them down the old-fashioned way."

He spun up the Gatling cannon and could feel it shaking beneath his feat as it moved. He keyed for the rounds to use explosive charge, and led his trio around for a strafing run. A light keyed green as the rounds were chambered, and Vincent's finger slid down to the secondary trigger.

Vincent teased the rudder and took up a position behind an enemy ship, its bulbous frame hiding the deadly munitions beneath. He kept his ship in a lazy spiral to avoid some of the tail gunners' fire, and squeezed off a burst from his cannon, the chemical-filled rounds stitching a row of miniature blasts in front of the bomber as it continued onward. Its armor took the brunt of the damage, but Vincent could see atmosphere draining from some of the holes. The Duchess's rounds punched through its cockpit, and with a muted flash, the bomber continued its run without pilots. Vincent and his wingmates charged forward through the sand cloud and other bombers. They moved fast, and the sand blocked the bombers' computer sensors from painting them with a target lock; the enemy gunners had to shoot them by sight.

The bombers' formation had pulled away from its floundering member and a well-disciplined gunner brought his lasers to bear on the Duchess. Before her armor could be overwhelmed, Vincent kicked his own ship sideways to take the fire on his port side. A quick flash of red bled into the green field of his HUD as the heat compensator protested, and Vincent diverted his starboard power to reinforce. The ablative armor could shrug off only so much before it slagged.

Vincent's maneuver opened an opportunity for Zombie, who had been further back, and with a quick burst of his own guns, the bomber disappeared in a torrent of muted flame.

"No man escapes the Reapers," Vincent intoned the squadron's motto. Duchess let out a whoop of exhilaration, and an undercurrent of gratitude and thanks poured openly through the bionet.

<*Tell the techs to get the paint ready. Score one more guppy silhouette for me,*> Zombie called across the net.

"Button up, Zombie," Vincent chuckled despite himself. The thrill was starting to overtake him; he was losing himself in the fight.

Their chase had taken them further from the furball and remaining bombers, and with a flick of the rudder, Vincent corkscrewed and pushed back into the chaos.

So far the dreaded alarm had stayed silent; no one in his squadron had been injured. For this, Vincent was grateful. Too often he lost good pilots to careless mistakes or chance. But today, he intended to congratulate eleven pilots in the debriefing room.

Chapter 7

The Exile

The pilots broke down completely when they saw the enemy bombers and their fighter escort. They were juveniles, and no amount of training could have steeled their nerves when they found themselves surrounded by the enemy. Exile's web couldn't break the hold of the fear that consumed them, not without it consuming her as well. She pulled her knife from its sheath once more, and stared down at the obsidian sphere nestled in the pommel. Her own blood would not be enough; she needed more power than she could pull from her own reserves. She needed a sacrifice.

The Shadow within the dagger thrummed with excitement, connected as it was to her emotions. It knew what she was planning, and it hungered for the release. Was it worth giving into the creature to save herself? For what felt like an eternity, she considered re-sheathing the dagger and letting fate choose her path.

Patience brings peace. The mantra came quickly to answer her silent question, and she felt the spear of pain from the ghost of her amputated arm. Her lack of faith was what forced her from the conclave, bonded her to the monster in her dagger, and stole her arm. She would never again allow fate to have sway.

Exile approached the first man who had moved to attack her. She had difficulty discerning humans by their physical features, but she remembered the imprint he had left in her mind. A pathetic, lecherous creature, which no one would miss, and yet she stayed her hand.

The dagger screamed in her mind, fighting against her to stab it into the human's blood, to give it the power it so craved. Exile's hand trembled as she lifted it over her head. *Lose one, save many.* The dagger plunged down into the man's chest, and Exile felt every inch of skin that split, every strand of muscle severed, and the scream of sated hunger when the dagger found his heart.

Though he had been incapacitated by her attack, the human screamed, his voice raw from the terror and pain. It was not just the physical shock of the steel in his heart as the Shadow spread from the wound and exchanged blood for darkness. Within moments, it spread through his body, consuming him as though he were skewered with flame. The man was no more, and a being of darkness lay in his place.

The dagger clattered to the floor as Exile pulled away, and the Shadow slipped away from the body. Then the black energy twisted into a point and shot out of the cargo hold. Walls, atmosphere, the vacuum beyond—none held sway over the creature. He was darkness given form—an elemental made of absence. Exile sank to her knees, the overwhelming knowledge of what she had unleashed too heavy for her to keep on her feet. One man was not enough for the monster to come fully into the world—it would have minutes at best, but minutes were more than enough. Her shuttle would be safe, but fate would take those who got in its way.

Chapter 8

Vincent

Alarms wailed as Vincent's world became a swirling miasma of nausea and fear. His control board was dead, and his fighter was out of control. The Duchess and Zombie took up defensive positions around him as Rover came alive. Springing from its position, it skittered into Vincent's view and crouched down beside the damaged thruster. From beneath Rover's eye-shaped sensors, a laser played across the exposed wires and rent metal, assessing the extent of the damage. The enemy strike had punched through the port stabilizer, grazing enough to cut through the control lines, and without regulators attached, the powerful thruster was pushing well past its safe limits.

<Sir!? Are you alright?> Duchess called, worry permeating the unspoken connection.

Vincent fought to stay alert as the spin pushed him into the seat, his suit rippling and tightening to keeping his blood flowing.

"I was hit by a fighter, watch your six," he said.

<It wasn't a fighter, sir. Whatever hit you destroyed half the bombers.

40

It's some kind of super weapon.>

"You need to get out of here. Take the Reapers back to the ship," Vincent ordered.

<We're not leaving you.>

"There's nothing you can do."

<We will come get you.>

"Damn it, Duchess, take the others and get out of here. Protect the *Inferno*."

Whether it was fear for his pilots, or his home, or something else, Vincent did not know, but it was enough to force him to key the command he never thought he would use. His AMI sent the data packet that overrode Duchess's system, and twisted her fighter back to the safety of the *Inferno*. The other Reapers followed in her wake. He made sure they could still maneuver — he wouldn't forgive himself if they were killed because of his order — and then he cut off his incoming communications to focus on his own crisis.

He struggled to make out the HUD's readout of the damage, but his vision blurred and he nearly blacked out. He tried to reach out for his control board, but the spin was too great. He cut short a groan, and with a short mental command, the lights in the cabin flashed colored lights to alert him of the damage severity. When a red light washed over him, fear threatened to grip the edge of his mind. The grav prop had automatically throttled back to its lowest setting, keeping the artificial gravity as well as inertial compensation active. If the prop stalled, the g-forces would tear Vincent apart.

Vincent shut his eyes to the swirl of stars visible through his canopy and waited. He regretted it immediately as the nausea flared, and opened his eyes to another blaster flashing across, close enough to draw spots in his vision. Another mental command and his canopy darkened, obscuring the laser that came close enough to strip his ship's paint.

Vincent concentrated on Rover, who was clinging to the rotating ship with its six magnetic clamped legs. The bot lifted its front right leg and reached back into a compartment on its shell, and exchanged its configuration for a short laser-cutter. Rover's arm shot in and out of the damaged hole with robotic precision as it probed and cut the damaged wires. Once finished with the wires, it stopped and played out the diagnostic beam again. The controls to the cockpit were slagged, almost unsalvageable, Rover informed Vincent through the AMI, but the bot continued anyway. After cutting away the destroyed sections, Rover unfurled a pair of precision manipulators from where its jaw would be. The miniature claws grasped the burnt and mangled ends and pulled them together. The material that surrounded the wire was able to self-repair to a degree and started reattaching — though for Vincent, not nearly fast enough.

Rover reached its larger left claw down and clamped the ends, securing the connection. Its tail rotated, bringing a nozzle to bear. It snapped into the hole with its fore claws and twisted through a series of deft movements, spraying an insulation membrane that coated all the remaining wires. The lights within the cockpit flashed to yellow, much to Vincent's relief. Rover had given him the most basic of controls back, enough to stop the sickening spin.

Immediately, Vincent grasped the joystick and attempted to arrest his death spiral. Even at its lowest speed, the grav prop had still dragged Vincent well past the battle's engagement zone. Not far out of the planet's gravity well to begin with, Vincent found himself falling towards the planet as he attempted to secure control of his ship. Rover's hasty repairs weren't enough to ramp up the engine and pull out of the dive. He was going to hit atmosphere.

"This is Reaper One, I've been hit, cannot maneuver, impact with Bastogne imminent. I say again, I am beaching my fighter," he called.

<Eject, sir!> Duchess screamed in his mind. She had overridden his com blackout.

"Negative, I can land it." Then he keyed the command sequence to reroute all communications through the AMI. No distractions, not if he was going to pull this off.

On his wing, he could just make out Rover jamming the armor back into alignment. The bot exchanged both its foreclaw tools for clamps and grasped the rent armor. All along the robot's spine, maneuvering thrusters fired off to keep it firmly latched to the ship as it pulled the armor back into place. Its tail rotated again, and a plasma welder swung down to attach the bowed metal permanently. The job left the armor bulging and ugly, but intact, and hopefully it would keep the ship intact for reentry. Let the repair crew worry about aesthetics; Vincent just needed to land.

A countdown to impact flashed onto the corner of the HUD. The planet grew until it all but filled his screen, and he could see the fires that ravaged the surface even as far out as he was. The research colony was gone, destroyed by the blaze. Maybe that's why the Separatists had arrived — to salvage intel. Vincent shook his head. He needed to focus. He briefly released the stick to run his thumb over his father's multitool.

The transition from vacuum to air was gradual, and without his sensors telling him how far he'd gone, he wouldn't even know when he hit the upper layers. His grav prop cut off automatically once the atmosphere was too thick, and he lost shields and inertial dampeners. Gravity reoriented so that he was falling face first.

The front of his nose and wings took on a cherry glow from the friction as the ablative armor deflected most of the heat. Alarms screeched in his ears, and Vincent snapped to mute them. The patch job Rover had done wasn't taking the strain, and the little bot had to stay nestled in his mount or would be ripped off the hull.

Vincent reached up for the levers above him, knowing there was a fair chance that what he was about to try would lead to his abrupt and violent death, and then he twisted and pulled straight down. Tiny detonations rocked the hull as the armor panels were jettisoned from the craft, and the no-frills frame of the Chimera fighter was revealed. Thin nose, cockpit, engines, and wings; no armor, weapons, or navigation equipment. Just enough to fly. *The way Dad taught me.*

Vincent was far enough down now that he could see the ground clearly as it rushed up to greet him. Pulling back lightly on the stick, he tried to get some air under the stubby wings. Pull too hard and they would snap off, not enough and he was a burning wreck on the ground. Since problems always came in threes, the only place to land below was on fire.

Maybe I should have ejected.

Chapter 9

The Exile

Regardless of the distance between them, the Exile could feel the glee and savage hatred that warred inside the Shadow. It was a creature of destruction, and it tore through its enemies like a house pet with a toy. The bombers and fighters it encountered didn't stand a chance against its invisible strikes, its weapons born of darkness. Exile shouldn't have been able to sense the minds of the pilots anymore, but she was connected to the Shadow, and so she felt all their terror and pain as their lives were snuffed out.

Again and again, she reminded herself that it was necessary, that she had bonded with the monster for a reason. Whatever that reason, it was washed away in the wake of the pain and anguish that assaulted her. She had no defenses against it, no barriers to erect that would withstand the pounding blows. The iron reek of human blood penetrated her senses; the blood the Shadow had not soaked up was pooling around her as she lay collapsed beside the body. The wet, thick texture around her hand was almost gentle against the throb behind her horn. She needed to move the body. She wouldn't have the strength to purge anyone's mind if she was found unconscious beside the victim with a murder weapon in her hand.

She forced herself up from the ground and then to her feet. She would not have the strength to move the body, not while her mind still throbbed. She ran her hand over the horn growing from her forehead and concentrated on the arm that wasn't there. She could always "feel" it—the phantom pain that reminded her of what she had lost—but she searched for something else, something more tangible. *A calm center, a clear mind.* The words from her conclave training bubbled to the surface.

In the same way her Web could reach out and connect with unsecured AMIs and influence thoughts, she could draw her Shell to enhance and protect her body. The energy lurked on the fringes. It was something she did not spend nearly as much time using. The Web allowed her to keep tabs on anyone around her, and when she released it to draw her Shell, she felt as though she were blind.

Still, she forced the switch, and her perception of the unconscious crew members around her and the thoughts of the pilots fell away. The pain from the Shadow diminished slightly, but did not disappear. Its power was not limited to what she could sense.

Her body tingled as energy wrapped around her, and a blue ethereal shape pushed out from her shoulder. An arm formed, then a wrist, and then fingers. Her arm was gone, but the Shell remained; she twisted the ghost fingers into a fist, and could almost imagine they were there. Unlike the illusions she cast with her Web, the Shell was as solid as her, and she wrapped her ghost and flesh hands around the fallen man's uniform.

An ice pick of pain lanced from her spine to her feet as she lifted the man. Somehow she kept her grip, and despite the Shadow's distraction, she was able to drag the body towards the airlock. Trapped with only her own thoughts and the Shadow's disgusting, monstrous glee, she felt like the journey took an hour. In truth, it was less than two minutes. She could barely maintain her Shell, let alone use the power fully.

Once she unceremoniously dropped the man's body into the airlock, she looked back at the trail of blood she had caused. That would pose a problem. It wouldn't take a CSI team to figure out what had happened. She might be able to conceal her actions with a clever Web illusion, but the effect would only last as long as she concentrated on it.

The pain continued to throb in her head, and she had a difficult time remembering what to do. She needed a plan. Not just for the blood, but for moving forward. For the first time in years, she was on her own; she had only herself, that cursed knife, and her entire race willing to kill her on sight. She had taken a serious gamble going to Bastogne, following the rumor of a secret testing facility. The wildfires had forced her back into space, and once she was aboard a fleet ship, things would only get worse.

She ran her hands over the man's pockets, searching for anything useful. From one she pulled a date cube. Though he was dead, his AMI unit still functioned enough for her to dig his passcodes out and activate it. She brushed her fingers over him to make the contact — it was the only way to maintain her Shell and connect to the AMI. Spreading out her Web would cost her time. Once she accessed the cube, she searched for the man's purpose for going to the fleet. Was he a colonist escaping the fires below, a scientist, or a sailor? No — he was none of those things. He was a Special Forces soldier on assignment there, and he was being recalled.

This was something the Exile could use.

The Special Forces were their own worst enemy when it came to tracking their soldiers. They did not keep detailed records of their operatives, which could expose them. Instead, they worked as cells, only dependent on the most immediate chain of command. They were ghosts. Ghosts with powerful resources and no ability to check if she belonged. Once she disposed of the man, she could take his place, and any new command could be conned into believing she was their commander. The box had only the name of the platoon he was meant to command: The Condemned. How fitting.

She also found a number of weapons on his person, including a set of explosives. Now the Exile had a plan. She would make it to the fleet unhindered after all.

Chapter 10

Vincent

Vincent fought the stick for every meter as he careened down toward the surface of Bastogne. The raging fires below wreaked havoc with the air currents, and his already harrowing descent on emergency wings was made that much more difficult by the turbulence.

"I really need somewhere I can land. Somewhere not on fire," Vincent called, and he felt the acknowledgment as his AMI pushed out the sensors to find somewhere not completely engulfed. What was left of his armor would probably withstand most of the heat, but if he was going to repair his fighter, or be rescued by a tug, he needed somewhere he could get out of the cockpit.

What had caused so much destruction to the planet? The fires had to have spread hundreds of thousands of kilometers. He had been briefed on the situation, but flying above it gave him a new perspective.

<Three possible locations found, engaging automated control,> the AMI unit chirped in his head.

"Negative," Vincent snapped. "Just put it on the screen." Not a chance he was putting his fate in the hands of the computer.

Boxes appeared on his display tracking; they grew ever smaller towards a point in the distance. Vincent tapped the rudders to bring him inside of the first projected box, and aimed for the second. Just like playing a video game. When the whole craft dropped a meter on dead air and shuddered, he reconsidered the thought. It felt like being strapped into a rollercoaster, trying to fly a fight simulator with a busted stick. Without his grav prop to compensate, he felt every g of force. Even with his tightening nano-suit and the padding, the restraints still cut into his shoulders, but they kept him firmly in his seat.

Vincent's wrists ached as he tried to keep the sticks in line; the fighter seemed to want to go anywhere except where he was directing it. The basic frame wasn't meant for this kind of flying. That's why he had an atmospheric configuration sitting back in the fighter bay. For all the good that did him.

The heavy armor frame could have handled it too; all the frames could adjust on the fly, assuming you didn't slam into a gravity hard enough to melt the armor off. His was somewhere behind him, a shower of flaming debris from his reentry. The term *FUBAR* sprang to mind.

He was far enough down that if he ejected he would survive. Rover's survival routine would kick in, and the two of them would float down somewhere and hopefully land outside a hot spot. Vincent knew if he lost his fighter he wouldn't get another one anytime soon. The Chimeras were in short supply, they were prototypes after all. There certainly were none to spare. Best case, he would be taking another pilot off the line; worst case, he was on a shuttle back to Fleet HQ for reassignment.

No, he was going to land, and hopefully he'd live to brag about it.

He leveled out best as he was going to manage, the stumpy wings barely catching the air. It was little better than a nose dive. His air brakes were open to their max, and he was still moving fast enough that the ground was a blur. What he wouldn't give for some science fiction antigravity. Why couldn't the gnomes have invented that?

"Come on baby, hold together,"

Vincent readied the command in his mind; he couldn't let go of the stick long enough to flip the trigger. He ignored all the instrument panels and alerts from the AMI unit. He knew his ship, and he waited for the perfect moment.

When he triggered the command, the thrusters fired off below his nose and directly ahead of him. He jerked forward against the restraints, feeling like he'd just been slugged in the gut. His speed slowed dramatically over the course of a few seconds, and his ship bucked like an animal. He kept a white-knuckle grip on the sticks. He was almost there — the trees below were close enough to see the individual leaves — and then he saw it ahead of him. A soot-covered lake, maybe a kilometer across.

"A lake?" he yelled. "The ship isn't going to float!"

<The craft is sealed against vacuum. The water will pose no danger while you await rescue.>

Vincent wished the AMI had a neck he could throttle, but he didn't have the time; already, the water was beneath him, and with one last burst of his thrusters, he crashed into the surface. It was like hitting a brick wall, his right shoulder gave a sharp pop as he slammed back into his seat. Collision alarms flared, and he watched the water bubble up over the cockpit. He had to work to drop the controls, his fingers refusing to give up the grip, and he winced as he dropped his hand, his shoulder screaming. He grabbed at it, making things a thousand times worse, and could feel the gap between shoulder and arm beneath his suit. Dislocated, definitely dislocated. He hit a button on the chest harness to harden the nano-suit arm into a makeshift sling.

The pain didn't diminish completely, but at least he wouldn't move it. His craft hit the bottom of the lake with a thud. He didn't seem to have sprung any leaks, but as he looked out into the murky water, he felt oddly claustrophobic. Somehow, the vacuum of space seemed less dangerous than sitting beneath however many feet of water.

His emergency beacon was on and transmitting. Now all he could do was wait, and hope the battle above came out with the Joint Fleet on top. Otherwise the Separatists would be the ones fishing him out.

Chapter 11

Johnston

Admiral Johnston was not pleased. It wasn't enough that the Separatists had broken the treaty and forced his hand; they had also unleashed some sort of "magic" weapon that damaged one of his fighters, and blew up half of their own bombers. The damage to the enemy was not his concern, though any loss of human life was a waste in his eyes. What troubled him was how fast it had torn through them, like a wolf tearing open its prey. The ships' husks floated on their inertia, some with drives still active, only their hulls were torn open like tin cans, and the pilots within skewered.

Johnston was no stranger to forces he didn't understand. No admiral worth his salt would blink at the sight of an elemental, crystal, or dragon. Those were enemies they had faced down and could defeat. They were enemies that could be seen. Magic or not, impossible or not, they were at least a known quantity. Whatever had damaged those ships was certainly not on any fleet report.

"What the hell have you done?" the Russian admiral demanded, his com signal now reconnected.

"That weapon originated from the civilian shuttle, the same shuttle that came from the planet you claim is under your jurisdiction. What sort of facility is down there?" Johnston asked, a deadly edge to his voice. The Multi-Verse war was enough without the Separatists experimenting with magic.

"You think we would shoot down our own ships?" Kolchak's face shone red.

"You were quick enough to endanger our relief efforts, and it seems we have discovered why."

"I will make you regret this," Kolchak blustered, and then cut the connection off again.

"Sir!" Sensor called. "The Russians are maneuvering away. I have Alcubierre drive signatures."

"Have they recalled their fighters?" Johnston asked.

"Negative. The closest ones are turning back, but the others will not reach them before they make a jump."

Communications cut in. "They are broadcasting so much that we had no trouble breaking their codes. It's all the same, sir; the pilots think they are being left behind."

"Bloody hell," Johnston muttered, then said in a voice that carried over the others, "CAG, stand down our fighters and pull them back to a safe distance. Do not fire unless actively engaged. If those fighters are abandoned, then we will have no trouble scooping them up. They'll die without their carrier."

"What are they thinking, retreating like that?" McKinley wondered aloud. Johnson quietly shared the thought. Whatever they had created down on that planet was enough to abandon half a dozen squadrons to capture. That did not bode well for anyone.

"Sir, one of the civilian vessels' engines detonated," Tactical said. "They are venting atmosphere."

"Destroyed?" the admiral asked.

"Negative, sir, they are still broadcasting an SOS."

"Dispatch a rescue tug immediately. Send a marine escort with them, those civilians need to be quarantined"

"Aye, sir."

"And send another to the planet's surface after that beached fighter," he added. He knew the chances of survival were slim, but he had already lost seven Vapefalcons and did not want to lose even one more. "Which pilot went down?" he asked.

"Barkhorn," the CAG said, and Johnston thought he saw a hint of a smile.

Interlude

Ele

Fire and heat raged around her. Branches cracked and fell, battering her with blazing gusts of heat and noise; trunks splintered and trees that had stood for a millennium bent to the unwavering heat. Each lungful she pulled in was more smoke than air, though she did not cough or lack for breath. The flames that licked her skin left no burns, and the torrents of heat that buffeted her did not so much as singe her hair.

Her entire mind was consumed with an anger that burned hotter than the forest. Fragmented and confusing thoughts struggled to be heard over the fire and her screams. Pain, hatred, anger, a swirling torrent of emotions and thoughts. She did not know who she was, how she had come to be in the forest, or why the fires left her skin unhurt.

She was barefoot, though as she ran through the trees, she did not feel the heat of the fallen embers. Each unseen rock cut into the soles of her feet, but there was no pain. Why was there no pain?

Everything ahead of her was flickering red and yellow. The fire had no end. Though her memory supplied nothing of where she had been, she knew it could not always have been that way. Slivers of images tried to rise from the fog of her thoughts. Warm fluid surrounding her, her hands pressed against a window. Muddied faces looking at her, and indistinct voices.

Then those memories were gone, replaced with the pain of needles lancing into her neck, back, arms. Lights flashed endlessly, and waves of sound made her sick. Anger clouded her mind again.

Around her, the fire exploded with intensity. Several trees erupted from the heat alone, sending splinters whistling out, and trailing cuts into arm and side. Trickles of multicolored blood oozed from wounds flickering red and yellow in the light. Still, she felt no pain.

The blood sizzled and smoked on her skin, and disappeared before her eyes in the impossible heat. The splinters ignited, and when they burned away, her skin was unbroken.

Again, she screamed. Why? Why was she unburnt? Who was she? Fear started to take form, replacing the anger. Her tears sizzled and dried on her cheeks.

A new sound hit her—a screaming louder than the roar of the fire and the snapping of falling trees. She looked around, then up, and saw a blazing trail as something fell from the sky.

She ran after it. Whatever was falling would crash down somewhere nearby, somewhere in the fire.

It took her much longer than she expected to reach where she thought it would land. Though her muscles never tired, and her lungs never hurt for air, it was harrowing to run through endless fire and smoke with only her anger and fear as distraction.

When she finally broke from the trees, it was not some falling savior that she found, but a vast blue lake.

The water felt cool somehow, though she was unable to feel the heat outside. She dove under the surface to escape. Bubbles erupted from all around her, the water coming to a boil as it touched her skin. Before long, she was blind beneath the churning waves. Memories of being trapped under water assaulted her mind, and the boiling water around her flashed into steam. She screamed and screamed against memories she did not understand, and when she opened her eyes, she was sitting at the bottom of an empty lake, all the water boiled away, with a large metal ship stuck into the ground across from her.

She had found the falling object. A hiss came from the ship, and a seam appeared as the top half of it cracked open. A helmeted figure pushed his way out, his body covered in a skin-tight purple uniform. He started to approach her.

"No!" she screamed. All the anger had boiled away with the lake, and only fear remained. She was sure she would kill the man, and then she would be trapped in the burning forest forever.

He kept approaching, his hands raised in front of him. He was saying something, but she couldn't hear him through the helmet.

He was only feet from her when she screamed again, "Don't, I don't want to hurt you."

He pulled the helmet from his head. A young man with deep blue eyes and a head of short cut brown hair. She recognized him. But how?

"Please," she begged as he came close enough to touch.

He dropped his helmet to the ground and knelt. "It'll be okay," he told her, then reached out to touch her arm.

His fingers touched her skin, and nothing happened. He was unburnt.

She collapsed into his arms.

Part 2

Chapter 12

Vincent

Vincent's worry that he would be trapped under the lake evaporated, along with all the water pinning his fighter down. He had not expected his entry to put off as much heat as it did, but between shooting through the upper atmosphere and the heat of his engines he supposed it would be enough. His computer screamed a warning at him as the lake started heating. It was slow at first—he didn't even notice it for a few minutes after landing. Then the water bubbled all around him and flashed into steam. Before he knew it, he was sitting at the bottom of a dried-out lakebed.

The way he had sunk left him with his nose in the air and a good view on nothing but the sky, so Vincent unlatched his restraints and pushed himself up to try and get a better look.

"Is that a girl?" He gaped at what appeared to be the figure of a young woman across the lakebed. He must have been seeing things. "Rover, how hot is it out there?" he asked, blinking.

"Ninety-eight degrees Fahrenheit, thirty-six Celsius, three

hundred and nine Kelvin..." The little bot droned.

"Alright, enough. I can pop the hatch?"

"Affirmative, sir."

Vincent reached down for the control, but hesitated before he pressed it down. What in the void was a girl doing in the middle of the jungle, and how hadn't she been killed by the fire? Vincent, like most of the fleet, had learned to be wary of things he didn't understand. It could be some kind of magical trap, though he hadn't heard any reports of portals this far out in fringe space.

"Rover, scan out a hundred meters, full frequency," Vincent ordered, waiting tensely for the reply.

"One life form detected, human," Rover answered, and Vincent didn't waste any more time. As soon as the cockpit was open he vaulted out, landing in a crouch on the dried lakebed below. It wasn't even wet. His ship had been burning hotter than he thought, or the lake was smaller than he thought he had seen. Thank the gnomes for good life support.

Vincent wasn't halfway to the girl when she called out.

"No!" she screamed, and Vincent saw immediately how terrified she was. She was young, maybe twenty standard years old, with long red hair that stuck to her in clumps. She was wearing what looked like a jumpsuit—orange with black lettering—only it was burnt off to the point that she was almost naked.

"It's okay, I'm here to help," he called, but she clearly didn't understand. He tapped the control on the side of his helmet to separate it from the nano-suit, then lifted his hands so she could see he had no weapons.

"Please." Her eyes were so wide he could only see the whites. Soot stained her olive-colored skin. She twisted her arms around herself and shook.

"It'll be okay," he told her, and then he reached out to touch her shoulder, to let her know he wasn't a threat. She collapsed.

Vincent lunged to catch her, just barely keeping her head from striking the ground. She was really pretty up close. The kind of girl he might look for if he ever made it home. He pushed her hair back behind her ear. They were round, Human. Thank god.

"Rover!" he shouted. "Med kit, now!"

The little bot scuttled off the ship and towards him, exchanging its tail and foreclaws for basic medical tools. As soon as it was close, it squatted low and played a beam from its sensor array across the girl. Its tail shot forward, stopping just short of the bend in the girl's elbow, and then a needle deployed and pressed into her flesh.

"What's that?" Vincent asked.

"Battlefield antibiotic, painkiller, and sedative to keep her comfortable until rescue." A compartment opened at the rear of the droid's shell. It dipped its tail, and with a small set of graspers, pulled out a square of silver cloth. "Emergency blanket."

Vincent rested the girl's head on his knee as he pulled open the thin blanket and wrapped it around her. It felt like foil, only less prone to ripping, and reminded him of the kind of heating blankets he and his father would use when they went camping in the mountains. Human tech.

"Is the emergency transponder activated?" Vincent asked.

"Roger, sir," Rover answered, as did the AMI chip. Vincent grunted in reply.

"I need to get her back to the ship," he told no one in particular. She was not difficult to carry, and he got her to the ship without issue. Once he was close, he allowed Rover to climb the side and latch itself on.

With its clamps turned to the side, the bot lifted the girl up and over while Vincent climbed up himself. Together they managed to seat her in the cockpit.

Vincent nodded and dropped down to sit on the edge of the cockpit's opening. The ship rocked dangerously with his weight. He made sure not to make any more sudden moves.

"Rover, go find some rocks or something and make sure our ship doesn't fall over. Try not to scratch the paint," he said as he looked over at the armor plating still flash-welded to the frame. While the rest of the heavy payload package was scattered around the planet somewhere, the emergency repair Rover had made in orbit had stuck.

The droid barked and the dog hologram shimmered back in place before it set off to comply.

"She must have been using the lake for shelter when the fires broke out," he mused, looking back to where he had found the girl. The fires around him had started to burn themselves out. Blackened husks of trees stood where a forest had once been, and smoke overpowered any other scent. *Funny. No matter how big, it always smells like a campfire.*

Vincent glanced back down at the unconscious girl. She looked peaceful now; the fear that had been twisting her features was gone, replaced by the dreamless nothing of medicated sleep. His eyes fell to her slow-rising chest, which was exposed under the poorly situated survival blanket. He twisted his head, admonishing himself for looking, but a scrap of orange cloth caught his eye again. The black lettering he had noticed over her left breast was still intact enough to read. He reached down and pulled the blanket over enough to see the whole word.

ELE, all in block lettering, with a string of numbers beneath. Vincent pulled the blanket over to cover the lettering and any of the girl's exposed skin.

"What in the void were they doing on this planet?"

Chapter 13

The Exile

Once the Shadow's energy ran out and it returned to the blade, it was simple for the Exile to finish her deception. Before she detonated the rear of the ship, she moved through and ensured that every passenger was secured against the sudden decompression, and as she did, she touched each of them and erased their memories of her. The ones who had been injured during her fight were still alive, and with a little basic first aid, she was able to keep them stable. Once finished, she slipped into one of the cargo hatches and blew the charge.

When the rescue crews arrived, they found a compartment full of unconscious but alive civilians, and with the damage to the shuttle's engines, there was no time to waste looking at blood trails or camera feeds. The Exile slipped past the rescue crews unnoticed, her Web causing them to forget about her if they looked. None of them were searching for someone hiding, though; they were too preoccupied with rescuing everyone aboard. She made it to one of the Fleet ships with no one even aware of her existence, and from there, she was just another body in a crew of hundreds.

She was still an alien to them, however, and even if there were a thousand sailors aboard she would stand out as a blue-skinned "nymph." But something was off, and when the rescue tug landed on the flight deck, her Web detected something she did not expect. Others — others of her kind. What were they doing on a human ship? They were allies to humans, yes, but her people kept to themselves, and the humans did the same. But there they were, as bright as spotlights in her Web. Her infiltration suddenly became that much more difficult. Humans she could trick, or hide from, but not one of her own.

Enemy mistakes are allied opportunities. The mantra sprang unbidden to her thoughts. A lifetime of training took more than banishment to remove. The ship was a mixed compliment, and that meant she would go unnoticed among the humans while hiding herself in the Web from the others. As long as none of them spotted her and saw the mark of the Exile on her, then she would have time to plan.

The first step was to gather intel, to find out what she could about the "Condemned." Where they were located, and what their mission was. The next step was to find them. A platoon of special ops soldiers would be a powerful tool in her mission.

Although… she did not really have a mission anymore. She was banished from her path, and the ideals she had trained for her entire life had been stripped from her. She was a completely free agent, stripped of her rank, her influence, and even her name. She had no obligation to continue.

She could steal a ship, take as many supplies as she needed, and leave human-controlled space. Everything she had done was for her people, and they had taken everything from her. The Exile ran her hand over the hilt of the dagger she lost everything for. She knew she needed power to combat power, and if she was to prevent what was coming, she needed every advantage. The Shadow and his ilk from beyond the portals were nothing compared to what destroyed her homeworld.

No, she had to continue.

The Exile found herself on a large hangar deck hidden from view by the numerous boxes and machinery that littered the space. She held her Web as close as she could, not wanting to draw her Shell, but knowing that any active pulse would alert other Psykin of her location. The Exile slinked across the bay, moving between shadows to keep out of sight, all the while watching the various crew members as they came and went, mentally mapping out the different routes in and out of the bay.

Intel gathering was simple: watch everyone, memorize patterns. An unsecured computer would allow her to find out more about the Condemned. If that man from the shuttle was moving from Bastogne to the fleet, then they must be either stationed on one of the ships or within a jump of the system. Before she found them, however, she would find resources. Weapons, uniforms, equipment. She was going to impersonate a Special Forces lieutenant, and she would need to look the part.

The Exile felt the analytical calm that took over whenever she set herself to a goal. The constant undercurrent of anger and betrayal was pushed aside for the details she needed to take in.

She could continue her search for the project Rebirth.

Chapter 14

Johnston

A headache had wormed its way into Johnston's skull. It sat right between his eyes, and throbbed whenever he tried to look at his console or even turn on the lights. All the enemy fighters had been recovered, the civilians in the disabled shuttle rescued, and Lieutenant Barkhorn had been found on the planet alive, and had managed to save someone himself. So why was his head splitting open? The ship was hardly damaged, and while the lost pilots were distressing, it was not enough to create such incapacitating pain.

He had experienced these kinds of headaches in the academy, after nights of no sleep and constant study, as though his body were rebelling against him. It had to be stress, only Johnston couldn't figure out what was causing it.

A chime sounded outside his door, and his AMI informed him that it was Commander Belford.

Just what I need. The admiral sighed, a heavy sound in the dark room, and then he pulled a pain reliever from the drawer. He pressed the applicator into his upper arm, and barely felt the pinch of the needle with the pain lancing between his eyes. Thankfully, humanity's allies, the shogoths, were masters of chemical manipulation. His painkiller didn't addle him or cause the euphoria most painkillers did; the shot he took simply blocked the nerves from screaming.

He would need to be careful not to do anything to hurt himself, as he wouldn't even feel a broken bone. The rest of his crew was forbidden from having such powerful medication on hand, but he was the captain, and he couldn't afford to be anything other than one hundred percent.

He keyed the mental command to open the door.

"Enter."

Belford blustered in, and Johnston was immediately thankful he had taken the pain suppressor. He was not going to enjoy this conversation.

"William, I need to, uh..." Belford started, but Johnston nipped that in the bud.

"*Captain* will be fine," he interrupted.

"Uh, right, Captain, sir." Belford's train had been derailed. Johnston hoped he would make it short.

"The article fifteen I submitted for Barkhorn was pushed back." It seemed he had found his track again. "I have submitted it twice. Why are you, uh, pushing back? Sir?"

Johnston rubbed at the spot behind his eyes. He could have sworn he still felt the pressure. Perhaps he had discovered the cause of his stress.

"Commander, your pilot's actions not only saved the lives of every civilian aboard that shuttle, but exposed a dangerous weapon without taking casualties. He then managed to land a heavily damaged fighter and rescue another civilian, and you want permission to discipline him?" Johnston had long ago mastered the technique of monotone delivery. He would let Belford string out his own rope.

"He left his post. He disobeyed orders!"

"The com recordings show you ordering him not to protect the civilians or intercept the enemy bombers?" The captain was swiftly regretting his decision to open the door, and he gave Belford a disapproving look while he activated his AMI and contacted McKinley.

<Belford cornered me in my office, need immediate evac,> he sent.

"That flyboy is going to get someone killed. He didn't even destroy any of the enemy, okay?"

"Lieutenant Barkhorn is the only squadron leader who brought back all his pilots and ships. And their flight logs clearly show they had several confirmed kills. I fail to see how that is criteria for discipline."

"They must have altered the logs. He's always toying with the ships."

"Assisting the overworked repair crews with the complicated prototype fighters?" Johnston corrected.

"You don't understand, um, he's a dangerous..."

"Commander, that is enough. We will not diminish this ship's morale with an investigation or discipline. Am I clear on this?"

"Sir, he is already ruining the morale of the troops. His squadron is full of wildcard pilots who don't follow orders. He used a, uh, command override during the battle."

Now that was interesting. Johnston knew the lieutenant was against tech reliance. He was the only officer aboard the ship who wore an actual cloth uniform, not just the more convenient holocammies like the rest of the fleet. Not to mention his "dog," which the admiral had turned a blind eye to.

He would have to look into that; it was out of character for the lieutenant. Still, Johnston wondered why McKinley hadn't summoned him yet and broken up the unwanted conversation. His XO was the only person on the ship he could lean on, and he knew all too well the problems Belford created.

"Captain to the bridge, captain to the bridge."

Finally, Johnston thought. "This conversation is over," he said to Belford. "You will take no action against the lieutenant." Johnston stood, forcing the commander to do the same, and left his ready room. The bridge was a short walk down the corridor and had an emergency bulkhead door that would only permit one person through at a time, thus preventing the commander from continuing his conversation without talking to the captain's back.

Johnston stepped through the hatch onto his bridge, and was pleased to see none of the chaos he had walked into hours before. Though he had not expected more difficulties, it was always a relief to see the calm and conserved bridge crew going about their tasks to keep the ship operational.

McKinley was standing at his own command console, his brow creased. With everyone engaged in their tasks, it took a few moments for the captain to be noticed, and he was able to step up to his XO without the bridge coming to attention.

"Thank you for the assist," he said.

The XO jumped, twisting around to see the nearly seven-foot captain standing behind him. "Jesus, sir!" Then he took a deep breath and shouted, "Captain on deck."

"At ease," Johnston called before most of the crew could take to their feet.

"How do you manage that?" McKinley asked him.

"A captain knows his ship," Johnston said conspiratorially. "Still, though, it took you a little longer than usual to pull me out."

"Sir?"

"Belford cornered me in his office. You found a reason to call me to the bridge?"

"Negative, sir, we had a pigeon from our recon unit on Aberdeen. The research colony there is under attack. They are requesting reinforcements."

Johnston's mood went from jovial to serious in a heartbeat. "Gather the officers. Download all the data to my com unit."

"Already done."

"When it rains it pours."

Chapter 15

Ele

She woke in an unfamiliar room, in a bed with white sheets. A machine was bleating behind her, a rhythmic chime that made her feel sick inside, though she did not know why. Above her was a dull gray metal ceiling crisscrossed with beams and wiring. She pushed herself up on the bed.

"You're awake," a voice beside her said. She turned, fearful that it would be one of the men in white. Then the memory was gone, and only the fear remained.

The man who had spoken was handsome, with piercing blue eyes and brown hair cut close around his ears. He wore a military uniform, and had a chest full of medals. He was smiling. The fear evaporated.

"We were worried about you, Ele," he said.

"Ele? Is that my name?"

"You don't know your name? It said E-L-E on the uniform you were wearing."

"I... I don't remember anything," she admitted. "Do I know you?"

"My name is Lieutenant Vincent Barkhorn. You can call me Vincent. I found you on the planet."

"Vincent," she whispered. "I remember seeing you. I recognized you though."

Vincent scowled. "You probably saw the posters. They put them up everywhere."

"Oh." She couldn't remember if that was the case. "I was afraid I would hurt you."

"Hurt me? How would you hurt me?"

"The fire, the lake, it boiled away when I touched it. I caused the fire."

Vincent raised an eyebrow. "Caused the fire? How? The lake boiled because my ship crashed into it."

Could that be true? She was convinced that she had made the heat, but another part of her knew that was insane. Could she have imagined it all?

"I couldn't feel anything. I wasn't burnt."

He smiled again. It was a kind smile, though — a trustworthy smile. He reached over, slowly, as if she would pull away, and moved the sheet from her shoulder. She looked down and her eyes widened. Her skin was pink beneath the sheet, and as soon as the sheet passed over, she felt the sting of the burn. She really had imagined it.

"How bad is it?" she asked.

"You were very lucky, it's like a bad sunburn." He lifted a mirror off the table beside him and showed it to her. The face in the reflection was a stranger's. Long brown hair framed her face, with brown eyes to match. *That's me? What did they do to me? Why can't I remember?*

"You don't remember anything?"

"No."

"You're probably just in shock. You must have had a terrible time down there."

"You saved me?" she asked.

Vincent rubbed his hand across his neck. "It was more luck than anything. I was sort of crashing."

Chapter 16

Vincent

Vincent found himself feeling out of place. He had been forced to come to med bay, and been prodded and scanned in every way possible before the blasted corpsman had admitted that nothing was wrong. He seemed surprised by it, but Vincent wasn't. His ship was mostly intact; you could barely tell he had crashed. When he saw that the girl he had saved was waking up, he wandered over, and hadn't really thought any further than that.

So he found himself in a conversation he felt like he maybe shouldn't have been in, and thought maybe that corpsman should be examining her. The poor girl was probably in shock, spouting off all sorts of wild ideas, like that she had started a fire that could be seen from space. She seemed genuinely concerned about it.

Weirdest thing was, he remembered rescuing a red head down on the planet. But this was definitely a brunette lying on the cot, and there weren't any other pretty civilians lying in the sick bay. The fires and the "emergency landing" must have thrown him off.

"Where are we?" she asked.

"On a ship called *Inferno*. Like that poem," he explained, then wondered if that was supposed to be classified. She was an experimental new ship, but they'd also painted the name in forty-foot letters along the side.

"A ship? So we left that planet?"

"Yeah, I found you at a lake. You must have been running from the fire. I'm sure your memory will come back to you."

"Why don't I remember anything?"

"I think I can field that question." The corpsman had finally arrived. Vincent stood up from the seat beside the bed and moved back.

"I'll come check on you later, okay?" Vincent said without thinking. She smiled at him. *Slag, she's pretty.*

"I have it from here, flyboy." The corpsman pushed him towards the door. Anyone else and Vincent would have said something, but corpsmen could get away with talking to an officer like that. They were arrogant, but completely necessary, and untouchable. Vincent barely heard him as he was ushered out of the med bay.

He was halfway back to the hangar before he even thought about where he was going. He shook his head. Why was he so distracted? Then he felt a wave of guilt; it had been a long time since he thought of his father or Rodrom. He still hadn't written that eulogy.

He didn't have the luxury of time to grieve, though; he needed to get back to his fighter and start repairs. Otherwise the mechanics would start on it, and who knew what sort of damage they could cause in the short time he was away. He picked up the pace, nearly running as he hopped through the emergency bulkhead doors. Hopefully Rover had kept the mechanics away. He would try and sort out the stuff in his head when everything else settled down.

Chapter 17

The Exile

The Exile had no trouble hiding in the vast ship named *Inferno*. The crew stayed in the main corridors, or in the rooms they connected, never straying into the maze of subcorridors that led everywhere, where wires and ducts connected the various systems. These engineering crawlspaces were used almost exclusively by droids, and they didn't notice her.

Crawling with only one arm proved a challenge. And though it would have been far easier to draw her Shell for support, the Exile steadfastly refused to be limited by her disfigurement.

Her Shell looked more and more promising as she continued, as the ship was absolutely filled with unsecured AMI units, and it felt as though she were hiding in a concert hall full of people screaming.

Each presence, each unimportant passing thought was like a gunshot through her mind. An overbearing cacophony that caused her to become disoriented. So many people on the ship so woefully unaware of what they were doing. She tried to hold her Web tighter, but the pressure was too strong, and the crawlspace was oppressively small. The tiny space seemed to close in on her as she lost herself to the Web.

The duct she was in opened further ahead into one of the human waste rooms. A momentary release of her tightly held Web to probe inside revealed no one was beyond the vent, and she kicked out the metal between her and the room and slipped inside. Once she was through the hatch, she locked the door and concentrated on drawing in her sense of self once more. With so many errant thoughts crowding into her mind, it was difficult to know which were hers.

With her back turned to the door, she slid to the floor. Her horn shuddered beneath her hand when she reached up to rub her head. She released it to pull her knife from its sheath on her back, and once she pulled out the blade, she ran her finger over the edge. As her nerves called out in protest against the cut, and she lost herself in the physical pain and the power of the Shadow, she was able to shut out the voices that screamed loudest in her mind. She allowed herself only a moment's reprieve, however, before slipping the knife, and the Shadow, away.

Drawing herself off the floor with a grimace, she moved to the sink across the room. She reached out and twisted the handle to fill the basin with chilled water. A sigh escaped her nose as she dipped her hand into the cool water and splashed it across her face. Looking up, she examined herself in the mirror. Again, she wondered how humans could find themselves attracted to such trivial details. If she squinted, she was able to make out the litany of old scars crisscrossing her skin. The green lines barely stood out against the natural blue of her skin. They traced her exposed neck and face, and as she stared at them, she thought of the wounds that had caused them.

A calm center, a clear mind, the Exile thought, knowing the undercurrent of anger would never leave her mind clear. She sighed again, dipping her hand into the water. She concentrated on her fingers, on the palm of her hand, and on the feeling of the cold water moving across it. She extended her effort, and in a feeling quite unlike any of her other abilities, she willed the water from the basin into a floating ball, creating a rough sphere of rolling liquid that connected to the sink only by a thin thread of water. She looked over the creation, feeling the smallest drop of contentment as her strange power created a swirl of mini currents.

"What a useless parlor trick," came a voice from behind her. Her concentration wavered and the water splashed down across the porcelain and onto her. The Exile whirled around.

Standing in the corner beneath a flickering light was a shadowed androgynous figure, its features further obscured by the changing light. Two squinted eyes glowed vibrantly, bright yellow holes that bored into the Exile.

She shuddered, and cast out her Web to touch the new arrival's mind so that she could communicate with it. She pulled out the knife as she did. Her fingers burned when they touched the obsidian crystal. When the connection was made, a sharp agony coursed through her like lightning and she dropped to a knee. How had the Shadow taken form with so little of her blood?

"Now there's the proper greeting for your master," it purred. Exile fought the urge to retaliate. Despite the pain both in her mind and arm, Exile again cast out her Web to take a tentative hold on the fringes of the monster's thoughts. There was no AMI unit, of course, but the knife made communication possible. Once contact was made, Exile placed a thought into the connection. The Shadow would hear it in whatever passed for its mind.

<How have you formed? I did not give you energy,> Exile pushed, still grimacing. The longer she stayed connected, the longer it would

burn.

"You have no idea the depth of my power. Soon I will have no need of you, and this partnership will end," the Shadow drawled, its voice undulating.

<*I could destroy your crystal. What do you think would happen then? How long until you are able to re-form on this plane?*> Exile allowed some of her anger into the thought; it helped dull the pain of the connection.

The Shadow's vibrant eyes closed for a moment as the figure stepped further from the corner. Light touched the creature, and a hint of red skin traced with swirling black tattoos blended in and out of the shadows. Smoke rolled up from wherever the light touched, lingering in a growing cloud around the ceiling, further obscuring the room.

"Do you not require the power I give you? Am I so easy to cast aside? You were cast out from your people. I am your only friend." The Shadow grinned impossibly white pointed teeth.

<*You are dangerously close to overstepping your contract,*> Exile threatened.

"You are but the gatekeeper. The gateway will remain without you," the Shadow said.

Exile was tempted to be rid of the creature for good, to destroy the link that allowed them to speak, that allowed it to even take shape, but it was right. She had given up everything for that power.

<*Tell me what you know,*> she asked, then pulled back to relieve the pain.

"The minds I consumed were terrified of something down on that planet. Something they created."

<*What is it?*>

"They did not know. They only knew it was dangerous, and they were terrified this fleet would find it."

<How does this information help me?> Exile was growing tired of the Shadow's games.

"Because that which terrified them was found, and it is here on this ship." The Shadow's voice dripped with enjoyment. Then it stepped back into the corner of the room and simply stopped existing. The Exile had to blink several times to convince herself that it was actually gone. Once she was sure, she re-sheathed the dagger and took several deep breaths. She needed to find weapons. Hiding wasn't going to cut it.

Chapter 18

Johnston

Johnston stepped into the ready room and looked at the men assembled: the various captains of the other ships in his fleet, all of whom fell under his command. Most of them were not actually present; their likenesses were displayed as holograms in a rough circle around him. The only other physical presence in the room besides his own was Commander McKinley. The captains were all standing when he entered the room, and promptly saluted. Johnston returned the salute, then waved his hand so they could relax.

"Alright, gentlemen, for those of you who haven't heard the news, the Aberdeen research station has recently fallen under attack from the Verdantun."

The other captains' reactions ran the gamut from surprise to anger, and enough of them were slow enough to react that Johnston was sure the information had already made the rounds. Nothing could stop the chiefs' network.

"How did this happen?" Captain Fredricks of the *Excelsior* asked.

"The facility was built around a portal, with buildings on both the near and far sides. It seems the Verdantun massed a sizeable force against the latter," Johnston answered.

"Didn't we have forces stationed there?"

"Was this facility unguarded?"

"How could the elves get the drop on them?" Several captains tried to speak up at once. Here was the inherent problem with having everyone in their own ships, without the physical presence of the others in the room.

"The *Inferno*'s own Special Forces Unit was on station to oversee the project, as our ship has a significant stake in their research. They sent a pigeon to alert us of the danger. A nearby element of the second fleet was detached for ground support, but their ground forces are only fitted with human tech. They managed to gain a foothold, but recent intel is that the scientists working there were not killed – they were captured by the Verdantun. This has been confirmed by ground forces."

The captains started arguing again, each offering their own idea of how to reinforce and rescue the survivors. The conversation moved away from the immediate logistics that Johnston had gathered them to discuss. He cleared his throat, forcing them all to look back at him.

"We do not have the time to argue over the whys and the hows," he said. "We need to discuss our actions going forward. I have outlined a plan; however, there is more on the table than the rescue of Aberdeen."

"What information is that?" Fredricks asked, but Johnston had a feeling they all already knew.

"During the fighting, one of our fighter wings intercepted an unknown energy weapon. One that destroyed several enemy bombers and severely damaged a civilian shuttle. Our sensor techs have analyzed the data and found that the source was far-side technology."

"Magic?"

"Out here?"

"How did intel miss this?"

"At ease," Johnston called. He was swiftly regretting the meeting. He did not technically need their input. He was an admiral and they were all captains, so the entire meeting was a formality at best. In the end, the decision and the responsibility would fall to him. It was courteous, however, something he had learned in the British navy, before he had joined the Joint Fleet and been exposed to all the other military cultures, alien included.

"We do not know the origin of the weapon, but we have our analysts working on it. You all know how unpredictable the portals can be. For all we know, one opened on the planet, unleashed a fire elemental, and then closed again. I think the more likely possibility is that the Separatists have been trying to research or engineer far-side tech for themselves, and that the fire and this weapon are a result of that."

"If the weapon could damage so many, how do we know we aren't also in danger?" asked Captain Torres of the *Pride of Brazil.*

"None of the Merlins have ever displayed that sort of long-range space weaponry," Gregor of the *Roosevelt* added.

"We have already moved the fleet to a high orbit. The shuttle was thousands of meters closer to both the planet and moon, and we have no reason to suspect the fleet is in danger."

"It sounds like you don't know anything," Fredricks said.

Johnston gave him a level stare. His patience was at an end, and already he could feel the pressure mounting between his eyes. He was close to cutting off the meeting without any of their input. Fredricks was quick to back down, however.

"That is to say, sir, should we not take a more defensive stance, at least until we know more."

"Yes, that is what I have called you all here to discuss. We now have two missions, both of sizable importance. The colonists planetside still require assistance. We cannot abandon the forces we have already deployed to assist the relief efforts. We also can't ignore the attacks on Aberdeen. I have outlined the following plan: The *Inferno* will leave a contingent of fighters behind, and will use the hangar space to transport ground personnel and equipment from the ships that will remain here. We will jump to Aberdeen, secure the research facility, and rescue the colonists."

Johnston expected them to protest, but the other captains nodded with him.

"Will you be taking any escorts?" Gregor asked.

"I do not want to leave this battlegroup in a position where it cannot defend itself. Aberdeen has an orbital weapons station, so the *Inferno* will be supported in orbit. I intend to only take the military transport ship and possibly two destroyers. These are the logistics I wish to discuss."

Before the other captains could comment, the power to the hologram shorted out. Immediately, the emergency power kicked in, but the connection was lost.

The captain keyed his AMI to broadcast.

<Captain to engineering, what's going on down there?>

Johnston held up a hand to his ear to show McKinley he was speaking across the bionet.

<Engineering, sir, there was a power fluctuation somewhere near medical. It doesn't look like there's any damage to the systems, though. Something must have come loose during the fighting. I've got crews en route now, but I'll have the power... Ah, there she is.> And before he finished

speaking, the lights were back on.

Johnston keyed back an acknowledgment, and then opened a line to medical.

<Doctor Kerrigan, is everything alright down there?>

<How do you always know the second something goes wrong?> she asked.

<It's my ship.>

<Right,> she said. <Our guest, the girl from the planet. She's gone, sir.>

<Gone? How did she die?> Johnston had been under the impression she was suffering from minor burns at worst.

<Not that sort of gone, sir; gone as in disappeared. We were trying to run some routine tests and she got spooked, and when the lights turned off she vanished.>

<I'm sure the ship's systems can track her. She couldn't have gotten far.>

<She doesn't have an AMI implant, and I didn't get a chance to scan her in. Unless she passes by a classified area's camera, we'll have to find her on foot. I've already dispatched some medical drones and ensigns to start sweeping.>

When it rains... Johnston thought.

<Let me know when you find her. Johnston out.>

"Get the other captains back," he told McKinley. "The sooner we are underway the better. When did combat become the easiest part of the job? Those colonists on Aberdeen don't have time for this."

Chapter 19

Rodrom

The world beyond his operating table seemed as distant as Earth to Derek Rodrom as he worked on the alien before him. Like the guard who stood watching, the Verdantun on the table was of the feral tribe. To the untrained eye, it could almost pass as human, but its eyes were too catlike, and its face held one too many angles. Its body was of humanoid shape: two arms, two legs, a torso, and a waist, though the muscles beneath the skin revealed the truth. These minor differences were easily missed, hidden beneath a thick coat of brown- and black-streaked fur.

Rodrom stooped over the right side of a tree root that served as his table, the Verdantun draped haphazardly atop it. Above them, more roots formed a ceiling, with hard-packed dirt serving as walls, in a space just barely large enough for Rodrom to stand upright in. The "room" had nothing in the way of décor or equipment, and the space where Rodrom kept his tools, as well as the table his wounded lay upon, grew straight out of the ground.

His gaze was locked onto the shrapnel wounds that peppered

the feral's right arm and chest. With unsteady fingers, Rodrom maneuvered a pair of forceps made entirely of wood. He pushed them into the ravaged hole and twisted, attempting to create enough leverage to push past the shattered bone fragments and grasp the metal beneath. Finding purchase, he carefully pulled back, only to reveal a partial fragment that he unceremoniously dropped to the floor.

Rodrom threw down the bloodied forceps onto the makeshift tray beside him and snarled. Across from him, the guard raised an alien eyebrow in an obviously practiced human gesture, unknowingly igniting Rodrom's fury.

"How do you expect me to save these soldiers without exposing the injury?" he called, knowing the guard wouldn't comprehend the words. The alien tittered out a string of words in his nonthreatening musical language; Rodrom's ire was understood, and the guard was threatening him back to work. Not for the first time, Rodrom cursed his inability to connect to the bionet. It would take only moments to download the translator patch he needed to understand and speak the Verdantun tongue—assuming the patch existed. On this side of the portal, he would have no such luck.

"Lorelei," Rodrom spat back. Although he butchered the name with an English approximation, the guard would understand. In response, the guard revealed pointed teeth in an animalistic growl, and moved through the gap in roots to find the healer who was responsible for Rodrom's conditional work. The other scientists of the captured research facility were imprisoned in a grove at the back of the compound. Rodrom was the only human permitted any freedom, if being made to work could be considered that. Despite their alien nature, the Verdantun had still been able to recognize him as a doctor, and the healers who traveled with the war party had put him to work.

The research facility where Rodrom had been working for the last six months had been overtaken by hostile forces. An army of Verdantun had appeared without warning, seizing him, his months of research, and the other scientists as well. Joint Fleet had mounted a counter offensive, and fierce battles raged across the planet's surface as ground troops vied for control, but Rodrom remained within the forest camp. He and his colleagues had been captured for nearly two standard months, with no end in sight.

Crimson blood spilled from the wound where Rodrom had been working. He scrambled to press a handful of leaves onto the wound. Though they looked no different from the kind he saw back on Earth, no terrestrial leaf would bind to a wound the way a Verdatun's did. The wound was sealed, and whatever shrapnel he couldn't get was still trapped inside.

The other scientists called the Verdantun by the more common Fleet nickname *elves*. With their pointed ears and musical language, it wasn't too far of a stretch, but their abilities were what truly set them apart from humanity. The adhesive leaves were the least of their medicine; and some of the advanced things they did seemed impossible to Rodrom.

If one of the elves placed their hands upon a wounded person and sang, the wounds would knit themselves back together. Of course it was a result of the Verdantun coming from beyond the portals and not truly being a part of humanity's universe, but after seeing a decapitated soldier be brought back to life, it was hard for Rodrom to call it anything but magic. He constantly had to remind himself that what seemed like magic was only technology he couldn't yet comprehend.

The Verdantun beneath Rodrom shuddered as the doctor probed the other wound with gloveless fingers. The alien felt no pain due to the same magic, and Rodrom had become accustomed to his patient's irregular twitch, not that it helped the barbaric surgery. In a proper lab he would have access to his equipment, and the AMI unit within his brain would also be able to access the bionet, where he would have all the medical knowledge of generations with a simple thought. He didn't necessarily need the information, as he had enhanced his own mental faculties. But regardless of his own prowess, with such an alien species he had no point of reference, and currently felt more like a med student than a practiced surgeon.

His painfully naked fingers felt more fragments within the Verdantun's arm, but no amount of careful extraction could remove them through the tiny paths from which they had entered. Rodrom grunted in frustration, once again formulating the argument against the oppressive and detrimental rule of the Verdantuns not to use blades to open their patients' flesh. When Rodrom had suggested that he might need a scalpel blade, he had been tossed back into the prison pits with the others. At first, he assumed they feared he would use it as a weapon, but to his amazement—and horror—they never used such tools at all. They took the concept of "do no harm" to incredible lengths.

Rodrom looked up sharply from his patient at the sound of footsteps, his breath catching in his throat like it did every time. Ducking into the dim sourceless light of the chamber was the most beautiful woman he'd ever met. She was alien, without a doubt, but with graceful curves, and with her uncharacteristically soft features, she nearly looked human. Her pointed ears and catlike pupils gave her away as Verdantun, and her skin had the unbroken amber color of a non-feral elf.

The only clothing she wore seemed to be vines and foliage that grew straight out of her skin. Flora wrapped around her arms and legs, and along her torso. All the amber-skinned Verdantun wore such attire, which appeared tied to their powers.

When she spoke, it sounded as though at any moment she would burst into song, and even the harsh inadequacy of English could not blunt the beauty of her alien voice. "DerekRodrom, we have a great many warriors to attend to, why have you called me here?" she demanded.

"Lorelei, this soldier will never regain the muscles in this arm, and will probably die from the shrapnel in his chest if you do not allow me to operate," Rodrom said simply, attempting to keep emotion out of his voice. Alien or not, Rodrom refused to lose a patient over asinine rules.

"Leave us," she ordered, pointing the guard who had followed her out again. Rodrom thought for a moment that he would protest, but the Verdantun discipline held fast and the guard complied. Lorelei remained silent for several breaths, staring at Rodrom as he continued his futile efforts. "What would you have me do DerekRodrom?" she finally asked. It was the bluntest Rodrom had seen her be since coming to the camp.

As usual, his mouth moved faster than his considerable mind. "A cheeseburger would be nice, or setting me free," he muttered. He pushed another leaf onto the wound to forestall any bleeding.

Lorelei ignored his comment. "Should I step outside this tree and tell these soldiers I am allowing a human to break our code? When so many already argue against you being allowed to treat?" Lorelei held up her hand to prevent him from speaking, a gesture she had learned from Rodrom. "My personal thoughts on the matter aside, my people have done things this way since long before our war, and the words of their enemy will not sway them."

Anger overwhelmed his forced calm. "So you will let him die?

Just to maintain outdated and dangerous ideals?"

"Your own people consider us to be creatures of myth who wield forces beyond their comprehension. Yet despite what you have seen, you insist the only answer is to use your own methods to cure these men." Lorelei glanced outside the tree, then lowered her voice further. "You have a sharp mind, you could..."

Her voice was lost in the din of a massive explosion that rocked the camp. A moment later, a wolf's howl rose above the roar, and the noise within the camp shifted dramatically.

"They've broken through," Lorelei whispered. Then louder, "We must prepare to receive the wounded."

Chapter 20

The Exile

"**Look, ma'am**, I don't care if you have orders from the bloody king. I am not going to release anything without the proper forms," the human in charge of supply spat out. Between his massive bulk and offensive odor, the man maintained a putrid aura the Exile found repulsive to even briefly connect to.

To further her frustration, his thoughts were not on the papers in front of him; instead, he was busy contemplating the scores of some game. "We've got half a continent burning down planet side, and I can't just be handing out supplies to every Butterbar who walks into my armory." He used the mention of rank as an excuse to look at her lapel ranks, and then slid his eyes below them.

<*The papers are in that pile, I'm sure of it...*> she projected with emphasis only a mind connection could muster. She looked down at the ranks pinned on the man's lapel and cursed herself for not remembering their meaning. He caught her glance and the rank bubbled to the forefront of his thoughts. <*...Chief,*> she finished.

The man glanced down at the papers in front of him, his mind turning. He knew she was probably right; the papers hadn't moved in over a month, and if she pulled his superior, he was going to have his work cut out for him. He looked up again and after running his eyes down her frame one last time, sighed and said, "I suppose a medium will suffice, Lieutenant." The last word he spit out, as if calling her anything other than an insult brought a sour taste to his mouth.

<Yes, that will be fine.> Exile waited as the man moved from his desk and stepped over to place his thumb on a door lock behind him. It chimed, and the hatch beside it swung open to reveal a room filled with supplies.

Before he could turn back toward her, the Exile reached out and touched the forefinger of her left hand to the base of his neck. Her connection to him flared and she sent a mental blast through the man's synapses. As he slipped to the floor, she grabbed him and awkwardly pushed him into his chair. She took a moment to prop him against the desk, so it appeared as though he had only fallen asleep. A moment's search through the desk resulted in a bottle of hard liquor, which she pushed into his hand.

Another touch—to his forehead this time—and Exile delved deeper through the AMI into his mind. She found the memory of their encounter and destroyed it, erasing her presence completely. She added some muddled thoughts to fill the space for good measure.

Her trail effectively covered, she stepped past him into the room beyond.

The bile rose in her as she stepped away from him. At her back, the dagger was pulsing with enjoyment. Any suffering, however slight, fueled the monster within.

The Exile found herself in a storage room with the walls

separated by dividers; one section was devoted to racks of the holographic uniforms worn by the naval personnel, and the other to various equipment. A generator sat back against the wall where the suits were given their initial charge. Exile quickly stripped out of her simple traveling gear and tossed it onto the ground, then grabbed one of the uncharged uniforms, which was nothing more than a gray silken lump, and placed it inside the generator. The machine thrummed, a green light sparked, and a test hologram shifted across the fabric's surface before it reverted back to blank.

She had first begun her infiltration of the fleet ten standard years ago, whole of body and ready to serve her people's agenda. She did not need to hide her face or features, as her people were falsely considered to be members in good standing with the fleet. However, finding the appropriate role had taken practice. Low-ranking enlisted members were easily ignored but often questioned as to their movements, and the higher ranking enlisted were often given piles of work to occupy any free time. High-ranking officers were too few in number to go unnoticed. None made for adequate infiltration roles. The lowest of the office corp, however—the second lieutenants—went unnoticed and ignored. They held enough rank to go unquestioned by any enlisted soldier, and not enough rank to mean anything to other officers. As a spec ops officer, she would be completely invisible, as well as untouchable. A ghost.

It had taken her more than one nearly failed mission to realize this, but with failure came knowledge. She only had to program the uniform to display the appropriate rank and insignia. The humans used AMI units to do this work, of course, but despite her ability to interface with and control them, she had no artificial intelligence of her own. It was no problem, however. Humans were redundant creatures.

Her gaze fell on a small space on the wall that was devoid of any equipment. She stepped over to it and touched the empty space. A slit appeared, and a keyboard slid out before her. The blank space flickered and then a screen appeared with the symbol of an eagle with its wings spread out over a spaceship. The words "Joint Fleet" were inscribed below it.

She used holographic keys to flip through the different items until the desired object appeared: the multipurpose unit, a wrist-mounted device that would accept oral commands, but in the case of an emergency, could be controlled by touch. Exile looked down at where her right arm had once been and shook her head.

She looked to the shelf the inventory listed. She found several roles of tape. After another three minutes of searching she spotted a bank of drawers labeled "M.P.U." Exile's horn ached with frustration. How could the conclave deem humans so important when even simple things were beyond them.

She pulled one of the devices from the drawer and looked it over. It was larger than a wristwatch, about half the size of her forearm. Most of its length was taken up by a projector that would display a holographic screen and controls, and underneath was a slot where a battery would go. More hunting and she found the batteries half a room away from the units, and once she plugged one in, the holographic screen blossomed outward.

"Multipurpose unit operational and ready. What devices will you synchronize?" the unit intoned.

Exile set the unit down on the shelf. She concentrated on her lost arm, and after a moment, a shimmer of blue emerged from the metal cap below her shoulder and coalesced into the shape of a forearm, then wrist, hand, and fingers. She used the spectral fingers to lift the device and place it on her true arm, fastening it in place. It had taken a lot of effort to draw her Shell. Too much effort. She had trained with these abilities all her life, as all Psykin did, and her affinity for Web work was no excuse.

Centering herself again, the Exile used her ethereal hand to tap out controls on the MPU to connect to the uniform she'd pulled out earlier. As she touched the holographic keys, the suit before her came alive, shifting colors as it activated. It imitated her hand and the floor beneath, then the cabinet behind her as she lifted it. Another key tap and it became a basic lieutenant's uniform. Exile slipped it on and looked herself over. She tapped a few more keys to let out the seams at the stomach so it hung looser around her figure. *Let them stare now*, she thought.

The lights across the room cut out, and Exile was left in total darkness. She collapsed to her knees. If the ship had been wounded enough to lose power, then the vacuum would get to her. She would be lost in the endless void. The walls started to pull closer.

Almost immediately, the lights came back on, and the Shadow pulsed with contempt for her weakness. Or was that her own self-loathing she was feeling? She pushed herself to her feet. It was best not to think about it.

Along another wall were racks of gear, including various types of rucksacks. One was a light weight version made of collapsible mesh that could expand to an enormous size. Exile lifted one off the wall and pulled at the straps to open it. She tossed in her old set of clothes, then walked over to the wall and pulled down three more of the uniforms, and tossed those into the bottom of the bag as well. After the uniforms went a backup communicator, four multipurpose unit batteries, and a holographic balaclava. Then she spotted the lock at the back of the room.

It was set into a thick door, and made of a kind of metal composite. She couldn't sense anyone behind the door, which she knew led to an armory. She looked over it for a moment and bent to examine the keypad. With a glance back to the still unconscious guard, she lifted her hand to the handle and pressed against the mechanism. With the same will she had used to lift the ball of water, she reached out and clicked the mechanism free from within. The door swung freely on well-maintained hinges, exposing a brightly lit armory. Within it were rows upon rows of advanced weaponry. Stacks of standard infantry Gauss rifles with high-powered scopes, miniature grenade launchers, rail-gun sniper rifles, and crew-served laser weapons were all stored neatly before her.

It was a room full of brand new weapons—not ones she had taken from a downed adversary, or that she'd rebuilt herself from parts. For once she would be able to arm herself in the manner she saw fit.

She stepped inside and lifted a weapons rig from the wall. It was made of similar material to the rucksack. She pulled it over her shoulders and fastened the straps around her waist and legs. Next she grabbed two handguns and holsters and placed them on her hips. The guns remained visible on her uniform, so she called forth her spectral hand and keyed another command into her MPU, and the guns vanished beneath the hologram. She grabbed one of the sniper rifles that folded down into a convenient size, then strapped it to her back. Finally, she added a belt of grenades and a Gauss rifle to her mobile armory and rolled her shoulders to test the weight. The familiar weight of heavy weapon's was more a comfort than anything she had found so far.

Beneath each type of weapon was a crate of ammo. The rail gun's ammo was the lightest—small blocks of metal that, when fired, would shave off a sliver and accelerate to a fraction of the speed of light. The Gauss rifle was the heaviest as it used pre-shaped rounds that were accelerated by rotating magnets. Regardless, she still grabbed several magazines and clipped them to the magnetized bolts on her rig. Then she grabbed a half-dozen handgun battery packs to power the miniature blasters.

Once all her ammo was in place and the weapons were slung tightly across her body, she coded a command into the MPU. All of the weapons shifted in color to blend in with the surroundings. They wouldn't be completely invisible, but they would certainly draw less attention than walking around with more weapons than a frigate.

She took a last look around the weapons room and with a slight sense of longing stepped out of the door, slung the rucksack over her shoulders, and walked back out into the room where the guard lay slumped. She shook her head. Things were so much easier on her own.

With the MPU linked to the ship's communication net, Exile was able to quickly download a map of the station. A few more commands allowed her to begin searching for the *Inferno*'s destination. *Human security never ceases to impress*, she thought. Within hours, she would infiltrate their ranks once again.

Chapter 21

Vincent

Vincent ran a hand across the rag on his belt, leaving a trail of grease. A similar streak darkened his brow. He straddled the portside wing of his fighter, the engine laid bare before him, as he tried to repair the damage the junior tech had left for him.

"I'm going to need more copper wire, Rover," Vincent muttered. A cheerful bark acknowledged him. Vincent glanced down to where the bot was sitting with its nose pushed into the toolbox. After a moment it sat back with the wire seemingly attached to the end of its nose. Vincent rolled his eyes.

Vincent had put the mechanics in a tough spot, though he would never admit it to them. By reattaching the armor with a plasma torch and then reheating it at reentry, the repair crews had been forced to spend hours stripping away the outer layer of metal and laying the pieces again. On a Falcon it would have been a simple fix, but the Chimera and its shifting parts made for difficult work. The mechanic's inexperience with the ship, coupled with the complicated procedure, left for an agonizingly long strip job.

Vincent was able to hold back his comments and ire during the initial strip job, as it was a tough thing for even the most inexperienced mechanic to botch. The moment the rebuilding began, however, Vincent was pulled from the flight deck by his pilots with threats of bodily harm and several choice curses echoing in his wake.

He was unable to change the senior chief's decision, so Vincent adopted a routine. The junior would fix this or that, often causing several extra hours of work with each new "repair," and then Vincent would come down during third watch to correct the damage. Between him and Rover, they were well on their way to bringing the fighter back to her usual self, and if Vincent was able to add a few personal modifications while he had her stripped down, so much the better.

Rover skittered up the side of the ship and dropped the bundle of wire in front of Vincent. He cut off a piece one-third of a meter long before reaching back into the engine, and started splicing his new length in. Once the copper was entwined with the severed end, he pulled another tool from his pocket and spread a fast-hardening insulator gel over the entire job. He moved the wires back to their mounting, and spread the gel liberally along that as well, to insulate against the EMP bursts and radiation his ship so often endured.

"As I live and breathe. Is that our kapitan working with a robot?" a deep voice exclaimed from behind Vincent.

"I fancy it is," came a second.

"Is that the sound of someone volunteering for scoring detail? I'm sure Tanker would love the company," Vincent replied over their laughter.

Pilots Tesla and Forge passed beneath him into view. Despite having served with Tesla on a multispecies ship for nearly six months,

Vincent bristled when he saw the diminutive Grelkin.

Like any Grelkin — or gnome, as the fleet liked to call them — Tesla looked more or less like a man, only significantly shorter. He came in at just under a meter tall, and the only other big differences were his oversized head and the extra fingers and thumb on each hand. In general, he had a frail appearance that all his people shared, and as always, he had on his goggles. The massive black lenses hid nocturnal eyes that couldn't even stand the hangar's artificial light. The goggles also helped distract from his lack of a nose. Gnomes smelled from their ears, though Vincent wondered if Tesla was lying about that.

Tesla's real name was a series of gestures the gnomes used when interacting with their own. Upon his arrival on Earth, however, he had adopted the name Franklin Faraday. One of the more history-savvy members of the squadron had deemed the call sign "Tesla" most appropriate.

"You might want wipe your face, sir. Lord knows how expensive space grease is," said Forge.

He was the gnome's polar opposite: seven feet tall, and his skin was a dark brown from years of exposure to roaring fires, which contrasted with Tesla's pale white complexion. Yuriy "Forge" Kovalchuk had earned his moniker because his family had owned and operated a colonial-style working museum, where Forge had been a blacksmith before the war pulled him in.

Tesla punched Forge behind the knee — it was the highest he could reach. "Why would you go and ruin the fun?"

Vincent sighed. "Forge? What is on your back?"

"It is uniform. I do not understand joke."

"Rover, help him out."

The bot skittered back down the ship to behind Forge. It lifted one of its front claws and telescoped up to snatch something from his back. It held up a paper sign with the words "Kick me" written on it.

"By the void. Really, Tesla?"

"It's a classic!"

"How many times do I have to tell you two to stop the pranks?"

"We didn't mean no harm, sir. Just foolin' is all." Tesla gave a big smile to reinforce his desire to avoid the scoring detail he'd already been threatened with. Somehow, after living with human's for twenty years, the gnomes still spoke a mish-mash of English from across every generation since the invention of the radio.

The lights across the bay dimmed and then switched off, and several yells of surprise and grunts of pain rang out in the second before the emergency lights came on. The gentle hum that sailors learned to ignore hadn't stopped, so Vincent knew the Inferno's engines were still active.

"What happened?" Tesla wondered aloud.

"We have lost power," Forge offered.

"No shit, Sherlock."

"Who?"

"Read a book."

Before the two finished arguing, the lights came back on.

"Someone must not have paid the antimatter bill," Tesla quipped.

Forged slapped him lightly on the back of his head. "Anyway, sir, we thought you might need help getting her back operational," he said to Vincent, patting the fuselage. "They are saying word that we are to be redeployed."

Vincent leaned back and cocked an eyebrow. "Heard that through the chiefs' network?"

Forge grinned, then made a forced stoic expression. "Nyet, sir. No such breach of OPSEC exists. Although if it did..."

Vincent sighed, knowing he shouldn't indulge. "Go on."

"A major elf offensive. We're being re-tasked for support."

Vincent rubbed his chin, unknowingly smearing more grease on his face. "That would be preferable to this LRRP mission," he mused, referencing the ground forces term for deep reconnaissance. *Not that Belford would deploy the Reapers anywhere intuitive.*

"So we thought you might... What is expression? Let loose the reins and let us help you get ship fixed," Forge pressed.

Vincent paused, weighing the options. On the one hand, they were working with a rumor, and he already had to deal with one set of unwanted hands on his work. Forge and Tesla were no strangers to Chimera ship repair, however — almost all of his eleven test pilots had come from a background in mechanics, just as Vincent himself did. The Chimeras had a tendency to break, and it made sense to cross-train the pilots.

Vincent admonished himself for allowing personal desires to get in the way of his mission. He might have only been a squadron commander for a few months, but he was determined not to make such rookie mistakes — not after the example his father had set.

He pulled his multitool from the pouch on his belt and ran his fingers over the engraving along the side as he nodded and gestured for the two pilots to join him. Forge unceremoniously grabbed Tesla by the back of his uniform and hoisted him onto the wing opposite Vincent, and while Tesla examined the patch job, Forge dug into the toolbox. Each item he cast aside was a toy in his massive hands. Not for the first time, Vincent seriously wondered if Forge had been a part of the Beserker Project.

"Boy Howdy, boss, you've got a swell number of modifications in here," Tesla called out from inside a panel.

"Nyet. Be less loud," Forge snapped, throwing a wrench at him. Tesla snatched it before it struck his oversized head. "The kapitan is knowing more about these ships run than anyone. If he swallows distaste long enough to fix something, that something needs fixing."

Vincent choose to remain silent. Anything he said would make its rounds through the squadron. It was well-known that Vincent was no admirer of complicated technology, as he was just old enough to remember a pre-contact earth. Fortunately repairing a spacecraft, no matter how complicated, still involved wrenches and grease. The grease might have been exponentially more chemically complicated and expensive, and the wrenches might have had computers that ensured the proper torque, but it came down to wrenches and grease all the same.

"Sorry about that, boss. I didn't mean to... blow... Uh, who is that?" the gnome asked.

Vincent and Forge turned.

"That is example of prime striking," Forge rumbled.

"What?"

"You know, strike when iron is hot. Because she is... never mind."

Vincent craned his neck as Ele walked into his view.

Chapter 22

Ele

Ele was unsure exactly how she had stumbled into the large room filled with little ships, nor could she figure out why all the orange-suited people were staring at her. She was wearing a uniform the same as theirs — the doctor had called it cammies — so she didn't think she should have stood out. It seemed a little tight, like a second skin, but still. Her memory was still patchy, though. She just wished she had some clue about what had happened.

"Ele?" a voice called out to her.

She turned and saw Vincent sitting on one of the many ships. Ele hurried to him.

"What are you doing here?" he asked her.

One of the men with him was smiling at her. Vincent grasped the side of his ship with one hand and hung down before dropping to the floor. He was a lot taller than she remembered.

"Ele, why isn't your hologram on?" He sounded concerned. She didn't know what he meant. He looked her up and down, then his face turned red. "Your AMI turns on the suit to hide your, uh... to show a uniform."

"Humans are always so testy about modesty." The tiny man—a grelkin? Ele couldn't remember—said.

She looked down at the uniform. It was very tight, and looking at the other women working she could see that theirs were much baggier, distracting from their bodies. Ele wondered why the doctor hadn't told her.

"Who's Amy?" The man beside Vincent threw back his head and laughed.

"Slag. Rover, help her out before Forge's head explodes."

The other man looked away. "I am not the only one who is seeing." He laughed.

There was a loud bark, and an animal came trotting towards Ele. She knelt down to pet it. Halfway down she wondered where she had gotten that impulse, but the...dog didn't seem to mind. It's tongue rolled out of the side of its mouth as she reached for its head, and then her hand passed right through it.

She pulled back and landed on her backside with a yelp. Vincent slapped a hand to his face. "Hologram off, Rover."

The animal grew fuzzy, and then it was gone. A metal creature sat in its place.

"Sorry, Ele, this is just Rover, my droid. He won't hurt you. I promise."

The droid lifted one of his legs toward her, and a small wire poked out. She lifted her right arm tentatively, and when the wire touched her suit, it sparked slightly. She pulled back again, but only a little, and let the droid do whatever it was Vincent had told it to do. After a few seconds, the suit she wore became fuzzy like the droid, and then a blank, much bulkier uniform appeared in its place. It didn't feel any different, though. Ele felt her cheeks warm.

"How did you get in here?" Vincent asked again.

Ele shrugged, and the fake uniform moved with her. "I don't remember. The doctor told me I might have short-term memory loss from a concussion."

"Did you cut your hair?" He had a confused look on his face.

"No?" She reached up to touch it. It was hanging down to her shoulders, with tufts sticking up randomly.

"I could have sworn..."

"Smooth, sir," the grelkin said.

"Scoring detail," Vincent snapped, and then he touched his hand to his ear and looked down.

"Vape it all, I have to go to a briefing. Tesla, Forge, you two make sure she gets back to medical. Ele, I'll come check on you later, okay? Sorry to run off." And then he did just that.

Ele looked over at the other two, who were smiling at Vincent's retreating back.

"So, you're Ele, huh?" said Tesla. "How did you and Lieutenant... I mean Vincent, meet?"

Chapter 23

Rodrom

The sounds of battle echoed around Rodrom. The guard at the entrance was shouting out orders, though even in his distress, he sounded like he was singing. Lorelei fired off a reply before running out just as two more of the elves moved in. The two newcomers grabbed the wounded off the table, supporting him between them. The first guard roughly grabbed hold of Rodrom, and in the confusion, forgot the hood Rodrom had been forced to wear during every other move. Relieved to finally see beyond the root walls of his prison, Rodrom drank in the details.

The "camp" beyond the walls he had spent months staring at looked more like a forest park than a military compound. Massive trees with raised twisted roots stretched as far as he could see; they all had openings like the one he had just left. Between the trees was a flurry of activity as the elves responded to whatever Joint Fleet force had broken through. Amber-skinned elves sprinted by in their humanoid forms, some helping the wounded, others moving toward the chaos with weapons and supplies. Perverse versions of Earth animals — the feral elves — moved across the camp as well. An impossibly large bear covered in what looked like natural bone armor thundered between trunks smaller than its legs; a porcupine with forearm-thick spines along its back scampered low to the ground; and a bull with midnight-black horns growing from both its shoulders as well as its head charged forward.

Rodrom knew the animals to be the same species as the alien he had just been working to save; their "magic" gave them the ability to shapeshift into immensely powerful analogs of once unremarkable creatures from his home planet. Of all the strange abilities he had witnessed, this type of transformation disturbed him the most. Being reminded of what happened to earth, seeing the animal's he had grown up knowing twisted into weapons. Horrible.

Rodrom looked away deliberately; he would be a fool not to take advantage of this chance to see the camp's layout. He wasn't just distracting himself He mentally alerted his AMI to store anything his organic memory didn't capture in the unit's storage, and methodically looked around the camp to draw a mental map. It didn't look very impressive compared to the technology-heavy colonies or ships that human's lived in post-contact. Even the more mundane human designed equipment was a far cry from the trunks and roots that filled the muddy clearing

Between the trees, smoke clouds billowed; Rodrom assumed this location was their version of a forge. They didn't use metals in their armor or weapons, but favored crystal, as well as what seemed to be impossibly dense wood. What sort of process went into repairing crystal swords? And how did they maintain any sort of forge fire inside a tree? Rodrom tore his eyes away from the smoke clouds. There was no time to contemplate these questions.

Another explosion buffeted the air above him and he staggered down into the mud. His guard kept on his feet, and dug sharp nails into Rodrom's bicep as he jerked Rodrom upright. The guard's eyes had glazed over; the beast inside him was clawing its way out. From the color of the guard's downy fur, Rodrom knew his bestial side was a wolf—all speed and savagery. The wolf-guard pulled Rodrom harder, gesturing towards the rear of the camp, away from fighting. His fingernails were sharpening into black claws. Rodrom knew he was running out of time.

Chapter 24

Vincent

Vincent jogged out of the bay. The message that had pulled him away from his ship was as follows: <*Priority transmission from Commander Belford; All squadron commanders are to report at their convenience to the briefing room for an operations order.*>

"At their convenience" usually meant "Drop whatever you are doing," so Vincent hurried back to his room to strip away his coveralls. The same mechanism that deployed his nano-suit would scrub away the "space grease" and whatever other contaminates he had picked up during repairs, and recycle them back into use. The grease was expensive enough to warrant it.

Vincent pulled a set of holocammies from his footlocker. Normally when he attended briefings or the officers' mess, he chose to wear a legitimate cotton and polyester uniform he had obtained for no small price. While there was no regulation against wearing actual fabric, most of the fleet chose to don the far more comfortable and practical holographic uniform, which could display any image the user chose. The uncomfortable collars and hours of measuring were a part of wearing the uniform though, one that Vincent refused to let go the way of earth.

Slipping on the holocammies, he keyed for one wall of the room to become a mirror while he projected his uniform in his mind's eye. His AMI generated a perfect copy of the United North American Air Force dress uniform, with all the medals and flair. Wearing full dress uniforms onboard a ship had always been far too great a hassle, but the brass liked to show now that it was as simple as slipping on an image. But since the AMI generated the uniform precisely to the personnel file specs kept on the bionet, it was no longer up to Vincent which medals he displayed. His chest looked like a furball, all chaos and color. It felt wrong to display every medal he had been handed throughout the war. Medal meant less than the hologram they were made of if the man wearing them didn't truly earn them.

Vincent stepped out of his room to a shared latrine down the corridor, where he quickly relieved himself; he wouldn't have a chance once the briefing started. He washed the small smear of grease off his forehead and chin, then examined himself in the mirror. He gave a satisfied grunt. *Good enough for government work.*

He exited the head and made his way toward the elevators. The briefing room was toward the front of the main ship; the only connection between it and the flight deck sphere was two decks above him. The sphere that encased the five docking rings only connected to the main ship across four decks. It was designed to be detached from the main prow of the ship, allowing the carrier portion to deploy and recover fighters as a stationary base, while the forward portion of the ship maneuvered. In practice, the feature had never been implemented; the naval officers continued to treat the ship like a carrier from the days of the wet Navy.

Inside the lift, Vincent keyed in his officer override code. The other officers would arrive as they normally did, in dribs and drabs. But Vincent and Flight Commander Belford had had one too many arguments for Vincent to arrive anything but early.

As he moved down the length of the super carrier, Vincent allowed his AMI to download and unpack the critical mission brief document he would need to have read before the briefing. The entire conference could have been done telepathically, but tradition was tradition, and Belford struggled to prove he was in charge without lording it over the pilots.

Vincent's lift stopped halfway through its journey to admit two Vapefalcon pilots. Both wore the uniforms of the Britannic Union. They nodded politely to Vincent, then resumed their heated conversation.

"How in the bloody hell could you think we're diverting to anything but combat?" the blonde-haired lieutenant said. "We've been taking on ground troops, 'aven't we?"

"Oh, shove off. What sort of fight would the JFC jump a super carrier to without her escorts?" the second junior-grade lieutenant, this one a brunette, countered. "Besides, they never send us anywhere important anyway. We're basically an R&D ship at this point." Both pilots glanced at Vincent; they knew which squadron he commanded.

Vincent couldn't help but agree. Despite his pilots' victories, the Joint Fleet Command was reluctant to send an experimental super carrier with mixed crew armed with prototype fighters anywhere critical. Vincent made no move to comment, however, and before the awkward moment stretched on too long, the lift stopped and opened onto a corridor. Both pilots were quick to exit, Vincent a few steps behind. The lift exit was only a few meters from the chamber where they were congregating.

As with any starship, space was at a premium, and the designers of any military vessel would have a lot of people to answer to if they designed an amphitheater-style room for the sole purpose of briefing. As such, they now gathered in a multipurpose room that could be reconfigured for use as a zero-gravity training room, gym, storage, and for other purposes. Today, the weight sets and equipment had been moved aside, and several benches had been arranged in a ring around a holographic projector.

Vincent took one of the seats closest to the projector. He might not have been well liked by the commander, but that didn't mean he had to hide. He glanced around the room. All of the other squadron leaders were human, though they wore different uniforms. Despite Joint Fleet's success at combining the nationalities on warships, Vincent's was the only squadron on the *Inferno* with a mixed-species crew. Eventually the Fleet would need to adopt a standardized dress uniform, but everyone was reluctant to accept that the fleet was anything but temporary.

Vincent turned back toward the projector and tried to focus on the mission at hand. It was only a few minutes before Belford himself entered the chamber, and all the pilots rose immediately to the cry of "Attention!"

Belford didn't just enter — he sauntered. A grin was plastered across his sagging face as he stepped up to the podium.

He remained silent for a few moments, the grin stretching wider as he looked around at the men standing rigid before him. Finally, he said, "At ease," in a tone dripping with arrogance.

"I can't help but notice how well our Falcon pilots did during the last battle," he began. "I was one of the first to pilot that craft, you know." He slurred a little at the end of each sentence, like he was chewing on the words instead of speaking them. "So I take it as a personal, ah, accomplishment when my pilots do so well."

Eight Falcons had been lost in the last battle. The after-action report had shown that Belford was forcing them to use only the tactics he outlined. Vincent was sure that more would have survived without his intervention. He bit the inside of his cheek.

"This carrier has some of the best pilots in the fleet, so we need to keep following the protocols that keep us flying." He shot Vincent a look. Vincent felt a strong urge to punch the smirk off the commander's face but kept his own face passive.

Belford pulled a bench over and lifted up his foot on top of it in an awkward position. He leaned into it anyway. "Any pilot who goes out there, okay, and starts showboating, is going to find himself grounded." He started to sound angry, like he was building himself up. The brief was going nowhere. "This fleet isn't looking for flyboys, alright? They are looking for pilots. When I was a lieutenant, they taught us to follow orders, not fly by the seat of our pants. I know things might be different with your, uh, training and whatnot nowadays, but that doesn't mean you can just do whatever you please out there, mmkay?" Vincent clenched his jaw; any moment, the marbles the commander must have been holding in his mouth would fall out.

"The enemy bombers got killed because they didn't listen to orders, okay? They probably flew too close together, and uh, didn't follow the flight path, probably—no, definitely. Shot each other out of the sky."

Vincent gritted his teeth. His squadron had brought home more enemy kills than any of the others combined. Belford had neglected to mention a single one in his reports.

"When I was uh, growing up, my dad used to tell me this story..."

"Commander Belford." A voice like thunder rolled through the room. The pilots all looked up to see the old man himself standing in the entrance. If Vincent's chest of medals were a furball, then Admiral Johnston's was a supernova. Vincent had never seen anyone with more medals. He nearly had to double over to come through the door, and though his dark features were blank, Vincent could tell he was not pleased.

"Uh, yes, sir?" Belford stumbled out of his tirade. "I was just about to, er, start the oporder."

"You are needed on the hangar deck to ensure our fighters have adequate supplies for their stay."

Belford pulled his leg off the bench, and rubbed at it absently while he spoke. "Sir, I was just going to, er, start the brief. I can send one of the others to..."

Finally, the blank slate cracked and the old man's eyebrows slid down. "I told you this needed to be done yesterday. See to it, Commander."

The air seemed to deflate right out of Belford, making the folds in his skin all the more noticeable. "Aye, sir," he slurred, and moved out of the room. Once he was gone, a collective sigh passed through the room.

Chapter 25

Johnston

"We have limited time before we enter warp to discuss all the details of this next mission," Johnston began. "It seems Joint Fleet has decided our unofficial shakedown cruise is over." He paused as cheers went up around the room.

He raised a hand for silence. "The following is classified secret. Six months ago, a portal opened on the military testing world of Aberdeen. Due to the portal's dimensions and permanency, a research facility was constructed on both the near and far sides of the breach. That facility has been paramount to Joint Fleet's understanding of these damn tears. Two weeks ago, the Verdantun appeared in the jungle and captured the entire scientific contingent that facility housed. These forces attacked Aberdeen from the portal, and our own forces sustained heavy casualties before pushing them back." His blunt words fell like stones. The loss of a facility like Aberdeen would cause major production problems for the fleet. Alien technology might power their engines and keep them mobile, but human tech gave the war machine its teeth.

"How?" Andrews, a Falcon pilot, asked.

"We are unsure of the specifics, but it appears as though a second portal opened less than a hundred klicks outside the far side research facility. By the time the colony was able to send a distress signal, it was already too late. However, we have reason to believe some of the scientists may still be alive. The research facility is the highest priority to the fleet, and our own Spec Ops platoon was dispatched through the gate. The intel they sent back is the reason we are pulling in troops from our escorts."

Johnston paused as he accessed his AMI, changing the hologram from a full-planet view to a grid square with various symbols for units on the ground.

"The situation is as follows: The Verdantun have entrenched on the opposite side of the portal." He pointed at the hologram, where a blue line separated the graph. "The recon platoon has sent back intel stating that after the initial Joint Fleet push to take back the facility, the enemy set up a forward operating base and appear intent on keeping the territory. They're fighting with everything they have, and Fleet thinks the planet in contention—code name 'Hecate'—is some sort of portal hotspot.

"Holding Hecate could be the beachhead we need to seek out the Verdantun home world. They're drawing a line in the dirt because they can't afford to allow us any further. I will stress the importance of finding their home planet. If we were to capture it, then we would be one step closer to ending this war and getting these damn elves off earth."

Johnston slammed one fist into the opposite palm, but he needn't have bothered; he had the room's undivided attention.

"Recon believes there to be a brigade-sized element of feral Verdantun along with their support contingent. They have Stormcallers and Pyromancer artillery. No reported corporeal elementals or dragons as of yet."

The room breathed a sigh of relief.

"They seem to be a mainly arboreal feral tribe, with a large number of bear and wolf analogs. Their air support, if any, has remained grounded thus far. They have been sending a steady volley of artillery fire at the portal, and they are shielding their camp from ours. Aberdeen Colony, as I'm sure many of you know, is built in a woodland valley between several large mountains. The portal exits at the base of one. On the elf side it opens into a dense jungle under a solid cloud cover created by the Stormcallers."

A new wireframe map of what Vincent assumed was the far-side facility spun into view behind the admiral. It comprised a dozen or so rectangular buildings, plus a dome-shaped one, around an oval representing the portal. Small dots appeared among the buildings.

"Since receiving this message, the portal has exchanged hands five times, and our forces on the ground are evenly matched. Two brigades of the 101st Infantry are on station supported by the 64th Tank Battalion. The troop deployments were downloaded to your AMIs, and the battalions were deployed with friend-or-foe emitters. Study them before our arrival. The last burst transmission that we received outlined our forces dug in the hard buildings, though we have been unable to push any further. A shield has been erected and it is stopping a majority of the enemy artillery. This was a rush operation, and there are no advanced tech assets available. These brigades were being rotated back core-ward for refit and resupply. They have little, if any, droid, walker, or mobile armor support.

"The portal dirt side is low to the ground, and too small for any warships to traverse. A fighter, however, will have more than enough room to maneuver. The atmospheric pressure on the far side is far denser than Aberdeen, and Fleet Intelligence has decided that the only ships that can reliably make the transitions are the Chimera." Johnston looked at Vincent.

Stunned for a moment, Vincent blinked, then managed to choke out, "Yes, sir, the Reapers can do it," before Johnston continued.

"The Chimera will be re-outfitted for atmospheric maneuvering, and the *Inferno* will descend into the upper thermosphere where you will be deployed. The 101st has retaken the landing pads at the colony and they will serve as your forward base while operations continue dirt side." Johnston turned his attention away before Vincent had time to argue, or even agree. "There is a good chance they will need direct air support the moment you break dirt side. So be prepared to enter the portal immediately."

The map twisted and changed again, this time showing a slightly more familiar view of Aberdeen Colony City, with another portal off to the side. The wire frame zoomed in on the portal and a series of arrows appeared.

"Your ships will have to dive and enter the portal at an angle in order to clear the buildings on the far side. This particular portal screws with momentum, so how you traverse this obstacle will be up to you. The Falcons will be deployed as well; however, they will remain on the Aberdeen side. Patrol routes will be mapped out and executed. If the ferals do have an aerial presence we don't need to be caught off guard.

"Be prepared to execute movement no later than one hour after we break warp. You have from now until then to brief your men and ready your planes." Johnston clicked off the hologram and the room snapped to attention. "Let's show them what *Inferno*'s fighters can do." Then he marched from the room.

Chapter 26

Vincent

Any pride Vincent might have felt at the captain placing him as the spearhead of the operation was lost in a single repeating thought. The Aberdeen scientists had been captured. Derek had been at Aberdeen. He had been presumed dead in the fighting. If the elves took captives... Vincent hurried back to the fighter bay. He needed to plan, needed to do everything he could to ensure the mission was successful.

You had better still be alive, Derek, or I'll kill you myself.

Chapter 27

Rodrom

The wolf-guard managed to keep the animal within him contained, and dragged Rodrom along just far enough for them to get caught by another mortar. The blast tore them both from their feet, and a sharp pain shot behind Rodrom's eyes as his ears screamed in protest against the pressure. Disoriented, he tried to blink away the haze that clouded his sight, only to have it choked off again by the rising cloud of black smoke from the impact crater. A vicious howl cut through the ringing sound as the guard's bestial form took hold. The tone of the call changed to a fearful whine, and Rodrom dragged himself towards the alien.

Beyond the smoking crater, a larger-than-life wolf lay with its back to Rodrom. The telltale bone spikes along the spine left no doubt of its alien nature. Rodrom could also see an additional spike—a metal shaft that pinned the wolf's arm and a portion of its chest to the ground. With a deep breath to ward off the sudden nausea from moving, Rodrom dragged himself closer. The wolf's chest rattled as he tried to breathe around the shrapnel.

Buffeted by another wave of nausea and the pressure of a third nearby round, Rodrom pressed himself low into the mud. Fortunately it wasn't close enough to actually harm them, but the shockwave on his already-wounded brain proved too much. Rodrom retched uncontrollably, throwing up the gruel he had been forced to consume earlier. *Concussion. I most definitely have a concussion,* he thought as he shuddered and wiped his mouth. There was no time to waste, so he struggled forward again, unable to avoid his own vomit as he crawled.

When he reached the wounded wolf-guard, Rodrom pushed himself up to his knees and tried to catch his breath. Just as he had seen from far away, a twenty-centimeter length of shrapnel had punctured the Wolf's right upper appendage and continued far enough to pierce between two ribs on the right side, and most likely into the lung beneath.

Rodrom leaned down to press his ear against the wolf's chest, mentally commanding his AMI to begin filtering through the noises of battle for the creature's heartbeat and the sound of air moving in the lung. Almost immediately, it was clear to Rodrom that the shrapnel had pierced the lung tissue, and without the proper interventions, the wound would begin trapping air and a tension pneumothorax would develop.

Rodrom looked up and searched his immediate surroundings for a healer, or, save that, something he could use to improvise a needle. He wiped his brow as he searched his surroundings, though he was sweating so profusely that it hardly made a difference. The elves were still running back and forth between the trees, but none were close enough for Rodrom to call.

When Rodrom turned back, the look on the wolf-guard's face was one of pure terror. It looked for all the world a wounded house dog. How similar the two of them were, Rodrom thought, despite coming from different worlds, different realities. The elves feared death just the same.

Alright, Derek, you're running out of time. Time to MacGyver something. "Brilliant advice," he wheezed aloud.

The wolf-guard's respirations came faster and more shallow. *Damn it.* Rodrom grasped the piece of shrapnel and pulled it from the wound. A gush of dark blood accompanied the movement. Working as swiftly as he could, he jammed his naked fingers into the wound, pushing the lung tissue inside away from the hole, and allowing air to escape as he worked his fingers back and forth. Almost immediately, the wolf-guard's breathing improved, and a whimper escaped between ragged breaths. He stared up at Rodrom.

"Sorry. The jewelry clashed with your coat" Rodrom muttered as the air escaped, feeling some of his own anxiety bleed out with the quip.

The danger of the wolf-guard asphyxiating momentarily abated, and his own nausea and dizziness swept away by the adrenaline coursing through him, Rodrom was finally able to think clearly. They couldn't stay where they were, as the rounds had already found their mark. And no other elves were within shouting range, not over the din of battle. Rodrom rolled his shoulders, the decision made before he had time to reconsider.

He tore off a piece of the rags he wore, and using nearby stick as a windlass, he created an improvised tourniquet. He tied the whole thing around the wolf-guard's upper arm, and as he twisted it tight, the creature yipped in pain and snapped his teeth. Rodrom shifted and maneuvered his knee between himself and the animal's neck, preventing unwanted bites, and continued to work.

Any hemorrhage was effectively ceased by the compression. Rodrom took hold of the shrapnel and pulled it fully out of the creature's flesh. The moment it moved, the wolf-guard yipped a final time and lay silent and unconscious. Rodrom tossed the metal aside, and after scanning his surroundings a final time, he reached under the beast and pushed most of its bulk onto its right shoulder, twisting his own body to gain leverage against the animal's near hundred-kilo bulk.

Rodrom had spent most of his time in a lab or surgery ward, and his time in captivity had not helped strengthen the muscles he had, but adrenaline and six and a half feet of stubbornness allowed him to lift the creature up and across his back. Grunting, he pushed up from his knees to take his feet.

He wouldn't be able to support the weight for long, so he took off at a lumbering gait, trying to find enough balance in his barely controlled forward momentum to keep going. He headed back in the direction he thought the healers would be, putting his back to the sharp retorts of rifles, and the gut-clenching concussion of falling mortars. His ears deafened to anything but his own heartbeat and the coarse bellow of his struggling lungs. With each stumbling step, he grew more sluggish, his blood thundering in his ears as it tried in vain to fuel his straining body.

Rodrom made it almost a hundred meters before he spotted another elf running towards him. Relief flooded him immediately and he collapsed in a heap to the ground to lay pressed between the warm mass of slow-breathing fur above, and blood-stained mud below. He gasped for air; he had pushed himself too hard. As darkness encroached on the edges of his vision, he looked down at his arms. Blue blood oozed from his numerous cuts, mixing with the red blood of the wolf-guard above him.

Damn, he thought. *He's more human than me.*

Interlude

The Duchess

Something was wrong.

She couldn't say what, exactly, but the Duchess knew in her horn that the ship was in danger. She had learned long ago to trust those instincts; it was imprudent to ignore such obvious divine intervention. Cloaked in the protection of her Shroud of Faith, she moved through the cargo hold. Whatever force was guiding her had led to that bay, and planted a sense of "wrongness" in the back of her mind. The same sort of feeling she had whenever she was near heresy.

Her Shroud muted each footstep. She would catch the monster unawares, force it to bend to the unwavering power she was a conduit for. Send the heretic back to the dimension that spawned it.

She knew the beast must be close, and with her Faith, she felt strong. All around her were neatly arranged crates of supplies that kept the super carrier around her running. This particular cargo bay held engineering supplies, spare weapons, hull plating, and scrap metal. The room was massive, so her quarry could easily stay hidden.

The Duchess needed the high ground to survey the entire scene, but she did not dare lower her Shroud to extend her Sense. Besides, her

Sense would likely not even register the monster, as its kind was so impure.

Gathering her Shroud around her legs, she crouched down, and felt the rush of power before she kicked off and soared into the air. She easily cleared the four meters and landed without a sound on top of an equipment rack — the fourth rack out of eight, in the center of the room.

<All pilots to the ready room for briefing,> her AMI chirped. She ignored it. Once she uncovered the heretic, she could explain away her behavior. Until then, exposing the full range of her abilities would only hinder the mission. From atop the fourth wall, she used her vantage point to look across the bay.

<All hands prepare for jump, I say again, all hands prepare for immediate jump,> came a ship-wide transmission.

The Duchess knelt down, pressing her fist against the steel equipment housing, and willed her Shroud to anchor her. The whole room rocked around her, but the strength of faith kept the Shroud from wavering. They were jumping. The mission must have been more important than she thought for them to jump so soon without her knowing about it. Still, her need to eradicate the heresy came first.

She stood up from her crouch, strength coursing through her, and leapt from one vantage point to another, scanning for her prey. She never saw the blast before it took her in the side.

Her Shroud softened the impact, but her breath still erupted out of her with a *whumf*. She twisted in the air, her trajectory unchanged. She hit the next equipment rack at the wrong angle, then tumbled to the ground.

The monster was close. She drew in her faith, forcing herself to believe in the solidity of the Shroud around her, and took off running between the racks.

Another blast slammed into her side, kicking her off her feet and down to the cold metal floor. She slid to the side and snapped her eyes forward. Her Shroud wavered. The prey she was hunting was one of her own.

The Psykin was wearing a blank fleet duty uniform, and had weapons strapped across her back and both hips. She had a single horn in the center of her head, and her right arm ended just below her shoulder. Everything about her screamed danger, from the way she stood to the dagger she held in her remaining hand. Even with her Shroud held tight, the Duchess could see the other's wretched aura. She was tainted, a fallen one.

<*Heretic.*> She forced all her hatred and fear into the word.

The Exile only stared. <*How did you find me?*> she finally asked.

The Duchess glared at the dagger in the other's hands. Was that what she had come to find? <*I was led here. The gods sent me to eradicate your evil.*> Then, without another word, she launched herself forward with all the power of her Shroud. She crossed the distance in an instant. She used that same power in her fist as she visualized punching straight through her opponent. The Exile made no effort to move, and a wall appeared between them.

It isn't real, the Duchess reminded herself, *just like training.* Still, she felt sick when she passed through. The Exile had stepped to her right, and slashed out with the dagger.

The steel bit the Duchess's shoulder, and then a terrifying cold ran down her arm, as though the blade had sucked the very life from it. She hit the ground with an awkward stumble, her arm hanging limp at her side.

<*How could you go against your people? How could you abandon the mission?*> the Duchess screamed, forcing the Shroud to strengthen her

arm. She lunged again, close enough that the Exile had no time to distract her with another illusion. Her fist shot in, catching the Exile in her chest with enough force to slam her backward.

<Everything I did, that I do, I do for our people. You know nothing. You are all the same, blindly following the orders of a council of fools.> the Exile spat back. She took a step forward. Darkness swirled around the blade and her arm as she slashed again. The Duchess leapt to the side to avoid it. The weapon seemed to suck in all the light around it.

<The heresy is turning your mind. Cast aside the blade and repent,> the Duchess cried, then gave an enhanced kick at the other's arm. Her foot slammed into the darkness like it was solid, and the crack echoed in the silence.

<The last time one of your "Chosen" tried to take my power, seven lost their lives. They managed to take only my arm.> Another step forward. The Duchess could barely keep on her feet as she tried to dodge each swipe. She used her forearms to catch the Exile's arm before the blade could slice her again. With two arms, she had the advantage, and managed to force the Exile back a step with a series of Shroud-enhanced blows.

<My faith will protect me. I am of the Chosen, destined to rid this realm of your taint.> The Duchess lunged her head forward and their horns cracked together.

The Exile wavered, and the Duchess pressed forward, lashing out with her fists, once, twice, and then she hit a wall.

The Exile had turned the blade around in her hand, and pressed the steel into her own flesh. The air shimmered over her skin even as the blade sucked in more light. The Exile's shroud enveloped her, and did not stop at her disfigurement. It continued down and took the shape of an arm, of a hand. Impossible, the Duchess thought. How could she surround herself in faith when she was a heretic?

In that moment, the Duchess wavered. The speed and strength the gods had blessed her with was sapped from her limbs, and the crackle of energy left her flesh.

<You truly know nothing. Your books and prophecies aren't the future. They are the same as the elves or dragons: a blending of realities and nothing more.>

<You aren't strong enough to stand against the gods. The conclave will destroy you.> But the Duchess had nothing to back up the words.

The Exile opened her mouth and darkness poured forth. "I am more powerful than you can possibly imagine."

The Duchess's mental scream tore through the ship, sending every living creature into a moment of brain-splitting agony. Then there was silence.

Part 3

Chapter 28

"All hands report ready for jump, sir," said Navigation.

"Aye, you may engage. All ahead full." Johnston tightened his hands around the grips on his console. The young pilot sitting at the front of the bridge nodded and twisted in his chair to type in the final sequence.

The com officer keyed a ship-wide transmission. *<All hands prepare for jump. I say again, all hands prepare for immediate jump.>*

After the countdown ended, the pilot grabbed a large lever set into the console and pressed it forward.

Johnston's stomach lurched as the Alcubierre drive kicked into gear. It only lasted a second, and then they were trapped in their own bubble of space-time. Space compressed in front of them, and expanded behind, and with math Johnston couldn't hope to comprehend, space moved around them. Or something to that extent. Johnston did not trouble himself with all the details. He understood the tactical and logistical impact the Alcubierre drive gave to his ship, and left the physics to the physicists.

"Status report," he said after they had been underway for a few minutes. Each of his stations checked in. No one had been hurt by the sudden acceleration, and engineering reported the reactors to be in the green and steady. Johnston had never had an issue entering warp, but he had heard enough bad reports to always be wary. They were underway, however, and the ship was as safe as she was going to be.

"Commander McKinley, you have the bridge," Johnston said, then stepped away from his console and moved towards the corridor and his ready room beyond.

"Willia—Captain, sir?" Belford called out. Johnston whirled on him. It was bad enough that the man tried to call him by his first name in private, but on the *bridge*? *His* bridge? He mentally located the nearest airlock.

"What is it?" he asked through clenched teeth. The commander did not seem to notice the murderous look carved into Johnston's face.

"I wanted to discuss the, er, engagement stratagem you briefed the fighter pilots on. The Chimeras aren't ready for that sort of challenge. I was a Falcon pilot, you know. I know what they can do. They should be the ones to lead the assault."

Military bearing and a lifetime of discipline were all that saved the sniveling man from Johnston's wrath. All the other members of the bridge crew turned their heads down to their consoles with obvious haste as the captain drew himself to deliver the ass-chewing the commander deserved for questioning his orders so publicly.

Then a mortar went off inside his brain, and he collapsed to the ground. The pain was like nothing he had ever felt before, an agony that did not just flare his nerves, but infused him with hopelessness. He would fail his mission, his ship would be destroyed, and he would go down in the annals of history as a colossal failure.

Johnston cried out against the anguish, but his voice was drowned in a sea of despair. Every other member of the bridge crew screamed with him.

Then, just as unexpectedly as it had arrived, the feeling was gone. Johnston pushed himself off the floor without a moment's hesitation, and although he was reeling internally, he forced calm over his features.

"Tactical report," he ordered, though he could see that no one else had gotten to their feet yet. The usual sharp metallic tang of the air on the bridge was replaced with the acrid stench of sweat and terror, and a touch of ammonia.

"What... what was that?" Belford cried.

"An attack," Johnston said simply. "Take your feet. We are not out of danger."

Several of the other crew had shaken off their fugue and turned back to their stations by now. Some of the bridge officers were calling out reports. Whatever had hit them had hit the entire ship.

"How could we be under attack?" McKinley asked. "Nothing can get to us while we are in warp."

"The attack did not come from without, Commander."

"Christ."

The nymph ensign who had first warned him of the enemy weapon on the shuttle was slumped in her chair, still unconscious. Johnston squinted at her, his brow creased.

"Open a com channel to the ship," Johnston called, then turned to his station and broadcast: "Attention all hands, we have been assaulted by an unknown force. All hands to muster stations, full head count. All Psykin personnel are to be taken to med bay for treatment." He released

147

the broadcast switch. "Now patch me into medical." When the patch went through, he spoke swiftly. "Doctor Kerrigan, I have reason to believe the attack we all suffered was Psykin in origin. Be prepared to receive their wounded. I will dispatch you additional help."

"It's more than that, sir," Kerrigan answered. "One of my nurses is a Psykin. She called out as she collapsed, and it came across all the AMI units because one of them was wounded. This wasn't an attack. It was a death scream."

Johnston turned back to his bridge crew. All of them were back in their seats and alert, save for the unconscious nymph, and Belford, who was still writhing on the floor. "All hands to battle stations. We have an intruder on board."

"Sir! I have reports of a fire on deck six, frame forty-five."

"Close the emergency bulkheads."

"There are civilians there, sir, and several of our crew members."

"Dispatch fire-suppressing crews. Scramble the marines. Those civilians are top priority, we will not lose them," Johnston ordered. Then, in a voice low enough only he could hear, muttered, "What the hell did we pick up on Bastogne?"

Chapter 29

Vincent

Vincent stumbled into the bulkhead, drowning in a wash of emotions. Grief, loss, and anger all vied to overwhelm him. His father's death, losing Derek, his inability to prevent either tragedy. He collapsed to his knees and tears streamed from his eyes as he curled his hands into fists.

Then it was gone, and only the soft echo of pain remained.

"What in the void was that?" he rasped, then wiped a sleeve across his face. He hadn't cried since the day he lost his father. This was no natural grief; some sort of magic had to be responsible.

The red washout of the battle station lights confirmed his suspicions, and Vincent took off running down the hall, leaping through the emergency hatches that split the hallway.

"Status report," he called between breaths.

<Fire on deck six, frame forty-five,> his AMI reported. *<Civilians and military personnel trapped, fire suppression crews en route. Unknown enemy on board.>*

Before the details even finished downloading into memories,

Vincent was already activating his squadron sense, connecting his mental chip to theirs so he could sense their positions.

Tesla and Forge were in danger. Vincent doubled down on his speed, sprinting wildly through the corridors as if the fire were behind him.

"What... caused... the fire?" he puffed between breaths.

<Unknown. Suspected battle damage.>

Vincent didn't waste his breath with further questions. He hadn't appreciated the length of the ship until he was forced to sprint the distance. He didn't dare take the elevator, not if there was a fire.

He took far too long to get there—long enough for him to consider the worst possible scenarios. Then he heard them.

The distinctive spray of the firefighting foam packs was the easiest to hear; then, as he got closer, he heard the grunts and shouts of the crews themselves.

"Connect me to their bionet," Vincent ordered. His rank would allow him in. The connection was made and a flurry of communications came flooding in.

<Damn it, Trevors, attack it from above.>

<Does anyone have eyes on the wounded?>

<Negative, I can't see anything.>

<Keep pouring it on.>

All the firefighters were launching off. Vincent was disoriented by all of their thoughts.

Ahead of them down the corridor, fire licked at the walls and ceiling. Closer to Vincent, foam coated the walls to stop the fire's advance. Vincent knew firsthand how devastating a ship-wide fire could be. If it got into the life support line that pumped the atmosphere, it would get far worse. There were automatic cutoffs everywhere, but they could fail, and sufficient heat would find a way to spread.

The firefighters were gaining ground, but the foam only did so much. Force fields and oxygen denial were far more effective.

Vincent saw an extra pack on the floor behind the rearmost fighter, and he scooped it up and pushed his arms through the straps. He hadn't kept up on the training since the academy, but the principle was simple enough, same as with a weapon. Business end towards the enemy. He grabbed a respirator as well and fitted it over his face.

The corridor was only wide enough to support three men abreast, and five firefighters were already crowding for space. Vincent slipped in between the rearmost two and lifted the nozzle of his foam gun to arc it over the men ahead of him.

<Who the hell is that?>

<Lieutenant Barkhorn. Saw you needed help,> Vincent answered.

<Christ, Jenkins, it's an open channel?>

<Cut the chatter, keep the pressure on.>

The tool churned in his hands as the foam blasted from the front. Flecks hit the three men ahead of him, but most arced over their shoulders to splash onto the flames. Between the six of them, they managed to press the fire further down the corridor, and then one of them broke off to access a panel on the wall.

<Updating AMI data directly. It's contained to the corridor ahead with hotspots in two chambers.> A stream of data accompanied the words.

<I'm running low,> one of the fighters ahead of Vincent called. The man directly behind him grabbed the lead firefigher's shoulder and pulled him back, then stepped up to take his place. Vincent found himself alone in the back row, though not for long; another called out for a switch a moment later.

Vincent pulled him back and stepped up. He was barely a foot away from the nearest flames. The view from his plummeting snubfighter filled his mind, forcing him to grip the tool with the same intensity as when he'd plunged into the fires on Bastogne.

<Flareup!>

It took Vincent a split second to remember what that meant. It was a split second too long. While the other two men around him twisted to shield their bodies, Vincent took the blast of heat full on. Every exposed inch of flesh screamed like a blanket of needles had pressed into it, and even with the respirator on, he could smell his own cooked flesh and singed hair. He screamed into the plastic of his mask, dropping back a step. The other two stepped forward to pick up the slack, but Vincent forced himself forward, still spraying everything with foam.

<Keep moving.> Some of his pain and fear had broken through. It hurt, more than he thought possible, and he was terrified that it was far worse than it seemed. What was it Derek had told him? The more pain, the worse it is? Or was it the opposite? He was always talking about one medical thing or another.

Vincent was starting to lose it. The wandering thoughts, the lack of focus. It didn't help that he knew. Didn't help at all.

<Chamber to the right. Clear for civilians.>

Vincent saw the hatch in question. It was closed off to the fire. He turned his stream on it until it was completely covered. The foam would help to dissipate the heat so they could open it. He remembered that much.

At the end of the corridor, a force field shimmered. They were close to extinguishing the blaze completely. The fighters they had left behind to exchange foam packs had returned, and with the combined effort of all six, they pushed the blaze inexorably back. Vincent dragged behind and moved for the door.

He grabbed the handle—it was cool enough to open. He twisted and pulled. No fire came rushing out to meet him. As he pulled it open, it occurred to him just how dangerous that choice could have been.

He looked inside, and found his pilots and Ele huddled in the corner.

"Jiminy Christmas!" Tesla yelled. "You got it out?"

"Do you not see, Tesla?" Forge cried. "It is the Kapitan!"

"Are you wounded?" Vincent called, and just moving his lips made his nerves scream again.

"Ele was burned."

"Give her to me. I'll take her to medical."

"All respect due, sir, but vape that. We will take you," Forge told him, and then pulled the foam nozzle from Vincent's hand and lifted his arm over his shoulder. Vincent opened his mouth to argue, but sank silently into the support instead.

"What were you thinking, dude?" Tesla muttered.

Vincent didn't give an answer. He didn't have one. He hadn't stopped to think about it.

Chapter 30

The Exile

The Exile had little time. She had not wanted to fight the other Psykin, had intended to keep hidden until she could find more intel, steal a shuttle, and continue her mission. But no matter how tight she'd held her Web, no matter how much of the ship was between them, the other had kept following her. The Exile hadn't had a choice.

Now she had several problems. The ship had lurched into a warp jump right before they battled. So the Exile was trapped inside the ship until they exited the bubble of space-time wrapped around the ship. The second problem was the death scream. The kill had not been clean, in more ways than one. The Psykin's chest was torn open from the inside out, as though both her hearts had erupted. The Shadow had taken over, had twisted the Exile's emotions with its power and forced her to go further than simply ending the other's life.

The Shadow—or was it her?—took sadistic pleasure in murdering the other. Exile was having trouble deciphering whose emotions were whose. She felt like laughing and retching at the same time. Only the knowledge that she had little time kept her from unraveling.

The ship would know of her presence now. She needed a plan. Already the red lights washed across the room. She tuned out the distractions and focused on the task at hand.

Tension causes panic, panic breaks control, came the mantra, though the Exile knew she was well past tension. The ingrained teachings were the same as the Psykin before her: dead, useless things that came from an organization of fools.

Focus, she told herself. *Don't lose the edge. Make a plan.*

The ship would be on high alert. They would take a muster and discover who was missing. Then armed marines would move through each deck until they found her. She couldn't blow up the compartment to get rid of the evidence, and she wouldn't be able to clean up the mess that the Shadow — that she — had made.

She looked around. The cargo containers on either side were large. Far too large for her to move, even with the assistance of her Shell.

She was out of options. Save one.

Her stomach churned. Every time she leaned on its power, it seemed harder and harder to separate herself. But she had no choice. Time was short and any minute they would discover her. She pulled the blade from its sheath, and the hunger filled her.

There was not much left in the dead Psykin's chest cavity, so she could not plunge the dagger into the heart. Instead, she pressed the metal into the soft area beneath the jaw. There was almost no resistance, but she could still feel the scrape of every bone scraped the splitting of each muscle. Hunger screamed inside her, as though she had been starving for months, and she sank the dagger in to its hilt.

Darkness blossomed from around the pommel, growing

branches towards the skull. Each one pierced into the Psykin's flesh, creating green bruises on the bluish skin as blood vessels burst and were shoved aside. The darkness slithered over and into everything it touched until a head of darkness remained.

Like wax dripping from a candle, the Shadow descended. First in drips and drabs, but then faster, pouring down from the skull as though it were a wellspring to fill the chest cavity beneath. The Exile had hoped the Shadow would eat away the flesh, that it would focus the hunger and take everything.

Then the chest cavity filled, the ribs pulled back towards the center, and the Exile realized her mistake. She tried to pull the dagger back out, to stop the Shadow before it was too late, but the very instant her fingers brushed the leather hilt, she was overwhelmed by a pain more excruciating than anything the Shadow had inflicted upon her before.

The head of darkness twisted around to look up at her, and the jaw clacked together, though no words came out. The swirling, dripping darkness was still pulling the chest back together, and spreading down to coat the dead Psykin's arms and legs.

The Exile shook with a mixture of revulsion and terror, helpless as the Shadow did not destroy the remains, but became them. The screech of tearing metal assaulted her ears as the Shadow's fingers dug into the floor, and then, without warning, it sat up and turned to look at her.

Every second that passed, the monster took on more and more of the features it had consumed. The twin horns along the head, the bluish tinge to the skin, the glint of anger in the eyes.

"This body will serve for now," it rasped, then it coughed violently before it spoke again, but in the Exile's mind this time. <*I had forgotten that your species is too weak to properly communicate.*> It was the deceased's voice, tinged with the monster's horrible inflection.

It reached up and pulled the dagger from its lower jaw. Drops of Shadow fell from the wound before it cinched itself closed. The monster twisted the knife around and held it out, hilt first.

<*You'll have need of this,*> it said. <*I have not finished with you yet.*>

Chapter 31

Rodrom

Rodrom's eyes fluttered open. A light bounced above him. As his mind sharpened against the fog of an unnatural sleep, he groaned. A fear stemming from the unknown buffeted him as he looked around fervently through unfocused eyes. Physical pain awoke as he did, and it was all that stemmed the terror. His head and back were aching, too much for him to be dead.

Rodrom, think. What's around?

He could just make out the vague colors of the inside of tree shelter above him. The smell of wet dirt and foreign foliage filled his nostrils. He was lying on a nest of woven branches and leaves, which were still green. Groaning again, he pushed himself up into a seated position.

"Don't strain yourself, DerekRodrom, you've been in the dreamscape too long to be moving so swiftly," Lorelei said from beside him. Rodrom turned towards her, slowly, his eyes finally adjusting enough to make sense of the room. Lorelei was seated on a similar nest, her legs tucked under her body with her customary staff resting on her thighs.

"Wha..." Rodrom began, his voice cracking. Lorelei lifted a pitcher towards him and he struggled to grasp it, his nerves still deaf from the long sleep. Lorelei leaned forward to cup her hands around Rodrom's and lift the jug enough for him to drink.

The cool water splashed down his parched throat, a flood through a dried riverbed, and though Rodrom drank hurriedly, he tasted the undercurrent of something too bitter to be water. If they wanted him dead, they would not have nursed him back to health, so he swallowed the last gulp and nodded slightly, wondering what sort of Verdantun magic they had infused into the water. Lorelei lowered the empty pitcher.

"How long?" Rodrom asked, not trusting his throat with a longer sentence. The headache he had felt so acutely upon waking was beginning to diminish. A healing draught, he concluded.

"I am unsure of how your people measure time," Lorelei explained. "However, the sun on this world has crossed our camp twice since the attack."

The average day on the unknown planet was roughly Earth Standard. "Two days," he muttered, knowing Lorelei would not understand the words. "You healed me."

"I did."

"Why?"

"Your efforts on Dirus prevented his passing. The healers consented to my treating you before those who suffered less fatal injuries." Lorelei extended her arms outward, palms up, to emphasis her point.

He knew all too well that when priority of treatment came up, it

159

was easy to overlook enemy combatants in favor of friendly forces. "Leaving him would have been rude," Rodrom snipped, unsure of what to say.

"Wars are rarely fought against an enemy that is uniformly evil. It would seem your actions are proof of that. We underestimated you."

Rodrom remained silent. What was Lorelei getting at?

"Your blood is different from the other iron-bloods," Lorelei said. She gestured to a handful of broad leaves soaked with blue. Rodrom looked down at his arm where he had been injured, and found only the white pucker of scar tissue.

"I had it replaced when I was young," Rodrom said, knowing he would not be able to explain synthetic blood any better than he could explain the leukemia that had necessitated it. Lorelei seemed to accept that answer. She remained silent for a time, staring at Rodrom with her oversized emerald eyes. She ran her fingers absently over the white stone on the end of her staff as she swayed to unheard music. Rodrom thought she was humming, though the low sound continued as she spoke.

"I do not believe we should be fighting this war," she whispered. "In every battle the wounded are dragged or limp back, only to be healed and sent back to the fight. You see us as monsters, we see you as metal demons." She paused, looking out of the shelter with her eyes unfocused. "You could have run."

"He was injured. I could not leave him in agony," Rodrom said, though he wondered all the same why he had done what he did.

"Your orders are to attempt to escape when presented the opportunity, are they not?" she asked.

"Derek Rodrom, Social Security number 046-72-8754 of the 82 Fleet Medical Corp," Rodrom recited. "I am to ensure the continued care of wounded fleet soldiers in any capacity. Hoo-ha and roger. I have not been following fleet regulations up until now. Why muddle things worse by escaping? I may also have been wounded," he admitted.

"You had strength enough to lift a"—Lorelei trilled out a musical name in her native tongue—"who weighs more than a full grown Verdantun. You had strength enough to run."

Rodrom's mind was slow, still clouded from the probable concussion. After a moment, he understood. His decision to help the fallen wolf-guard, Dirus, was not something she could comprehend. His actions had become a catalyst for something greater in Lorelei's mind—a pebble tossed into a pond, whose ripples were wreaking havoc on her view of the war, and of humanity and its allies.

He took a moment to compose his thoughts. He could recognize her disbelief and fragile new thoughts because they closely mirrored his own. It was not uncommon for soldiers in a war of such proportions to demonize an enemy. Killing someone who was someone else's father, son, or brother weighed heavier than killing a faceless monster, killing an idea.

Men who grew up surrounded by computers and machines fighting against a people who changed their bodies into animals—it was no wonder each side demonized the other. Rodrom steadfastly refused to believe the Verdatun or any other race's "magic" was anything more than technology misunderstood, but when faced with something so foreign that it made the aliens that comprised the Joint Fleet seem normal, he himself was swept up in the biased mindset that the Verdantun were an enemy beyond reproach.

His time in the camp had changed that. Each day he spent with them, he recognized more of the familiar, more of himself—and though the differences were staggering, he could no longer blind himself with the idea that they were a faceless evil that deserved to be destroyed.

"You took us prisoner," Rodrom said after careful consideration. "You could have killed us."

"You were unarmed, you were not a threat. Why would we attack?"

"Because I am so fearsome?" Rodrom muttered. "Unarmed opponents did not stop what happened on earth," he spat.

Lorelei's expression grew even more distant. "Not all Verdatun are of one mind. My leaders did not agree to what the" — Another incomprehensible name — "did to your world."

"You have separate goverments?" Rodrom pressed. Lorelei did not answer. It only made sense. Earth had spawned as many governments as there were planets, and all the unions post-contact had only slightly lessened that number.

He shrugged his shoulders and rolled his neck, the combination of physical and mental exhaustion forming a knot between his shoulder blades. In the silence that stretched between them, Rodrom could just make out the lilting of Verdantun voices. Healer songs weren't loud enough to travel that far across the camp. He looked past Lorelei to the entrance of the shelter, and found that night had fallen. The Verdantun had never allowed him or any of the other refugees to leave the holes they were kept in at night.

Considering the state of the camp when Rodrom last saw it, the singing seemed out of place. Lorelei had said that two days had passed. The realization gave him a sobering jolt. Anything could have happened in that time. Perhaps they had something to celebrate.

Rodrom broke the silence. "My own people have similar rules when it comes to war. They never told us that your people had similar conventions."

"We had our assumptions, though our leadership and yours do

not share the greatest trust. Your leaders seem to think we can bewitch them into some sort of agreement that would be less than beneficial for them."

"You are saying you cannot?" Rodrom asked, eyebrows raised. "I have seen your healers do some pretty incredible things with their... abilities."

"Our weavers can do a great many things, as can the ferals. Changing the minds of your human leadership is not one of them."

Rodrom tried to concentrate on the pain in his shoulders to maintain composure. Lorelei had never been so candid about anything with him. His scientific curiosity screamed questions in his mind: How did their magic work? What powered it? But his military training shouted other questions: What were their offensive capabilities? And how could fleet intelligence exploit them? He was torn between his two disciplines, but regardless of what he asked, he would need to tread carefully, lest he reveal his intentions and gain nothing.

"I have seen your soldiers take on the shapes of animals, as well as create fire and lightning from nothing." Rodrom hoped that by revealing something he already knew, he would lure Lorelei into explaining more.

"You have treated enough Verdantun to know the difference between our two peoples, DerekRodrom," Lorelei said with a wave of her hand, a gesture she had learned from him. "The ferals could no more change yours, or your leaders', minds as they could mend a battle wound, and the weavers, though powerful, cannot affect the minds of one another, let alone an outsider. Though the Verdantun are not without allies..." She trailed off, likely realizing that she had said too much.

Rodrom had already assumed that the Verdantun military had a two-caste structure, but he had not heard it so clearly defined, or known that the shape-shifting caste could not use magic the way their amber-skinned cousins could.

"Humans are unaccustomed to the abilities you and your kind display. Before the portals opened we had never seen anything like it," Rodrom offered.

Lorelei opened her mouth slightly and hummed a quick melody. Rodrom's sudden confusion cleared when she said, "You think my people are strange because we can sing trees into shapes and call upon the elements. Yet you come to battle in impossible metal beasts with black sludge for blood. You hurl beams of light, and thorns of metal from thunder weapons, and yet our taking one form over another is considered impossible." By the tone of her voice, Rodrom understood the melody to be the Verdantun version of laughter.

Rodrom smiled, finding that despite his situation, he was enjoying this new side to Lorelei. He found that he had nothing to counter her with, and reached his hand up to rub at a sore spot behind his neck. As he massaged the lump there, he became aware once again of the music beyond the root walls of their enclosure. Perhaps Lorelei was unaware of the music, concentrated as she was on him and his reactions? But no; as the music ebbed and flowed, she swayed her upper body in time. She suddenly seemed so different from the rigid-backed, no-nonsense healer who had been so adamantly opposed to him performing surgeries.

All of her actions seemed different now, almost dreamlike. Had she indulged in some sort of mind-altering drug? If the celebration outside the shelter was any indication of the other Verdantuns' mood, perhaps hallucinogens were commonplace in victory. His curiosity won out, as it often did, and despite his better judgment, he asked, "What are your people celebrating?"

Lorelei did not react to his words immediately, though her slight swaying stopped after a moment. "I believe I am mistaken of the word *celebrate*," she said.

"It means to express joy and praise for events people consider good. Such as a holiday or victory in battle," Rodrom explained slowly, the last words difficult to say.

"Tonight is no different from any other day. They are not... celebrating. Why would you think tonight is special?"

"I hear singing," Rodrom explained. "After all the fighting and wounded in the last battle, it seems out of place."

"Of course some are singing. They are not all painters or builders. Do some of your people not sing during their awakening?"

"What do you mean by awakening?" Rodrom asked quickly.

Lorelei looked at him. "Do all of your people enter the dreamscape each night?"

"Do you mean sleep? Humans have to sleep every night, or they do not function well. It is a time when our bodies heal damage and recuperate. I have seen Verdantun do the same. Your soldiers all sleep after they are wounded."

"Well, of course the ferals sleep." Lorelei waved her hand again. "They are connected with their beasts, and beasts enter the dreamscape. Surely not all humans are connected with beasts."

"So your weavers do not enter this... dream state?"

"The weavers do not enter the dreamscape, but the weaveroot is not the reason this is so." Weaveroot? Rodrom mentally filed this term away for later.

"What do the Verdantun do when they are not asleep... in the dreamscape?"

"For a healer you do not seem to know a very fundamental thing, DerekRodrom," Lorelei stated, but her tone was light. "They are awakened, of course. They spend their nights in song or with paint. It is a time for creativity and experiments. When else would our shapers and builders have time for music or art? Surely your world has art."

"Yes, we have art," Rodrom said absently, his mind wrapping itself around the concept of creatures without the need for sleep. The Verdantun were not so different biologically; their muscles and nerve connections worked similarly to if not exactly like humans'. Therefore they must have some need for a period of rest or recuperation. *Even the best engine needs maintenance.*

Dolphins did not sleep, though—not like humans did, anyway. Rodrom had entertained a fascination with marine biology in his grad school days, and could not help but draw the parallel now. Perhaps Verdantun functioned similarly, using unihemispheric slow-wave sleep, only shutting down a portion of their minds at a time. That could possibly explain Lorelei's behavior shift—if a different part of her mind was in control at night than during the day.

Rodrom was only making half-assed guesses, though, and without thorough research, he would be unable to find the real explanation for what Lorelei was attempting to explain. But in this moment he did not care. The pain between his shoulders had moved past the point of a dull ache to genuine pain, and was sprouting wings of agony that cloaked his upper arms and neck. Dropping any pretense of continuing the conversation, Rodrom reached both his hands up to massage the pain, his face contorting in a grimace.

Lorelei pushed herself to her feet and lighted over to Rodrom. The discomfort he was showing no doubt puzzled her healer's mind—he had taken their draught, after all. As soon as her hand touched down on his shoulder, however, her eyes and nostrils flared and she drew back slightly. She shook her head as if to rid herself of an unwelcome thought, lifting her hand and touching lightly down again on Rodrom's bare shoulder. Her hands were strangely warm. "It cannot be," she whispered.

Rodrom's eyes grew wide, and he screamed as something tried to claw its way out of his back.

Chapter 32

Johnston

Johnston slammed his fist down onto the table, knocking coffee onto his datapad.

"How the hell have we not found anything?" he snarled, the words barely audible.

McKinley stood stock-still across from his deck, his eyes focused on a spot just above the captain's head, his hands at his sides.

"Relax, Chris." Johnston waved a hand at his XO. "You are the only bloody officer on this ship I can trust. Don't lose your spine on me now."

The XO followed orders by putting his hands behind his back and moving his right foot so he was standing at parade rest. Johnston knew this was the best he was going to get out. McKinley took the failure to find anything as a personal one, and it would take more than an order from Johnston to assuage that sense of pride.

"Everyone has been accounted for. We did the muster twice, and had the ship's AI check on every personnel AMI unit. Doctor Kerrigan

168

has positive ID on every one of her patients as well as Lieutenant Barkhorn, who was wounded fighting the fire."

"Barkhorn is on the fire suppression team?" Johnston raised an eyebrow.

McKinley shook his head, "Negative, he was in the corridor and assisted the team. He was burned by a… uh… backblast."

"I never know whether to give that man a medal or an arse chewing." Johnston sighed.

McKinley's lip twitched, the equivalent of an explosive laugh from the statue of a man.

"He does seem to put himself in dangerous situations, sir."

"Is he still flight-ready?" Every member of his crew was important to Johnston, but he found himself growing found of the young pilot and the strange quirks that brought him across his desk.

"Doctor Kerrigan has had to threaten sedation several times to keep him from doing just that, sir. Though she assures me he will be ready before we are out of warp."

"Well, definitely a medal, then." Johnston shook his head. "Did we discover the source of the fire?"

"Negative, sir. There was no break in any of the life support lines, and the engineers who went through the damage found no battle damage. They are stumped, sir."

"This stinks of magic," Johnston growled. "Double the watch, place guards on all sensitive areas, and make sure no one goes anywhere alone. If we have an infiltrator on board…" He did not need to describe how easy it would be to destroy their ship while they were underway.

"I'll make sure it gets done."

"I believe you will, Chris. Dismissed."

His XO snapped to attention and exited the chamber, leaving

him alone with his thoughts. The headache had wormed its way back into the usual spot, and he looked through his desk for the injector. He would rather fight against impossible odds with a terrestrial enemy than square off against magic he couldn't understand. Going toe-to-toe with another ship was easy; thinking of the thousand ways unknown magic could destroy his ship was another matter.

Johnston leaned back in his uncomfortable chair and thought about how to proceed. Vincent Barkhorn was really starting to come across his desk more than he would have liked. With a ship full of pilots and sailors, he really shouldn't have been seeing the same name time and time again. The Yank was more his father than he knew. Chase had been the thorn in more commanders' sides than Johnston could remember.

No one on board knew how important all the Chimera pilots were, not even Belford. The *Inferno* was much more than the first interspecies warship. It was the testing ground for the most experimental and dangerous research humanity had ever undertaken. Project Rebirth might win them the war—at the expense of their humanity. Already, Johnston was responsible for the Condemned, and he had never agreed with that practice.

In the dim light of his cabin, he wondered how history would remember him.

Chapter 33

Rodrom

"**What...**" Rodrom began, but a scream of pain killed the words on his lips.

"This cannot be," Lorelei said again. It was not fear, but awe that colored her voice. "You are ironblood—your blood is too harsh for the root."

Rodrom was unable to respond as a roar escaped him and he twisted back against the nest. Lorelei quickly bounced off her feet to come to him, placing her warm hands around his face. She pulled his gaze towards her, and just for a moment, Rodrom was distracted by bright green eyes streaked with gold.

"Look at me, DerekRodrom," she commanded, but the fear inside Rodrom surged when he realized she was no longer speaking English. The musical sounds of her language fell on his ears, and his mind understood. "You have shown the trees you are a true healer, and despite the iron, it has taken root within you." Her musical language was far faster than English, and Rodrom understood each word, though he knew not how. The pain had traveled from his spine to his hands and his head was crescendoing into a symphony of pain.

"The weaver's root is truly painful. Each of us has experienced it. It will pass soon, and you will understand my people as I have come to see yours," Lorelei cried, her hand tightening on Rodrom's cheek, her fingers burning hot against his cold flesh, her gaze unwavering as she stared into his darting eyes.

"Root...weavers?" Rodrom choked out.

"Grown from the life trees of the fallen, the weaveroot is planting itself within you, and will unlock your potential!" Lorelei's eyes were wide, her excitement evident.

Rodrom could scarcely believe what she was saying. "You planted a tree in my back?" he screamed, though his voice lacked any volume, as he could not draw enough air to shout.

"Calm yourself, DerekRodrom. It will not sprout as the tree. The pollen from the Life Trees has taken root within you. When the weaveroot takes hold it will change you. Already you understand my voice; soon you will be able to understand the songs of all living things. You will hear the weave."

Rodrom was too terrified to speak, the pain arching through him and replacing his spine with lightning. He jerked as he imagined the branches of the weaveroot plowing through him, carving paths to his bones as it burrowed along muscle tissue, wrapping around nerve endings and breaking through their sheaths. The pain that lanced down his back and through his arms and legs was excruciating, and left him numb. The pain moved out as a wave, the numbness in its wake, until finally Rodrom thrashed a last time and fell still, his head and shoulders now supported in Lorelei's lap. She cupped both her hands around his face.

Rodrom took a shuttering breath, his heart pounding in his temples as the blood coursed through him fast enough to rattle his eardrums. The deep thrum of each double beat began to slow as he concentrated on it. Then, to Rodrom's confusion, the sound was overlaid with a strange new noise — almost like a stringed instrument, but without a melody. He opened his eyes to find Lorelei's gaze turned upon him. As he tried to reason out the noise's existence, more sounds joined the first. The intermittent but steady deep bellow of a horn, the tinkling of small bells that lost form as more and more caught his attention. Each new sound fit perfectly with the others, and Rodrom shook his head, afraid of what the weaveroot had done to his mind, and why he could hear music that wasn't there.

"You hear it, don't you?" Lorelei asked.

"Why do I hear music?" Rodrom asked, noticing that the beat quickened as he spoke.

"It is the song of your spirit, the beat in your chest, the rush of your blood. It is the song that every living creature, every plant has, and the weaveroot allows you to hear it, and with practice you may change it as well. You are hearing the Weave."

Rodrom's fear waned as irrational excitement took hold. The pain was nearly gone now. "This is how you access your powers?"

"The weaveroot allows us to sing to the trees to help shape them into more practical things, and allows us to repair the songs of those who are wounded, yes, but it allows us so much more."

"Can you show me?" Rodrom asked, curiosity overpowering him.

"Of course."

Chapter 34

Vincent

The burns were not as bad as they could have been, but that did not stop the corpsman and the doctor from giving Vincent an earful. The one female doctor could be a real ice queen. He hadn't intended to get burned, he just knew his pilots were in trouble and he had done the only sensible thing. The medical staff adamantly disagreed. They were too preoccupied by the effect to care about the cause. They didn't see his act as necessary, but moronic, and they were more than happy to tell him that.

Once he had learned he would not be permanently disfigured, he had attempted to leave, which the staff found less than charming. It took more than a few threats and a visit from his pilots to confine him to the recovery room. They had come pretty close to strapping him to the hospital bed. In the end, he stayed, but only because they promised he would be released back to his unit by the end of the day.

Ele took up one of the beds on the wall alongside his, but she had yet to wake from her own injuries. Vincent couldn't help but feel responsible for what had happened to her. He was, after all, the one who had brought her aboard the ship. Not that he could have left her down on the planet below. He was also the one who had ordered his men to take her back to medical. If he had taken her himself and weathered Belford's annoyance, then maybe she would not have been injured in the fire.

Those circuitous thoughts were quick to turn to other sources of guilt; his father's and Derek's faces loomed in his mind. Two more failures to save the people he cared about. He had been there when his father had died, unable to do anything to stop it. Derek had been light-years, and maybe even realities away when he was captured.

Vincent couldn't bring himself to imagine Derek as anything more than a prisoner of war. Surely he had the skills to stay alive when his facility was taken by the elves.

Can't they see I'm fine? Vincent needed to get back to his fighter. He needed to finish repairs, install the atmospheric armor package, and prepare all of his troops for the upcoming mission.

Most of his pilots had already come by to ensure he was recovering, and he had passed on what needed to be said for them to begin preparations. Tanker had found an excuse to stay away, no doubt still angry about his additional duties, and Tesla and Forge had already been in medical when Vincent arrived. Only his own wingmates, Zombie and the Duchess, had not been by yet.

Both would be busy managing the squadron's affairs while Vincent lay useless on the crisp white sheets of his prison. He was able to do some of the planning he needed with his AMI and the datapad his pilots brought him, but it was slow going, and he would get far more done if he were on the hangar deck in person.

His thoughts were interrupted when Rover barked beside him.

Much to the medical staff's ire, the robot had adamantly refused to be removed. Vincent could have ordered it to go, but he enjoyed seeing his captors annoyed. He followed the direction of the bot's gaze to a disembodied head floating just outside the curtains that separated the room.

"Go to the light..." Zombie was doing a very bad impression of a ghostly voice.

"Your hologram stopped at the neck," Vincent muttered.

A look of disappointment crossed the pilots face. "Damn holocammies never work right."

Rover barked again.

"They work just fine." Vincent gestured to the dog.

Zombie stepped inside the room, and the Duchess came around the sheets to follow him. While he sat on the edge of Vincent's cot, the Psykin chose to remain standing.

Zombie was one of the youngest pilots to join the Chimera program, but he had more than proven himself capable. He had a mop of dark hair barely contained by a military cut, bright green eyes, and a constant smirk that was always hiding some inappropriate comment.

The Duchess, on the other hand, was serious, and a strong counterpoint to the younger pilot's bravado. She had the deep blue skintone of her people, a two-pronged horn growing from her forehead that swept back over her skull, and a thin line of a mouth that she barely moved. She rarely spoke, but Vincent knew she was not always as serious as she seemed at first glance.

Today, however, she looked positively stoic. She had none of the swagger all his pilots expressed, and her body language was rigid and tense.

"You alright, Duchess?" he asked.

She stared at him. <I am fine. Zombie wanted to visit you. We have a lot of work to do.>

"Don't mind her, bossman, she's just got a stick up her alien butt because she's been picking up the slack while you've been napping."

The Duchess glared down at Zombie, and Vincent grew concerned that maybe the mantel of command was too much for her. If anything happened to him—a real possibility when dogfighting in the black—she would be the next in line to take command. He had always thought she would take to it, and had enjoyed the idea of Belford having an alien as one of his wing commanders.

<We have a lot of work to do,> she repeated.

"I appreciate you guys stopping by, but they will be releasing me in a few hours and I can get back to work then."

"Won't have much to do by then, boss. Forge and Tesla already got your fighter up and running, and we're almost done with the atmospheric package refit. We're running them all through the paces now." He let out a boisterous laugh. "Man you should have seen the look on those mechanics' faces when we fired up the turbines and scattered all their tools. Priceless."

"You're already finished with repairs and refit?"

"Trained by the best, sir." Zombie gave a mock salute. "Maybe you can meet him yourself one day."

<Are you finished?> Duchess asked. <Really, sir, we need to get back to work.>

"Yeah, of course, just don't push yourselves too hard."
They offered well wishes and left Vincent alone to think about how angry the Duchess had seemed. Something was definitely going on with her. She was one of the most structured pilots on the entire ship—she had to be, in order to prove to all the humans that she could cut it. But

this was a whole new level. Vincent needed to get out of the sickbay and back to his fighter deck as soon as possible.

Chapter 35

The Exile

The Exile could sense the Shadow as it moved through the ship in the guise of the other Psykin. It could access all the memories and the appearance of the departed, and therefore appeared to have no difficulty convincing the humans all was well. No small part of her wished to reveal its deception. She had never seen the Shadow exert so much control for so long before. It was growing stronger by the day, and eventually she might not be able to control it at all. It was never supposed to have been that way. The dagger and its summon were a means to an end—a weapon against the enemy from beyond the portals. If it extracted itself from her control, then she had only created more of the very thing she had trained to fight. That she had been exiled for.

It would be so easy to convince the humans in charge of its deception. She could go to the captain of the vessel. Show him the memories that would condemn both her and the Shadow. Destroy it before it came to power. If it weren't for Project Rebirth.

She did not need to find the Condemned to continue her search.

The project the humans had hidden so deep, was on the very ship she found herself trapped on. Details on the project were as scarce as the trail it left. The important thing though, was that it's completion would lead to human augmentation. A way for the frail men and women of the fleet to stand up against the monsters they were at war with. If she ensured the project was a success, it could be the push that was so sorely needed. It would mean everything Exile had sacrificed was worth it in the end.

She had chased the trail all over space. She had heard nothing for months, and was unable to glean even the smallest clue to the project's whereabouts, or its progress. Until she saw the ports on the back of the other's neck. Two metallic spots on the center of the spine, one on top of the other. She never would have noticed them if it weren't for the Shadow's deception. The humans had never displayed that sort of cybernetics before. They had the AMI units, of course, but those were grown inside the brain with specific nanotechnology. The ports could only mean one thing.

The ship's computer systems were easy to crack—a few pushes with her Web to gain the necessary passwords, and she was in. The pilot she had fought was code-named the Duchess, and was part of an experimental fighter wing called Chimera. That was as far as she had gotten before the encryption became too difficult to crack. She needed someone close to the project, and luckily, that person was lying in a bed inside the medical bay.

She snuck into the maintenance shafts that ran along the entirety of the ship, including near enough to the medical wing for her Web to reach him. The Exile lay in the dust-filled access way, her body pressed against wires and conduits as she reached out for the wounded's mind.

The mental anguish of those lying in medical berths was thick. So many languishing in the void of illness. The Exile found it sickening.

She could feel the wounds they had sustained, and all, save one, would recover completely. But she did not care, not when she had been scared and thrown aside like garbage. Forced to flee, and float alone through the vacuum.

She was tempted to lash out, to send nightmare visions to those too weak to deserve their unaltered flesh, but she held back. She needed information, and already she had come to close to being discovered. Better to bide her time than lose it over anger. *Emotions kill swifter than blades.*

She focused past those AMIs, looking for the lieutenant who would have the passcodes she needed. It should have been a simple effort to separate his mind from the others', but something was off. The Web was muddled, filled with confusing and disjointed images.

She jerked inside the confines of the access way, her mind full of fire. Anger that overwhelmed her own rolled off someone inside the medical bay. That someone was not human. The Exile reached for her blade, but as her fingers brushed the hilt, she remembered. She could not give it more power.

The presence was so strong, and pressed such poignant visions into her mind that her blood seemed to be boiling in her veins. She pushed through, focusing away from that screaming mind. She just needed to find the lieutenant so she could get the codes and leave. Whatever creature was causing her all this mental anguish would have to wait.

It took all of her mental reserves to force away the alien emotions and focus on the man she needed. He was sitting upright in bed, thinking about his command and his recent interaction with the Duchess. So the Shadow had come to see him, and the lieutenant had not been completely fooled by the illusion. She made a mental note that he could be of more use in the future.

She formed a thought in the Web about the ship he piloted, and fired it into his mind. For him, it would feel as though he had been struck by a wandering idea, and would have no knowledge of her infiltration. Humans were disgustingly easy to manipulate.

Unfortunately, this pilot proved to be more difficult than his compatriots. His thoughts turned immediately back to planning, and some human who was trapped on the planet they were traveling to.

Derek Rodrom — Exile was surprised to know the name. Another large player in Project Rebirth. She had stumbled into the center of the operation. Now she only needed to ensure that all the pieces fell into place. Rescue the doctor, force him to put his research into practice, and finally give humanity the edge it so desperately needed in the war.

It was difficult to delve into the deeper recesses of someone's mind. Emotions and surface thoughts were simple, the flotsam constantly generated by undisciplined minds. Secrets were kept deeper down, not broadcast as easily or as often. Even humans had some practice in that regard. She fired a few more projections at the man, to see if she could switch the path of his thoughts, but he was concentrating all of his effort on the rescue of his friend. It seemed the pilot wouldn't be giving her any more intel.

No matter, she did not need the codes if there was another way to advance the project. The Condemned would be on the planet they were heading to, and with them she could find Derek Rodrom and ensure his work was finished.

Chapter 36

Rodrom

The weaveroot wasn't working. Or at least that's how Rodrom saw it. Lorelei seemed beyond reason with excitement over the notion that an "ironblood" could possess the gifts of her people. For Rodrom, all it amounted to was a constant influx of noise and bodily aches as she tried to show him the ropes.

"Concentrate, DerekRodrom, you have to allow the Weave to speak to you," she told him, a look of serene patience on her face.

"I have no trouble tuning in. Sorting out all the noise without my head exploding is the tricky part."

Every life around him was like a garage band trying to outdo every other kid on the block. The unintelligible, inseparable noises made his head spin. He felt as though he should have the mother of all headaches, but somehow it was the rest of him that hurt. It felt like tiny needles were being slowly pressed into every inch of his palms, and the same with the soles of his feet. He longed for a med scan to tell him what sort of physiological changes were happening to his body. What sort of damage, or enhancements, the weaveroot was making beneath his flesh.

His whole body was an exercise in extremes. While his joints ached and popped, his muscles felt larger and tighter. His pulse throbbed in his neck as though he had just finished a marathon, but his lungs had none of the burn he had come to associate with exertion. Somehow the weaveroot was allowing him to transport more oxygen — or barring that, it was making him use less when he moved. His artificial copper-based blood was only a quarter as effective as a regular human's, but it was the only way the Grelkins could cure him of leukemia. The procedure had altered him down to the bone marrow, and he had felt it ever since.

He couldn't handle flying like his father, couldn't pass even the basic physical exam for the military. It was only as a surgeon that he was able to join the fleet and continue his family legacy.

Great, just great, Rodrom thought. *Trapped behind enemy lines with some super-science parasite giving me auditory hallucinations. Kudos to me.*

"You must not fight it. The Weave is everywhere, like the air around us. You breath it in, but only use what you need. Treat the Root the same."

Rodrom had begun to notice a distinct change in Lorelei as day turned to night, and wished he could study other non-feral Verdantun to fill in the gaps of his hypothesis.

Lorelei had kept his transformation a secret, so he was still being treated with the same animosity as ever. *No,* Rodrom thought, *not exactly the same.* It appeared his failure to run in exchange for helping Dirus had made the rounds. The guards shoved him around with a little less violence, and snarled at him with a little less tooth. Heck, they were practically family now.

At least he could understand them when they spoke. That was

one part of his newfound ability he had mastered. It didn't seem to matter what the language was, either. The ferals seemed to communicate with a series of snarls and barks when they were closer to their beast form, but he understood just the same.

"Lorelei, there has to be more to it." Rodrom sighed. "A command prompt or a visualization technique."

"The weaveroot is not one of your machines. It is as much a part of nature as it is a part of you. It is the bridge that connects you to every living thing."

"Do or do not, there is no try," Rodrom muttered. Lorelei raised an eyebrow. "Never mind, human expression."

"Allow yourself to sink into the music that flows through you. Do not try to control it yet, only listen."

Rodrom bit back the comment he wanted to make. She was far less receptive to his snide remarks during the day.

He tried to do as she said, to sit back and listen, but it was like sitting in a room full of televisions all tuned to different stations. How could he relax in the center of all that? The more he concentrated, the louder it all became, until finally a noise came so loud and sudden that he snapped his eyes open in surprise. The look on Lorelei's face told him it was not the Weave that had caused the disturbance.

The Verdantun were once again under attack.

Chapter 37

Johnston

"Sir, we will be coming out of warp in two minutes."

Johnston stood at his command dais. The feeds in front of him showed nothing outside their bubble of space-time.

For all the tactical advantage warp travel provided, the inability to know where they would exit was detrimental. He would have no warning if an enemy fleet were waiting just off their bow, and with the peculiarities of gravity wells, he would not be able to jump back out if the fight were too one-sided. Without her escorts, the *Inferno* would be hard-pressed to survive any lengthy engagement. She was strong, perhaps one of the strongest human ships flying, but she was only one ship in the end.

The intel had reported nothing of an enemy presence over Aberdeen. All of the fighting had been contained to the far side of the ground side portal, but by now they had been in warp for nearly two standard days, which for the enemy was practically a lifetime.

Communications keyed a ship-wide announcement to prepare all hands to exit warp. Johnston had already called a ready alert—not to force his crew to remain at their battle stations, but to be close by in the event of battle. It was taxing for the crew to remain inside their gunner's seats and fighter cockpits just to assuage his fears. He would be cautious, but not at the expense of his crew's wellbeing. In all likelihood they would drop out of warp into an empty expanse a few light-seconds out from Aberdeen. Unfortunately, that cheery thought did nothing to relax Johnston's grip on his console.

"Preparing to exit warp," Navigation announced.

Johnston's grip got just a little tighter; purple veins stood out against his light brown hands, and a small strip of pale skin on his left ring finger stood in sharp relief despite all the time it had gone bare.

Pay attention, damn it, Johnston told himself. It had been a long time since he had slept. The headaches were growing more violent by the day.

"Surfacing in five, four, three, two, one. We have reemergence," Navigation called.

"Scan all frequencies, all contacts to tactical. Launch Voidfox squadron." Johnston was thankful that his voice did not betray his exhaustion. He looked down at his display as the data poured in and was processed by his ship's powerful AIs. So far so good, but the sensors could only scan as fast as the light hit them. They were not far from the planet now. A few million kilometers, but enemy vessels could be anywhere around them. From the launch tubes the tiny interceptor craft fired out, their craft barely more than a cockpit and engines. They would scout behind the nearby planets and moons.

After several long minutes, Johnston looked over the data and acknowledged that his ship was safe.

"No enemy contacts, sir. We are being hailed by Aberdeen orbital command. Shall I put them on screen?"

"Aye." Johnston turned towards the screen.

The weathered face of an army officer appeared. "JFS *Inferno*, this is Colonel Trast of the hundred and first. I can't express how glad we are to see you. We have a real situation brewing down dirt side."

"We came as soon as we were able," Johnston said. "Have you had any incursions to this side of the portal?"

"Negative, sir. The troops on the ground have managed to hold them off, but they were pressed back to the research facility. They need support ASAP."

"And they shall have it." Johnson gestured to Belford to give the shuttle launch order. "We will dispatch ground reinforcements immediately, and air support as soon as we can bring the *Inferno* inside the atmosphere."

"What sort of ground forces are we talking about?"

"I have a company of marines, an armored platoon with escorts, as well as a full squadron of atmospheric-ready fighters."

A look of relief crossed the colonel's face. "Those elves won't know what hit them." He smiled.

"We'll get those troops back, Colonel. Leave no man behind." It was one of the american army's mottos.

"The boys will be glad to see you, that's for sure. Colonel Trast out."

The screen showing the ground commander winked out and was replaced with a forward-facing view off the bow of the ship. Already the blue flashes of engines was filling the space between the *Inferno* and the planet beyond — the shuttles carried the marines and tanks that would hopefully make good on Johnston's promise.

"All ahead full," Johnston ordered. "Get us close enough to drop the Reapers."

Part 4

Chapter 38

The Exile

The moment the Exile's vehicle passed through the portal she was assaulted by the unfiltered AMI transmissions of countless soldiers fighting for their lives. The cacophony threatened to overtake her, the pain of so many open channels spiking through her.

She redoubled the defenses in her mind, and casting out her Web as far as she could reach, she combed the battlefield for the consciousness of the Condemned platoon. Voices continued to wash over her, but her mental bulwarks held against the strain. As she searched, a picture of the battle formed in her mind. She picked up the views of dozens of soldiers, each snapshot pulling away the fog. In her mind's eye she pictured the Terran forces, and the Condemned lit up like beacons as she connected to their AMIs.

The Joint Fleet soldiers were set up in the dozen or so buildings that made up the research compound. They were built around the portal in a full three-sixty defense. The jungle beyond the buildings did not acknowledge the Terran claim to the land, and the foliage pressed in close, giving the enemy advantage of approach. An energy shield dome, just barely visible to the naked eye, ended only a few meters beyond the furthest building's edge.

The Exile's battle map shuddered as a fireball slammed into the energy shield. Exile remained motionless, her attention focused beyond the vehicle she occupied and on those bright lights of consciousness that dotted the battlefield. The Condemned were the easiest to spot, their AMIs distinct compared to the average ground trooper, but the real difference came in the emotions they broadcast. Every soldier had some fear, no matter how veteran they were. The Condemned broadcast nothing — they were literally fearless.

Exile focused her Web onto one such light — the soldier repairing the shield generator. She spun her thoughts into a tendril and reached inside the soldier's mind, attempting to see the battle from his perspective.

The soldier crouched low as a fireball smashed into the shield overhead. The unearthly roar shook his skull, and with that distraction, she was in and experiencing everything he did.

***

<Cowboy, are you hit?> His platoon sergeant commed from behind the soldier's position. Cowboy ignored the question as the fireball's energy thundered in.

The wave of heat roared over Cowboy's exposed skin, and his nose was assaulted by the acrid wash of smoke and brimstone. As the worst of the heat dissipated, he pushed himself up and out of the mud, and reached out to wipe the monitor in front of him clean. He cursed as he cleared away the grime. Beneath the cracked glass, the numbers read too low, flashed too red to be accurate.

One fireball couldn't have been enough to take out a shield grid that large, he thought. *Damn elves must have ripped up a relay.* He squinted down the field and tried to judge the distance from his position to the next emitter: a hundred meters between buildings over open ground. The pounding rain wasn't making anything easier.

Snarling, Cowboy ripped soot-covered goggles from his eyes and spat onto the lenses. While rubbing them on an even dirtier sleeve, he took a less obstructed view of the battlefield. His team was hunkered down in the crumpled husk of a biodome, their position directly beside a company of 101st regulars who occupied the adjacent building. Behind his team, at the center of the compound, was the distinct blurring of air that marked a portal. The elves outside his shield were pushing them up against it. Soon they would have nowhere to fall back to, and they would lose the beachhead they had fought so hard to gain.

The 101st Infantry Battalion entrenched with them had pitifully little tech, gnome or otherwise. Most were still wielding the weapons of the last Terran war. Their M-4's cracked loudly and filled the narrow passages with the smell of cordite, while their crew-served machine guns that belched off streams of lead in sequence as they talked back and forth. Cowboy had been with the Condemned for so long he had nearly forgotten the sound of pre-contact weaponry. Pinned down and facing steep odds was not the time he wanted to hear it.

Truth be told, his own platoon wasn't faring much better. Their mission had taken them so far from supply lines that most of their tech had broken down or run out of power. When the original incursion had been pushed back, his platoon was trapped behind enemy lines, and only with this latest beachhead were they able to link back up with Terran forces. At this point they might as well be ground pounders for all the good their unpowered gear was doing.

Through the distortion of his shield, Cowboy could see maybe a meter into the foliage around the compound. It was a truly terrible place to defend, lending cover to the enemy as they filtered through the trees. Enemy artillery, or their bastardized version of it, pounded down upon their position as Terran forces attempted to discern targets through the forest, and the beachhead was far too small to move their own guns.

It was only a matter of time before the overtaxed shield fell and the elves pushed forward, and to make things worse, they had found a way to launch small projectiles through what should have been an impenetrable wall. The tiny black spears managed to stay intact beyond the shield just long enough to pierce through soldiers' bodies before the instability from their passing the energy barrier caused them to explode. At this point, the shield was actually giving them an advantage; Cowboy didn't think the projectiles would explode without it, but to lose the shield was to be overrun. They were outgunned, outmanned, and running out of time. Grimacing at the idea of close combat or being spiked down by one of the elves' shots, Cowboy mentally keyed his holocammies to camouflage and hoped he had enough power for the dash. Grunting, he darted out from cover and across the open ground.

***Exile pulled back from Cowboy's mind as another light flared. The platoon sergeant, codename Killswitch, was calling out orders to cover Cowboy's sprint.

"Lift fire!" he shouted, the words barely audible over the noise.

He lowered his binoculars to observe the gun crew. They were thirty meters down the buildings, manning the last powered heavy weapon. Beast, the gunner, laid down the trigger and a series of eye-searing plasma bolts tore across the space between the buildings. They passed easily through the shield and splintered the line of trees beyond.

Killswitch swore as the line of fire passed dangerously close to Cowboy.

<Lift fire, damn it!> Killswitch yelled again, this time using his AMI as well. Beast looked up and nodded, spotting the barely visible blur of Cowboy's camouflaged run.

"Daredevil, take up the slack," Killswitch shouted to the other gunner.

Exile could see that the other gunner was positioned on the only remaining part of the second story of the biodome. With barely enough room for himself, he was operating an old M240B, a belt fed machine gun that spat 7.62 rounds. His assistant gunner, Snowball, was crouching on a ruined pillar beside him, his eyes glued to a pair of binoculars, and calling out targets as they moved between the trees.

Both minds shone in Exile's Web as they responded to their new orders. The gunner traversed his weapon to lay down covering fire for Cowboy, his advantage in height allowing him to clear the sprinting figure. With each burst of fire the gun slammed into his shoulder, his mind flared with excitement. A touch of surprise dampened his light in Exile's Web. He pressed himself low, and a heartbeat later a thick black spike whistled past where his head had been. It slammed into the building behind him, where it detonated, taking out piece of a wall.

The gunner leaned forward again and continued firing, and the Exile pulled herself back to view the field as a whole once again.

She had only discovered her platoon's involvement in the beachhead a scarce half hour before she breached the portal. Once she had realized they were planetside, it was a simple affair to find a ride down to the colony. As a newly minted Special Forces lieutenant, she was afforded certain privileges, not the least of them the ability to commandeer a shuttle. Her Web ensured none of the other soldiers would remember her.

Though they were based on the *Inferno*, the platoon had almost no record in any of the computers she had searched. The best she had found was a list of fifteen code names.

She would need to dive into their minds for more intel on their capabilities, but she had worked with Special Forces soldiers before. Each was an army unto himself. These were the best the humans had to offer.

Her Web trembled, alerting her that Cowboy was close to a source of the energy the human's called "magic." He had not recognized the threat, so Exile dove her consciousness forward into his and flashed a warning in his mind.

***

Rounds peppered the ground as Cowboy sprinted across the last open space to the relay. He was unshielded, wearing no armor, and inches from the front line. A shadow of doubt touched him, though he shrugged off the feeling, knowing the barrier was still up, and his holocammies were keeping him somewhat hidden.

The relay itself was a scant meter from the shield; its disc-shaped antenna projected the energy barrier between him and the enemy. As he dropped down into the mud to check the diodes, he felt a sudden sense of foreboding, followed by a blood-thirsty roar.

Reacting on instinct, he threw himself to the side. He dropped his hand to his hip for his sidearm as the feral lashed out at him. Cowboy saw only a blur of white fur and savage claws before red sprayed into his eyes. Wiping the grime from his face, he scrambled to cover the wound.

It wasn't until he noticed the monster slumped on the ground in front of him, its side littered with bloodied holes, that he realized it wasn't his blood. The feral looked almost like an oversized wolf, with pitch-black claws and wicked-looking horns over its eyes. Along its spine was a row of spikes that extended down along a whip-like tail and came together at the tip. Tight muscles bulged beneath blood-matted fur as it heaved its death rattle from its chest.

Cowboy holstered his sidearm and vaulted over the dead elf. He reached with his other hand for the toolkit he kept on his belt, dropping it on his knee as he forced his shaking hand to hold steady. His heart screamed in his throat, vibrating his temples as he concentrated on the relay and not the adrenaline surging through him. *Too close a call*, he thought. *No way I could have gotten the shot off.*

***

Exile pushed down the anger that threatened to rise within her. *Distraction kills more than the sharpest knife.* Cowboy had ignored her first warning, and her second was too late to help him—only the swift reactions of his teammate had saved him. They were unaccustomed to her methods, too steeped in battle to heed her telepathic suggestions. She was unable to move forward while trapped in her vehicle, and so the battle would play out without her interference.

But the operators inside her vehicle had begun arguing, and Exile reluctantly listened in.

"The damned instant we passed through the portal we lost them, Sergeant" one yelled from the rear of the truck.

"How could we lose all the coms?" the driver called back. "They have damn near a thousand redundancies." A similar sentiment emanated from one of the Condemned.

***

"You fix the coms yet?" Killswitch called as he huddled low beside a soldier called Locksmith. He glanced over his shoulder at the platoon sergeant with a sneer and ducked as another spike whistled over them.

"I'm not a radio operator; I know how to turn them on and off,"

197

Locksmith spat. "That's all."

"I realize that, damn it, but I need coms and you're all we've got," the sergeant spat back. He shook his head and glanced down the field. "How could an entire battalion lose coms?"

"Magic," Locksmith muttered, rolling his eyes, then went back to his work on the radio. Of all the tech they had lost that day—blasters, motion trackers, thermals—it was the radios that hurt most. The device wasn't actually a radio, of course; radio waves hadn't been used since pre-contact. Honestly, Locksmith had no idea what the thing emitted, only that it could go through portals and get them reinforcements, and maybe some desperately needed counter battery.

Locksmith had no desire to be bent over the little unit in the middle of a firefight; he should have ben laying down rounds against the cursed ferals, but they needed to get heavy support, and soon. If only he could access the bionet like he was supposed to be able to, then his AMI could tell him exactly how to fix it, but no such luck. So he pulled the unit apart and gave himself a crash course in communications.

The gnome radio wasn't like anything he had tinkered with before. Locksmith was a breacher, not commo. He dealt with portals, doorways, and things with locks—physical or otherwise. He just didn't have enough experience to know how this blasted thing worked. Not for the first time, he bit back a curse rising to his lips. Another deep breath and he pulled another set of wires from the box. He would just push them together until something worked.

***

Despite her attention on her own platoon, Exile still sensed the general tide of emotions shifting across the entrenched soldiers. Despite the initial determination to establish a beachhead and push the enemy off their colony world, the troops had too little equipment to hold against the forces the elves had amassed. The dull thuds of detonating rockets had begun to wane as the 101st expended the last of its shoulder-carried launchers. The thunderous roars of machine guns had become the intermittent growls of a dying beast, and the cries of "Forward!" and "To victory!" had been drowned out by calls of "Medic!" and "Fall back!"

The truck that had been sent back through the rift to establish bounce relays was unable to reestablish a connection. The elves had found a way to shut down their equipment, not just jam the signals. And with no communications through the portal, they were cut off.

Her own men's consciousness seemed to shine brighter as the battle declined. She could sense hope and awe from the men closest to their building. Given that the biodome they occupied had the largest profile of all the fighting positions, her platoon was effectively the center of the resistance. There were too many soldiers on the field for her to affect them with her Web, but the platoon acted as a conduit, allowing her draw attention to their actions. She bent to the task of rallying the troops around them, still connected to each as she watched the battle play out from fifteen sets of eyes.

***

"How did this happen?" Snowball muttered. "Fifteen left, down three." A burst of fire tore between crumbling walls into the treeline beyond, and they heard a roar in response.

"Solid hit. I think you wounded one," he said, squinting into binoculars.

"You mean how could Intel be just so completely wrong?" Daredevil asked as he realigned his weapon.

"Yeah, how'd they miss the entire damn army out here? Traverse left three." Another burst.

"I stopped wondering that a while ago—they're wrong more often than not. Do we have a spare barrel?" Daredevil asked as the last link of his weapons belt clinked to the ground. He grabbed another can and tore off the cover. With a quick glance at the rounds, he lifted the weapon's cover and laid them in place, then slammed the feed tray cover down and tore back the charging handle. With a squeeze, he sent another burst down range. "I haven't used one of these in a while but I'm pretty sure if it turns red we need a new one."

"I don't think so, hold on. Widget!" Snowball called over his shoulder, prompting another soldier to come running up on the floor beneath them. "Damn it, Widget, stay low. Make contact with the 101st in that building next to us and get a spare barrel for this thing."

Widget nodded and ran back out of sight, Snowball shaking his head as he turned back toward the fight.

"You think he'll find one?" Daredevil asked, letting off another burst.

"I doubt it, but it'll keep him from losing it during the fight. You know how new guys are." Snowball shrugged best as he could lying prone and looked back through his optics. "You know I always said the pre-contact weapon training would come in handy. Right fifteen, up seven." His ear rang as the gun swung around and spat another string.

***

Cowboy realized instantly that the relay wasn't damaged, and none of the others down the line were responding to his pings. The shield was coming down—he didn't know why, but it was coming down whether it should or not. Cowboy stole a glance back at his team; they only had two guns up and Doc had established a casualty collection point deeper in the biodome. The 101st on either side of their building seemed to be running low on ammo, or were losing more men than could man weapons—across the compound more guns were falling silent. The ferals moving through the woods only meters from him seemed impossible in number. Too many would survive a full-on charge. As he tore back towards the building, he ran his hand over the hatchet at his hip. The fighting was about to get a lot closer.

***

"As soon as Cowboy clears the wall, I want that barrel red," Killswitch snarled from his position next to Beast. "He's got that look. The shield's going down. Things are about to get bad. Where's Blackout?"

His knuckles white from gripping his weapon, Beast replied through gritted teeth, "He was covering Doc at his CCP."

"Shit. I'll be back." Killswitch dodged behind the gun and moved further into the building.

Beast counted the seconds as Cowboy sprinted toward his position. After an eternity, he cleared the field of fire and Beast slammed down on the thumbpads. The weapon shuddered in his hands and he whooped with pleasure. He watched with a cockeyed grin as the plasma bolts destroyed the trees in front of him and sent fires springing up. As if to answer his blast, a trio of fireballs erupted from the forest.

"The shields..." Cowboy panted, ducking low as the fireballs detonated.

"We know. You got that look." Beast's face lit up with each burst, the illuminated grin giving him a demonic look.

"I set up a few surprises for them, but I think a charge is coming." Cowboy pulled a rifle off his back and hit the ground next to Beast. With a careful eye, he took aim along with deep breaths of air. As the crosshairs steadied, he watched for movement, then snapped off a shot between breaths. "Where's the rest of the team?" His question was

201

punctuated by a roar from the wounded.

"Locksmith's on the net, the other gun team is to my right." Beast paused to shoot. "Killswitch is getting Blackout, Rehab, and Doc. Still no coms with the away team, and I haven't seen Widget."

"Leave it to him to get lost," Cowboy muttered with another shot. "We're going to need to fall back after the first wave." Beast grunted in acknowledgment. "Do we have a rally point?"

"The back of the building, I think."

"Lots of room to move in here. Better than the streets, but still it'll give them an advantage."

"So we'll just have to kill them all here, then." Beast set his jaw and went back to his methodical firing.

"I see Killswitch now," Cowboy said after a glance back into the biodome.

Killswitch came up panting with Blackout, Rehab, and Doc behind him. Widget followed, looking crestfallen.

"Alright, get ready for a charge," Killswitch barked the instant he caught his breath. "Blackout and Widget, take up a position between the gun teams, and use the guns as long as you can. Then we get down and dirty."

Blackout grinned and reached up to touch a hilt that protruded over his left shoulder. Widget gulped and nodded, the fear obvious in his eyes.

"Doc, I want you with me. We're going to fill in the weak spots, and of course you take care of the wounded."

"I was taking care of the wounded, until you moved me," Doc countered, pulling a weapon from his back anyway.

"The 101st have their own medics. We'll need you soon enough," Cowboy cut in before Killswitch went off on him. Tensions were too high as it was.

Killswitch grunted and took up a firing position beside Cowboy. "You men had best pray to whatever god you fancy most," he muttered. "Though you'll damn well keep your feet. I won't have any of my men die on their knees, begging for help that ain't coming."

Exile could sense their resolve as they set their defenses against the oncoming charge. Each of them prepared to fight to the last man to hold the breach. The vehicle she sat in had emptied of its soldiers, having lost all mobility when a spine pierced three of its six wheels. She almost hadn't noticed, but she didn't have the option to run, anyway. The Shadow had grown too strong, and failing to rescue Derek Rodrom could mean the end of Project Rebirth.

Chapter 39

Vincent

Vincent watched as Ele was carried into the medical shuttle along with the other civilians the *Inferno* had been transporting from their burning colony. Ele had still not woken from the coma that had landed her in the medical bay in the first place. The doctor seemed torn between it being a psychological reaction to the stress of two near-death experiences in as many days, or an underlying condition. But they simply didn't have the time to treat such a critical patient with the limited facilities aboard the supercarrier, and they needed to care for fleet soldiers first. The doctors down on Aberdeen would see to Ele's treatment.

That wasn't what was bothering Vincent, though. It was something else, something he couldn't quite put his finger on.

"Sad your girlfriend's leaving, boss?" Zombie asked from behind him.

"You often fly in front of my sights, Zom, think about that."

He turned around. A huge smile was pasted on the pilot's face.

"Safest place I could fly, sir!" He snapped into a precise salute.

"I'm going to change your call sign to Joker. Then I'm going to see if the captain needs the *Inferno* washed."

"Pretty sure that names been taken already." Zombie was still smiling.

Vincent felt the corners of his mouth itching, but forced the angry look to stay on his face. "Why do I put up with you?"

"Because I am the second-best pilot this side of the galaxy."

"Flattery? That's new."

"Sir? I meant Commander Belford, of course." Zombie's smile grew, then he dropped down to the deck on his palms and started doing pushups.

Vincent growled, "Real clever. When we get back I'm going to invent a special punishment for you. Get up, we have work to do."

The younger pilot hopped to his feet, still bouncing with glee as Vincent led the way up the false horizon of the docking ring.

"All the fighters have passed their preflight checks?" Vincent asked, already knowing the answer.

"You bet, sir. I double-checked them myself. All the flaps, turbines, and air intakes are operating at peak conditions. The Reapers will finally get a chance to see what this armor package can do."

Vincent silently agreed. With all the training they had undergone in order to pilot the craft, it had been nearly intolerable to launch with the same configuration time after time. He absently rubbed at the ports on the back of his neck, thinking about everything he had sacrificed to fly.

"All the other pilots are ready?" Vincent continued grilling Zombie. The young pilot would presumably command his own squadron before long, though hopefully not due to the loss of his own leader.

The question seemed to give Zombie pause. "Well, sir, Duchess has been acting weird lately."

So it isn't just me. "Weird how?" Vincent asked.

"Just off, you know, like she's not all there. More than usual, I mean."

"Do you think she's fit to fly?"

"Oh, hell yeah. She's acting weird, not dead." Zombie smiled again. "She's been going over her ship like she's a day-one pilot. Must have checked everything three times. It's probably just nerves. Who knows how those nymphs think."

Their ships came into view as they walked further along the ring. It was still bizarre to see his pilots standing on what appeared to be the wall as the floor curved ever upward.

"Right, just keep on her when we're down there. We leave with twelve."

"We bring twelve home."

Chapter 40

Rodrom

The sounds of battle echoed strangely around the pit where Rodrom and his fellow scientists sat. None of the survivors bothered to cower in fear anymore; their minds had adapted to the stress, for better or worse. Instead they sat with their backs to one another for comfort and to keep them out of the mud. Having seen the Verdantun encampment in detail, Rodrom no longer considered his prison barbaric. The Verdantun dwelled within the living roots of trees, and before the Joint Fleet incursion, they were constantly on the move. The prisoner accommodations could be considerably worse, and the mud could not be helped. The planet's local climate was a constant state of damp.

Looking up into the canopy, Rodrom tried to concentrate on the noise of the oncoming battle. Lorelei had been pulled away when the fighting began in earnest, leaving Rodrom to contend with the weaveroot on his own. His hands still felt like they were full of needles. Closer examination of them gave him little extra information, what with the mud and low light, though he was convinced he could see the ends of minuscule roots pushing out of the creases in palm.

Rodrom kept to himself at the edge of the pit—consciously because the further he kept from the others the less he would be able to sense them, and subconsciously because the other scientists did not like how much time he spent helping the Verdantun and made no moves to engage him. More than a few rumors had circulated that he was going to defect, given the chance. Should they learn that a dangerous piece of the enemy's "technology" was now grafted to his spine, the reaction was sure to be less than pleasant.

With no distractions in the muddy pit, Rodrom was more or less forced to listen to the music that drifted from each of his colleagues. Most of it was nondescript, just the beating of drums with an unenthusiastic stringed accompaniment. He tried to ignore it best as he could, but was quickly interrupted. A symphony erupted when an amber-skinned Verdantun came into view at the top of the pit.

"You will come with me," the elf stated, pointing at Rodrom with a slender finger.

Rodrom knew better than to acknowledge that he understood their native tongue. There was a difference between the language, and what the weaveroot allowed him to know, and Lorelei had ensured this was clear to Rodrom. She had implored him to keep his new abilities a secret from the others, lest they both be killed, but Rodrom didn't need the encouragement. Feigning ignorance, he raised his hands in a gesture of surrender.

The Verdantun pounded the long staff it carried into the ground with what was clearly impatience. "Damn ironbloods don't understand anything," it muttered, then thrust its staff into the pit towards Rodrom so he could hold on to be pulled up. Rodrom begrudgingly reached out, wrapping both hands around the staff.

He regretted it immediately. The moment his palm touched wood, the ever-present music that so bothered him was washed away in the fiery dissonance of energy the staff contained. While the Verdantun and humans sounded like orchestrated symphonies, each piece of their anatomy playing in a sort of harmony, the staff sang a thundering heavy metal song. The roar of a forest fire, the rampant thunder of a lightning storm, the fury of an erupting volcano, all twisted into music over the cadence of war drums.

Power.

The music thundered and vibrated through Rodrom. This was the tool the Verdantun used to create their offensive magic.

It was his lifetime of delivering bad news and handling incompetent superiors that saved him. His surgeon's face could confuse even the most adept poker player, and while a moment passed as he steeled his features, the Verdantun above him was no master interpreter of human expression.

Somehow over the din of the music, Rodrom made out the guard saying, "Get on with it already, lazy ironblood." Rodrom obliged by gripping the staff with his other hand, allowing the Verdantun to hoist him with supernatural strength up and out of the pit.

Rodrom released his grip as his feet passed over the lip of the hole and immediately the song that thundered in his mind was gone, replaced by the soft songs of nearby biorhythms. Their music was a whisper in contrast.

Curiosity mingled with relief washed over him. The touch of such power was foreign to him, and not simply due to its extradimensional origins. Rodrom had always been a healer, and had set aside any pursuit of personal wealth or influence for the betterment of those whose care was entrusted to him. The lure of that staff, with such tangible energy, was difficult to ignore. The guard did not allow him any time to think on the matter, however, and roughly shoved Rodrom walking towards the camp proper.

It didn't take Rodrom long to realize that the battle he had been listening to for the better part of the day was not going favorably for the Verdantun. As he got closer to the camp, he sensed the chaos long before his ears or eyes could confirm it. The Verdantun forces were in shambles, with wounded soldiers streaming in from the battle, carried by others who could barely keep themselves erect. The trees specifically used for the wounded were filled, the songs of the healers lost beneath the cries for aid from unshifted ferals, and the roars from those still in the beastly facade. Wounded lay wherever there was room for them, and already there was a pile of the ones who could not be saved.

Rodrom was ushered towards the healers, though his path needed no bidding. The wounded occupied his mind so fully, he almost forgot he was in an enemy encampment with a foreign technology growing inside his body. He triaged each wounded soldier as he moved, estimating each patient's chance at survival, as well as what medical interventions he could use to save them. It was butcher's work, learned from his long practice on the frontlines and in ships' med bays: *Save as many as you can as quickly as you can, and ignore the ones you can't help or who will take the most effort.* The brutal numbers game war forced on the members of the medical corps.

"Bring the human over here." Lorelei's voice broke through Rodrom's concentration. She was standing at the entrance of a large tree, her hair matted to her face, and blood streaked down the leaves she wore like armor. Catching Rodrom's eye, she continued in English, "I need your help DerekRodrom. Too many will die this day."

Rodrom nodded, wasting no errant thoughts on his feelings

towards her. There was precious little time as it was; he didn't need to be asked to help. "Where do you need me?" he asked for her sake.

Lorelei nodded towards the wounded lying around in the mud. Another Verdantun approached and handed Rodrom the bag he had been using to treat the other wounded in days past. Wasting no time, he approached the first casualty on his mental list, dropped to his knees to search through the bag, and set to work.

Chapter 41

The Exile

Cowboy squinted through the cracked scope into the forest. The movement between the trees had ceased, and spines no longer peppered the human forces. A lull had fallen over the battlefield. His shield had maybe minutes left before it collapsed, and the fleet ground forces would be up against the full brunt of the elven army.

"Shield's down!" Cowboy called, seeing the all-too-familiar flash, and as he shouted the trees bent aside and a horde erupted into view. The roiling mass was the stuff of nightmares; as it escaped the obscurity of shadow, violent analogs of Earth animals boiled forth. Spike-covered wolves darted with obscene speed between the column-like legs of massive bears. Horse-sized porcupines launched their spikes across the field.

Cowboy tried to identify as many as he could: a bull here, a cougar there, a moose with razor antlers beyond. Over the unnatural fear of seeing so many monsters, Cowboy's logic told him there were no exotics among them — it was an arboreal unit.

The monsters charged the gap, with unmorphed riders sitting astride them. Cowboy squinted at the patterns on their skin to get an idea of the forms they would take, then saw a bow in the hands of the closest rider.

"Take cover!" he called as a thousand bows thrummed impossibly loud around them and arrows filled the sky. Cowboy pushed himself as close to the wall as possible while the shafts rained down. Those arrows would kill soldiers without armor just as swiftly as bullets, and Cowboy had no doubt they had some magic in them to make them more deadly. When the lethal rain ceased, Cowboy pushed himself back up on his elbows and let loose a round that caught a rider in the shoulder. The rider twirled to the ground and lay there shuddering.

The thunder of his shot drew his attention from the charge; the field was far too quiet. Too few guns were answering the roars of the elves.

The soldiers were paralyzed with fear.

"They're using a fear spell—snap out of it," Cowboy yelled and snapped off another shot. He cocked a fist and slammed it into the side of Beast's head. The larger man scowled, but as the unnatural fear was broken, the scowl transformed into a sheepish grin. His plasma cannon started blasting again, the air between the armies filling with glowing bolts as he let fly. His shots were the key. The closest soldiers quickly leveled their own desperate fire into the nightmare mass beyond.

***

Exile released a held breath as she broke through the spell that had immobilized the platoon. In Cowboy's analytical assessment, she had found resolve enough to combat the fear spell. Cowboy's punch had been the physical catalyst that allowed her to affect them all. As each of them snapped out of it, Exile used that same resolve and spread it out among the other soldiers. Freed from the paralyzing emotion, the 101st opened up on the approaching horde.

Beast's gun tracked the larger target that approached from the two corridors he could fire down. The bolts of superheated plasma splashed across an armored bear's hide, and it melted to slag. He immediately traversed to a wolf without releasing the trigger. The smaller creature darted around the incoming bolts and avoided harm. Beast's dissatisfaction was palatable on Exile's Web, and he turned his fire on the larger morphed elves again.

The gun would overheat before long, and they all knew it. Their position would be overrun before that happened. Daredevil added his own heavy fire to the mix, traversing back and forth as he sprayed a wall of lead. Smaller beasts fell left and right, but still, they came. His smaller metal rounds simply bounced off the armored bears. Only Beast's plasma could melt their hide.

The riders continued to fire their arrows, keeping the 101st's heads down and the Condemned annoyed. Those who had been struck sent waves of pain and fear though the Exile's concentration.

***

Another fireball crested the forest, splashing violently just short of the lines. Smoke billowed from the foliage it struck and further obscured the field. There was no need to aim now; they were blind through the smoke and rain.

The faster wolves darted ahead of the horde and came within meters of the buildings. Cowboy dropped a hand from his rifle to form a pistol with his fingers. He pointed as the first one disappeared in an amazingly bright flash. "Boom," he whispered, miming a shot.

The IED's explosion caused a lull in the arrows, giving Snowball a chance to peek over his wall. The riders were standing up on their mounts and launching themselves into the air. He yanked up his optics to take a closer look. The first elf he saw was spasming and shifting in midair as its arms contorted and reformed into wings. Legs bent and twisted, forming claws, and feathers burst out of its skin. The changes happened before he struck the ground.

Snowball pulled back from the binoculars to witness the flock of monstrous birds take flight over their position and disappear into the storm clouds above.

"Shit, they're airborne!" yelled Killswitch, dropping one from the sky with a well-placed round as he spoke. "Daredevil, shift fire, they're the bigger threat now. Beast, you keep taking out those bears. None of the one-oh-one's guns are getting through."

"Sure thing," Beast replied, his fingers never releasing the trigger. Daredevil pulled his weapon off the tripod and braced the butt of it against the floor beneath him. His shots would not be accurate, but with enough lead in the air, the birds might think twice before swooping down their lines.

"Blackout, stay with Locksmith, those coms are priority!" Killswitch called over the chaos that swelled as the screams of the airborne mixed with the roars of the ground forces. "We need to start falling back inside the building, or we'll get surrounded."

Snowball moved first, swinging off his perch with one hand as he gripped his weapon close with the other. Releasing himself, he dropped the seven or so feet to the ground below and rolled to reduce the impact. Coming up in a crouch, he snapped off potshots at the fliers in order to cover Daredevil's egress. The gunner's move was not nearly so graceful; he cleared the weapon, dropping it unceremoniously to the concrete below before gripping the ledge with both hands and swinging himself down. Once down, Snowball fired off the last of his clip as

Daredevil rushed to load and resume firing.

With the gun team down from their position, Killswitch started moving other members of the platoon further into the biodome, where the tight space would at least provide some cover to fight from while they were overrun. Widget went first, followed by Cowboy. They ran back between shattered work stations and massive broken machines before turning and planting themselves behind the best cover. Other 101st soldiers had flooded into the building from the back, no doubt hoping the Condemned would protect them. They seemed heartened to have the elite team fighting beside them. Regardless of their lack of powered armor, the mere fact that they were Special Forces fostered hope in the beleaguered troops' hearts.

With the rest of the team on the move, Locksmith grabbed the mess of wires and metal that had once been a radio and hoofed it towards the others. Blackout followed slowly behind him, popping off shots as he moved. Exile could sense an inordinate amount of determination stemming from Blackout, concentrated as he was on protecting Locksmith.

Beast stayed on his weapon until the entire team had moved, and when he realized he was alone, he shrugged and continued firing.

"Beast, move," Killswitch yelled out, already realizing the gunner would ignore the order. "He's not going to leave that gun. We need to make sure he can fall back when they take the wall."

The first of the monsters had already reached the 101st building. The sounds of close in-fighting, grunts and screams, and metal clashing against rock-hard claws and teeth grew louder in the absence of gunfire.

As the elf warriors reached the Condemned, Blackout threw back his head and let loose a roar to match theirs. Dropping his rifle, he reached behind his back and pulled a staff from the mesh of his web gear. He held it with both hands, forward and across his body, and thumbed a trigger near the bottom. Two metals spurs erupted from the top, deploying smaller and smaller slices until they formed the double blades of a battle axe. He swung the weapon in an arc, challenging the nearest elf.

A wolf that had made it through the team's fire turned and leapt over the wall into the compound. Two more bounds brought it within range of the platoon. Blackout swung his axe in a wide arc low to the ground, and on the upswing caught the creature across its flank. The blade tore through the fur, muscle, and bone with its micrometer-thick edge, coating Blackout in gore. He continued the swing, and with a twist of the blade, lifted the wolf and used the weapon's momentum to throw it towards the other shapeshifters.

"Fix bayonets!" Killswitch called as he too dropped his rifle and reached for the two K–bars he kept strapped to his back. Beside him, Cowboy pulled the hatchet from his own web gear, then touched a gauntlet on his wrist. The mechanism within the gauntlet whirred and a round shield extended. A moment later, it thrummed with power as the force field lay over it.

Doc had already dropped his weapon and was working on the 101st wounded who were using the building as cover. Widget stood over him with his rifle quivering. He fired sporadically, but his rounds hit their mark. Snowball pulled out a dagger from his gear and twisted the handle, extending the blade by a meter. He took up a fighting stance beside Daredevil, who continued to engage the fliers when they attempted to come inside the holes that spread across the top of the dome. None had made it inside so far, but Daredevil only had so much ammo.

Two more wolves crested the wall with a massive bull just

behind them. The muscles of its shoulders seemed impossibly large, and its horns gleamed black. The bull snorted, then lowered its head and charged, smashing through anything in its path. Simultaneously, the two wolves sprung out to the sides. Cowboy knelt down and lifted his shield up, catching the one that pounced at him. As the wolf connected with him, Cowboy grunted and pushed it to the ground. He slammed his hatchet into its skull.

The second wolf dove for Killswitch, who slashed out with his knives as he rolled to the side. The wolf's razor claws cut a deep wound in his arm that immediately gushed warm blood down his skin and over his blade. Before he could turn to slash again, Snowball cut the head from the monster with his sword.

Blackout stood completely still as the bull charged at him. He tightened his grip on the axe, and at the last second, slammed it forward into the beast's head. The axe glanced off the magically enhanced skull and slid onto the horn, which sparked against the blade. The beast's advance was unhindered, and Blackout was caught by the bull's horns and tossed to the side. As the bull thundered past, he rolled to his feet and squared off again, ignoring the bleed seeping from the wound in his stomach.

"Let's go, bitch," Blackout growled.

The bull thundered to a stop and turned, tossing its head. It pounded the ground with its front hoof, sending dirt flying, then charged again. The bull bucked its head, and Blackout was catapulted again by the horns. He came slamming down as his axe clattered to the ground a foot away. As soon as his breath returned, he let loose a stream of curses and grabbed for the weapon. He roared once more and swung at the bull's retreating back.

Killswitch regained his footing and glanced back to see a

massive bull crash to the ground with an axe embedded between its now broken horns. Blackout was standing beside it, blood-soaked, panting, and smiling. Killswitch shook his head and Exile heard a single word at the forefront of his thoughts: *berserker*.

The rage that stormed through Blackout's mind shocked Exile. Any confusion she'd had about him disappeared as Killswitch thought that word. She didn't know what *berserker* meant, but it was clear that Blackout was no normal human.

"How are those..." Killswitch started to ask, but Locksmith shot him a vicious glare. He looked away as the rhythmic sound of the blaster cannon ended. Beast was holding a grotesque cougar by its neck, his knife embedded in its eye. With a quick jerk of the blade and a shove of his boot, he pushed the creature off, then with a last look at his cannon, turned and bolted for the rest of the team. Steeling himself, Killswitch sprinted to meet Beast halfway.

Before he could reach him, he was thrown to the ground by a sonic blast from one of the armored bears. The beast closed its massive jaws to end its roar and thundered towards the two of them.

Beast looked down at himself; his melee weapons had been stripped away during the fight with the cougar, and only his knife remained. He set his jaw and turned towards the bear, while Killswitch gripped his Ka-Bars tightly. The bear's head erupted in offal and tissue, and the explosion was followed by a sharp crack.

"That's Trigger's gun!" Killswitch called, his heart pounding from the close call. His scout team had to be close, relatively speaking, for their sniper to engage the targets. A quick glance at the patchwork dome above him led Killswitch to believe Trigger was set up in a tree somewhere outside the compound.

***

Exile picked up more lights on the fringes of her Web as soon as she recognized the rail gun. The rest of her platoon was moving through the treeline to the right of the battle, bringing with them the only gnome tech that was still operational. *Will that be enough?* she wondered.

***

Doc slammed his fist in the dirt as the soldier he had been working on rattled his final breath. He spat out the needle cap he had removed with his teeth and pushed all feelings away. He would deal with them later, when there were no more wounded. The regular infantry didn't have the experience to bring melee weapons into battle like the Condemned did. They were attacking the creatures with rifles held like clubs, and with the straight blades they kept on their kits. The casualties were staggering.

He looked in front of him at the dozens of wounded lying across the floor of his hastily established casualty collection point, with far too few medics. They didn't stand a chance without technology. Doc bent down to help the next one, knowing he was only prolonging the inevitable. As he reached back for his med bag he cursed—a cougar analog was attempting to sneak through his position. Doc could just make out its outline; it was mostly camouflaged by magic.

"I see you," Doc muttered, then without a moment's hesitation, he dashed forward and slammed the syringe into the cougar's head. He got lucky—the needle slid into the monster's eye. He depressed the plunger, partially blinding it, then dropped it just in time to avoid the wild swing of Snowball's sword, which sliced through the creature's neck.

"Monsters to the front, monsters to the rear, today isn't going well," Snowball said as he squared his shoulders and held his sword at the ready. He looked back across the CCP. "How many did it kill?"

"Too many."

***

Desperation and anguish screamed out of Doc and Snowball. Exile's platoon had kept a tight lid on their emotions so far, allowing only small sparks of fear or doubt to escape before they were quickly covered with resolve and determination. But the pain those two felt after so much silence rocked Exile out of her Web and left her panting and clutching her horn. Swiftly, she went through her mantras: *A calm center, a clear mind.* She unsheathed her knife. *Emotions kill swifter than any blade.* She pressed her thumb onto the tip, releasing a rivulet of blood, along with the tension pent up in her mind.

She replaced the knife in its sheath and steeled her resolve. She had been tortured by monsters that made the elves seem tame, and she would not allow two men's revulsion for a necessary task interrupt her. She didn't have time. Without another thought she pushed her Web back out to encompass her platoon. Two minds flared. Locksmith had fixed his radio.

When Killswitch reached Locksmith, he was brandishing a bloodied wrench like a sword as he defended his undesired charge.

"Never again," he snarled at Killswitch. The sergeant ignored him.

"This is Condemned Actual. Any station on the net, this is an emergency broadcast." Killswitch released the switch and bent low to hear the reply. The radio shouted static back at him, which Locksmith responded to with a resounding whack from his wrench.

Killswitch roared in anger, but immediately shut his mouth when a garbled transmission broke through.

"Condemned, this is Reaper One, I read your traffic. Sitrep, over," a voice crackled.

"We are pinned down by a battalion-size element of ferals. Break," Killswitch said, letting his finger off the mic out of habit—the gnome tech com units didn't need breaks. "No gnome weapons remaining, low on ammo, we've lost most of our brigade. Break. We need reinforcement immediately. How copy, over?"

The staticky pause stretched on for an eternity. Killswitch tried to turn a deaf ear to the screams and roars of close combat.

"That's a good copy, Condemned Actual. Close air support inbound, coming in hot. On station in five mikes. Hold on, over."

"Roger that, Reaper One. We'll be here."

Killswitch twisted the dial dangling from the box.

"Condemned Four, Condemned Five, anyone, this is Condemned Actual, do you copy?"

"Roger that, Condemned Actual, this is Condemned Four. You guys look like you could use some help down there." Killswitch looked up at the familiar crack of a rail gun; another feral's head exploded.

"What's your location?" Killswitch demanded.

"Above you on the mountain side. We climbed up as soon as we could escape their scouts." Killswitch looked up through the holes in the dome towards the mountain range and saw a glint of light. Klepto was signaling him.

"The bird's going to be here in—" His transmission was cut short as a spike slammed into the ground beside him. His reflexes kicked in, and he rolled to the side, coming up with Ka-Bars in hand. His darted his eyes back and forth in search of the feral.

"Sergeant, there," Locksmith shouted, pointing at what looked to be a spiny ball rolling towards them.

"Shit! I need to get back on the radio."

"I've got you." Locksmith brandished his wrench. The hedgehog ceased its roll, popped open, and bent forward. Three more spikes came firing from its back at Locksmith. He dove low, missing two, but yelled out as the third sank deep into the meat of his left shoulder. He tore it from his skin and threw it to the side. Without the shield to destabilize, however, the spike did not explode.

"Sergeant, I've..." He dropped to his knees and stared blankly at his legs.

"Doc! Locksmith's hit!" Widget screamed as he ran over. He gripped his rifle with white fingers, and swung it wildly about as he stood over his teammate.

Doc looked up from the man he was treating and swore. He slapped a bandage in the wounded man's hand. "Hold this tight, I'll be back." He grabbed his pack and raced towards Locksmith. As he reached the fallen man, another spike skittered into the ground beside him, sending dirt into his face.

"Shit, Widget, shoot it!" Doc yelled, then turned away. Widget looked at the spiked monster with wild eyes.

***

Exile felt a sense of unhinged terror growing in the soldier. His thoughts flowed like water as the fear consumed him, pouring out without any of the discipline the others had shown. Nothing could have prepared him for this. None of the training scenarios had felt this way, been this real. He couldn't survive this...

Widget sited down the barrel and lined the shot. His hands shook uncontrollably as he took a deep breath. Fighting to keep from closing his eyes, he squeezed the trigger like he had so many times before. Nothing.

"It's jammed," Widget said to himself.

"Then fix it," Doc snarled around the syringe he was holding in his teeth. He probed Locksmith's wound with his fingers, then shook his head as he heard the rail gun fire. He didn't bother looking up; he already knew the creature was dead. No one escaped Trigger.

"Drop the damn rifle and help me," Doc said as he finished the injection. He hoisted Locksmith under his arms and started dragging him back towards the others. If he could get him to Blackout, then he would be safe — well, safer. Widget tossed the old M-4 to the ground and lifted Locksmith's legs. Together they managed to run him back to where Blackout was fighting.

All the while, Killswitch was yelling commands into the radio as he readied his team for the Reapers' air strike. There would be almost no way to mark the targets with all of their tech down. The best chance they had was to stay within the buildings when the fighters passed. If they could thin down the ferals streaming in, they would at least have a chance.

He looked down at his watch. Too little time. Killswitch hoisted the radio and ran back to his men. Snowball and Blackout were standing together on one edge of a rough square with Cowboy and Beast on the other; the four of them held off the enemy while Doc worked on Locksmith. Daredevil's 240 continued to keep the airborne at bay.

"Air support incoming," Killswitch yelled as he ran over. Blackout acknowledged him with a grunt as he slammed his axe into the head of a cougar.

"What about the birds?" Cowboy yelled, ducking beneath the claws of an overly brave hawk feral. Daredevil dropped it dead with a burst of fire.

"I'm sure they can handle them. We just need to worry about staying alive," Killswitch called, then looked out through the nearest hole towards the portal.

A roar cut through the battle as a snubfighter erupted from the portal, its nose towards the sky. It seemed to hang motionless for a moment before its screaming engines slammed it forward and into the air. More engines joined the first as more fighters warped through.

The sound of the engines was nothing compared to the chain gunfire that followed.

Chapter 42

Vincent

Commander Belford had provided specific order for how the Reaper would enter into the breach — orders that would have gotten them all killed. Vincent made sure those orders were not followed, and had a few choice thoughts of what he would like to do to Belford. He pushed those thoughts away though, he was already skirting orders as it was; best not to have treasonous thoughts while he did it.

As it stood, when the *Inferno* had swung low enough to kiss the gravity well, Vincent was at the rear of the Reapers' deployment. As his pilots slowly twirled down through the layers of atmosphere, trailing bright colors from the excess heat on their shields, he moved to the front of the pack.

They hadn't been able to launch until the *Inferno* nearly beached herself. Their atmospheric package couldn't maneuver in a vacuum. The fighters were airtight, but were basically rocks until they had air beneath their wings. Vincent had anxiously flicked his multitool open and closed as he waited for launch, knowing the ship would only be able to hold position for a few minutes.

His heart pounded as the transmission for close air support came in and they dropped towards the planet. Vincent's stomach pushed into his chest as he allowed his fighter to fall towards the portal with the grav prop off.

Portals were hard to understand for most soldiers, though the way Rodrom had explained it to him made the most sense. The portals were like a three-dimensional door, if you could picture a curved door. If you took a flexible bowl and poked a needle through it, the outside curve of the bowl was where you entered. Turn the bowl inside out so the convex became concave, and that's what the other side looked like. So in order to come out going straight up on the other side, Vincent had to dive on this one. The trick of doing it in atmosphere was to come out at an angle so the air could catch his wings and keep him aloft.

Distances being what they were on planets (compared to open space), Vincent didn't have a lot of time to consider what he was doing before the portal loomed in his viewport and he passed through to the other side.

In the heartbeat that passed between one side and the other, Vincent had the vague notion of being both surrounded by popping soap bubbles, and his stomach filling with razors. Before he could appreciate either sensation, however, he was through, and his world shifted from the diffuse hazy outline of a portal to a sky full of chaos.

Monstrous birds swarmed on his view port, coming in and out of sight from behind ink-black storm clouds, and warning tones sounded as his AMI crunched the enemy numbers. Vincent maintained his composure long enough to slam forward on the throttle and key his afterburners, his engines screaming as they recovered from the near dead stop in the air. Any other snubfighter would have torn itself apart,

227

but the Chimera was built for these sorts of missions. Vincent climbed past the danger point and into the awaiting swarm of ferals above.

"Multiple airborne hostiles," the AMI warned uselessly. Vincent had already begun firing. Two ferals, unrecognizable from the plasma burns, fell from the sky when Vincent's first two shots connected. His guns cycled, and another two followed. There were so many targets in the sky that Vincent would have a harder time hitting clean air. His friend-or-foe tag began to blink more reassuring colors as the rest of his squadron followed him. Lightning flashed close by, illuminating the hostiles, and Vincent spun his ship to avoid a direct collision.

"Reapers, spread out. Engage targets at will," Vincent ordered. The AMI would put the transmission on automatic delay so his voice reached each pilot as they entered. "Stay with your wingmen. Steel, take your wing on a bombing run, we need to cover those ground forces."

Vincent's board flickered eleven times as his pilots entered the fray over the next sixty seconds and acknowledged his order Their incoming messages were filtered by AMI to keep the net clear. His orders given, Vincent concentrated on making it through the swarm and into open air beyond. A fledgling might make the mistake of thinking the Chimera would make short work of flesh and blood, but Vincent had seen the aftermath of enough battles to know claws and beaks could tear through a fighter's armor like paper. And the ferals had unpredictable abilities to boot.

Not even his own considerable skill as a pilot would allow him to avoid all of the ferals littering the air, so Vincent let his AMI plot him a course by the fewest number of the monsters. They were deceptively quick, and given the chance, they would latch onto his ship and tear it apart. But he had no time to think on it; the computer had already altered his course, and he was racing through the cloud of flesh and feathers.

He didn't trust the computer's automatic safety on his weapons, though. Vincent glanced at his squadron's position in relation to his own, and finding none forward of his location, he depressed the plasma cannon's triggers once more. The rhythmic whine and chug of the cannons as they displaced air and enemy was oddly soothing.

A kill counter tallied each visible strike, ramping up a number in the corner of his viewport. Vincent released his grip from the left stick to swipe it away—fighting was one thing, but keeping score was another. Just as swiftly as he'd entered, Vincent found himself beyond the mass of ferals and flying low over the canopy. Banking in an arc far too wide for a vacuum pilot's liking, he brought his fighter and those following him back for another attack run.

"Condemned Actual, this is Reaper One. I am on approach, setting missiles for drop. We'll clear a path, over." Vincent keyed up the data gleaned from the first pass. Steel's wing had already done some damage to the ground forces, though it was nothing compared to the destructive power of an entire squadron.

"Copy that, Reaper One. We'll duck."

Chapter 43

Ele

Ele awoke to chaos. The nightmare she had escaped was nothing compared to the reality around her. Everything was shaking. Shaking so hard she thought the ground beneath her would tear itself apart. She was lying on a stretcher, and the sheets were burnt and smoking. The metal walls around her were covered in black lines, drawn without pattern or sense.

Wires hung and sparked from one of the lights above. The medical cabinets beside her were smoking, their doors hanging off the hinges. The bottles and supplies inside them were twisted and warped, and puddles of medicine dripped from the shattered glass.

It looked as though a bomb had gone off right where Ele was lying. She pulled the still-smoking sheets away and stared down at her body. She appeared to be unharmed.

Her heart rate picked up pace. It was happening again. Same as the forest, same as the hall on the ship. The fire was chasing her—she couldn't escape it.

The light above her sparked violently, and Ele's nose filled with burning ozone.

Other people were screaming — some from fear, others simply trying to be heard over the destruction. A red light blinked slowly just outside her door. It made the dripping liquid look like blood. Ele prayed it wasn't. She couldn't stand knowing she had hurt one of the people who seemed so desperate to help her.

Vincent! She had seen him right before she passed out. He had rescued her on the ship. What if he was with her now? She had to find him, to convince him to run. She was dangerous. There was no denying it. The fire was after her. It was some kind of spell, or curse.

Something nagged at the back of her mind. Like a dream she could just barely remember. White suits, glass tubes, needles, fire. What happened?

Ele pushed herself up off the bed, pulling the ruined sheet around her. Whatever uniform she had been wearing was gone, probably burned by the fire that would soon consume her. She padded on bare feet over the strangely warm metal floor and out into the chamber beyond.

It was far too small to be the same ship as before. She was on a shuttle, a shuttle full of people who wouldn't be able to run.

One of the people at the front of the shuttle spotted her — a naked young girl with fiery red hair and fear in her eyes. She pointed and screamed, "Monster!"

The other passengers pushed away from her, screaming, pleading, stammering.

"Get out of here!"

"We're not soldiers!"

"It's not my fault," Ele tried to tell them. She couldn't control it.

231

Whoever had taken her memory, those were the people they should fear.

One of the passengers, this one dressed in the same uniform Ele had come to recognize as the fleet's, stepped closer. Maybe he would help. Maybe he could convince the others she wasn't dangerous.

But then he pulled a lever on the wall, and the ground dropped out from beneath Ele's feet. It was the shuttle's ramp, which was designed to open downward and touch the ground when the shuttle was parked. Only this shuttle wasn't on the ground; it was diving towards a planet, and the air that whipped by was far too strong for Ele to fight against it. She tried to grab onto the struts that lowered the ramp, pushing her fingers into the metal grating of what had seconds ago been the ground, but she could find no purchase.

Her scream was lost in the roar of the wind as she was ripped from the shuttle and plummeted towards the ground.

Chapter 44

Johnston

"**Sir! One of the shuttles has taken damage.** Moving to tactical."

Johnston whipped around to the display.

The shuttle he had dispatched was magnified on the screen, the damaged portions overlaid in red.

"Hostiles?" he asked.

"None on the sensors. It appears to be internal damage, sir."

Johnston looked down at the data scrolling across his console. *Always more bloody problems.* No matter how much they planned, something was always falling apart, and now civilians were in danger.

"Dispatch a rescue tug, and get me a com line with them immediately."

Johnston clenched his jaw as Belford executed the order. He was sorely tempted to do the job himself. He needed to light a fire under that man, or convince the fleet to give him a new Flight Commander.

After an agonizing amount of time, Belford announced, "The, uh, tug is launched, Captain."

"When it gets close enough I want the feed from its forward sensors. We need to know what happened to that shuttle. Pull up the preflight checklist as well. Until they touch down planetside, those civilians are ours."

"Aye, sir, the tug will be on station in two minutes."

Too damn slow, Johnston thought. Those weren't sailors; they were women, children, the people he put on the uniform to protect. The kind of people he had left light-years behind to ensure they had a safe universe to live in.

Something tugged at the edge of his mind, and he turned to face his Psykin battle commander.

<*Sir, that anomaly I felt on the shuttle during the Bastogne engagement is back. I think it's what's causing the damage, sir.*>

"God help us," Johnston whispered. What had he unleashed on the planet below? Would Aberdeen be destroyed by the same fires that had ravaged Bastogne? He was running out of time, and out of options. He needed to know more before he could justify firing on civilians.

If he stayed his hand, allowed the shuttle to touch down, was he condemning everyone planetside? Or was the anomaly not what he feared, and he was throwing away lives out of fear?

"Damn magicians and their godforsaken spells." He slammed his fist against the console. Around him, the other officers looked up sharply.

"I need eyes on. We need to know who is on that ship."

"Sir! The shuttle opened her bay doors. The passengers are forcing someone out. It appears to be a woman."

"They're doing what?" Johnston yelled, twisting towards the sensor officer.

"They opened the loading ramp, and it looks like a woman is

234

falling out, sir! Wait, I'm getting something else... She's throwing off all sorts of radiation. Electromagnetic, gamma. I've never seen anything like this."

<*That's no woman.*>

Johnston turned to look at his Psykin battle commander.

Chapter 45

Ele

Ele screamed into the wind that blurred her vision. She saw the blue sky, then the green ground, and then the blue sky again. She flailed, screaming, no longer thinking. Screaming because it was the only thing she could do. She was going to die, and the terror was impossible. It filled her to the point of bursting, burning her skin, throbbing in her head, pounding in her chest.

When her scream finally drained her lungs, she tried to pull in another breath, but the wind tore any chance of that away from her. Then a flash caught her eye, and she felt a sharp crackle in her skin.

What was happening? Why? Why? *Why?*

Another flash, another snap against her arm. Like she was being slapped. She tried to twist her head around, but she was still twisting wildly in the air.

She didn't want to die this way. To hit the ground and be gone. Then, the idea that she might not die instantly drowned all her thoughts again. The sky flashed azure, and again she felt the stinging bite across her entire body.

Light poured from her body, so bright she was blinded, and her tumble ended. She was falling with her back to the ground now, and above her was the shuttle she had fallen from. She needed to get back there.

Her vision shattered open, and suddenly she saw everything: the trees of the forest, the insects crawling in the dirt, the scorch marks on the shuttle. All at once, like she was everywhere—a thousand fractal images, as if she were looking through a prism.

The pain was gone, and replaced with a tingle of energy that filled her being. Her entire body coursed with power, but she could not feel her hands or move her toes. But somehow she could "see" the pillar of blue crackling energy she had become.

Then it was over. Her body was whole again, and she looked out from two eyes set firmly on the front of her face. A thunderclap boomed around her.

She was on top of the shuttle and scrambled for a handhold as the wind tried to pull her from the metal. She caught a yellow-and-black handle with her right hand. Tiny blue snakes of electricity twisted from her fingers to dance along the metal, and she felt each bolt sting as it snapped between the shuttle and her. The handle grew cherry red, but she could not feel the heat. The spitting arcs of energy only grew more violent as she tried with all her might to hold on.

She squeezed her eyes shut against the impossible things she was seeing, and tried to muster the strength to reach up and hold on with her other hand. Again, a boom of thunder assaulted her ears, though it was not nearly as loud as before. When she opened her eyes again, she saw the panel ahead of her had been torn from its bolts, and the electronics and wiring beneath it were completely destroyed.

Her left fist sizzled and popped. Had she done this? Was she in control of this power?

What had they done to her?

The shattering. She saw everywhere again. Another ship was streaking down towards her. The people inside the shuttle were staring out the windows. The engines were sputtering and belching smoke.

Boom — thunder — Ele was whole again, and tumbling along the edge of the blunt wing that made up the shuttle's profile. Each time a part of her slapped against the metal, there were more sparks, more arcs of twisting energy. How was it possible?

She was human. Not a monster from the other side. They looked different, had powers no one should have. That was never her. Was it? She didn't remember anything. Anger bubbled up inside her. She shouldn't have been there, shouldn't have been torn from her home and sent across the galaxy. She shouldn't be able to shoot lightning from her hands.

Her body smashed against the wing one last time, and the shuttle passed her. Helpless, she tumbled through open air.

Her chest burned, and her skin flushed red. She screamed again, feeling as though she would explode at any moment.

Pain erupted from her chest, screaming down her shoulder and arms until her whole body was on fire with it. Then her skin darkened. First pink, then red, and then deep black. She was burning from within.

Her skin flaked away from her palms, and was whipped away by the wind. The fall seemed to last an eternity, but she was still miles from the ground. The red glow of embers shone from behind the broken flesh, and as her skin peeled away, so did the pain. Fire bellowed from her hands, burning the air red and orange.

The burning forest, then inside the ship, and now the shuttle. It was all her. The fire had not been chasing her, it had been trapped inside her. She really was a monster.

Like a blanket, the searing heat wrapped around her, burning away any shred of clothing that remained. Soon, she was a blazing comet the size of a girl. Her descent slowed, and then she started to rise, turning towards the people who had forced her change.

They had done this to her. They were responsible.

The fleet would pay for what they did.

Chapter 46

The Exile

The concussive force of the Chimeras' first pass was too much for Exile's Web. She sat back with a sneer, her connection to the platoon severed, and for the first time since she breached the portal, she took a good look around.

She had no idea how close to death she had been. The tracked vehicle she occupied was jerked up to the side and front, on enough of an incline that her seat's harness was the only thing keeping her from falling. The cab was empty, and though she vaguely recalled the soldiers evacuating, she did not remember what had created the gaping hole where the rear of the vehicle had once been.

It wouldn't be long before her platoon moved without her, so Exile summoned her ethereal arm and tugged at the webbing that kept her seated. It released all at once, causing her to spill to the floor. With a mild reprimand to herself for fumbling, she pushed herself to her feet and moved towards the newly made exit. Closer to the hole, Exile saw that the edges were uneven, and had the look of charred wood despite being made of composite metal. A fireball must have detonated close, she decided; the unnatural fire could make any substance burn like kindling. Any closer and she would have been roasted alive, though that torture would be a welcome death compared to what awaited her should she fail in her mission.

Careful not to touch the still-scalding edges of the metal, Exile leaned out and looked to the ground below. It had to be at least an eight-foot drop, and there was not enough room to roll.

Her Shell gave her great control over her own physiology. She had learned firsthand what made her so different from—and superior than—the humans she infiltrated.

Humans had massive potential energy stored in their muscles, but they could only use a fraction of it without harming themselves. They had enough energy to jump six feet into the air, or sprint at forty miles an hour, but that explosive use would break down their muscles, and as a result, their minds limited their bodies for preservation's sake. Her people didn't have that problem. The conclave called it a Shroud of faith, and claimed the gods gave them strength, Exile knew that was all lies.

Her muscles contained specialized organic capsules that, when accessed with her Shell, allowed her to exert explosive bursts of energy, effectively tearing open the capsules in place of the muscle tissue surrounding it and releasing the recovery chemicals inside. Given enough time, she would regrow those capsules and be as good as new. If she used them judiciously, she could operate at a more powerful level than normal for longer. It took year of training and massive willpower to force the break, and the Exile believed that whatever manipulation her species had undergone, it was intended for last resort.

Wrapping her Shell around her legs, she pulsed, breaking open

241

several of the capsules with a cold rush of energy. She kicked off, leaping six feet out from the vehicle, and landed in a crouch on the ground.

She glanced around and took off at a sprint, energy still coursing through her. With the arrival of air support, she had a good chance of making it to the Condemned, and once close enough, she could establish a stronger connection, pierce their thoughts, and make her presence known. All around her, vehicles like the one she had arrived in were scattered in various stages of destruction. The corridors between buildings had been far too tight for any real assault.

The boxy six-wheeled transports that remained were either destroyed, as hers had been, or covered in soldiers repairing whatever damage had kept them from retreating. Unlike the Condemned, not everyone in the field had stood their ground when the charge came, and Exile could not pick out any fully functional vehicles. Further down the road was a torn-up tank that had made it nearly to the portal. One of the massive bears lay dead beside it, a gaping hole in its chest.

As her Web expanded across the field again, she tuned out the sparking emotions of the soldiers outside of her platoon. The fear, anxiety, excitement, and determination of the remaining 101st soldiers was powerful, but the Exile was able to find the bright sparks of the Condemned without much effort. With her battle map once again outlined in her mind, she allowed her senses to intermingle; by creating outlines from a bird's eye view with her Web, she knew where to move.

Pinpointing the platoon's position relative to her own, Exile ducked off the road into an alley between buildings, and rushed to meet them.

Their emotions began shift from the bitter resolve of having their backs against the wall to the determination before a charge. Swiftly, she ducked behind a piece of rubble and reached out with a firmer grasp for the leader's mind. She was close enough to hear their voices, and peered around the rubble.

"This is the opportunity we needed, men," Killswitch called, wiping his Ka-Bars against the back of his pants. He lifted a fallen soldier's M-4 and pulled extra magazines from his web gear. "Those fighters have opened up a path, and as soon as they find where this elf camp is, we're going to push the pointy-eared Merlins back to the hole they spawned in."

The rest of the platoon followed Killswitch's example, each grabbing as much ammo as he could carry. Locksmith and Widget were wounded, but Doc had patched both of them up enough for them to continue fighting.

Exile had limited time before they charged into the battle beyond. She had to establish herself as their commander now. She stepped around the rocks, and found herself staring into the barrels of several M-16s. Chastising herself for her haste, she slowly raised her arm with her palm open, suddenly cognizant of the weapons on her hips and back. She didn't believe for a moment that the platoon would be fooled by the simple hologram she held in place, but the sudden appearance of a blue, one-armed alien probably spooked them more than the weaponry.

"What the hell is that?" one of the soldiers blurted. Exile reached out tentatively, taking care to not shift his already startled mood. It was Widget.

"*That* is a Psykin, and an officer to boot, Widget. Show some respect," Killswitch snapped, but his surface thoughts showed that his own opinions were similarly disrespectful. He swiftly clamped down on any errant thoughts, and Exile looked over at him in surprise. She could scarcely remember the last human she had encountered who was able to hide from her.

"X-ray protocol in effect. Try not to think too loud, it's like screaming for our new lieutenant," Killswitch ordered, allowing Exile to sense his displeasure for a moment before clamping down on his thoughts once more. Not content to be bested by a human, Exile shaped her Web and pushed deeper into Killswitch's mind. Somehow whenever she tried to pull a thought or emotion, it slipped away, leaving her searching. Killswitch had obviously been trained in how to avoid Psykin intrusion. With a quick look into the minds of the others, she encountered similar blockades, though they were not nearly as adept as their leader. *Impressive.*

Although she was unable to glean any information Killswitch didn't want her to know, she was still able to speak to him telepathically.

<How did you know I was assigned as your new commander?>

"We are the only tech platoon on the ground. Psykins aren't that common in the fleet, and if I'm not mistaken, you have four gnome tech weapons strapped to you." Killswitch let slip a touch of his distaste. "It's not my first day, and you're not my first lieutenant... ma'am."

Widget's thoughts were the least tightly controlled, and Exile sensed confusion rolling off him. He asked Cowboy a question, but she didn't pay enough attention to make out the words.

"Psykin can't talk; they speak in your head," Cowboy explained, giving Widget a shove. "Now fill up your ammo so we can move."

<We don't have time for introductions,> Exile pushed at the group.*<We're moving on the elf encampment. Mission is to free the captured prisoners.>*

"No offense, ma'am, but that was our plan long before you got here," Killswitch said. "If you wouldn't mind lending out the Gauss rifle, and maybe that rail gun, that might just increase our odds."

Exile nodded, using the simple human gesture as opposed to expending the mental energy. Calling forth her spectral hand, she reached over her head to lift and unclip the Gauss rifle. A chorus of grunts and inhalations sounded off when her ghost arm shuddered into existence.

Killswitch shook his head. "You can all be amazed and impressed by our new LT's abilities later, men. We have a mission to accomplish." Killswitch tossed his scavenged gun on the ground and took up Exile's weapon. A sudden thought jumped to the front of his mind, past his veils: <*And you and I can discuss why you were sent here in the midst of a battle on an enemy planet.*>

Exile declined comment, choosing instead to unclip the sniper rifle and hand it to Cowboy. It wasn't the first time her missions had taken her into the ranks of the Joint Fleet, and she had dealt with suspicious soldiers before. Not one who could slip around her thoughts, however. It seemed the Condemned would not be so easily fooled.

Chapter 47

Vincent

After releasing his payload and blasting a hole in the enemy lines, Vincent took his wing high above the jungle canopy into the storm clouds, a swarm of feral birds in his wake.

"Stay loose on the stick," Vincent commed. "The elf encampment is out here somewhere, and they'll see us long before we see them."

Vincent dipped his ship into the churning black clouds above the massive trees of the Hecate jungle. The clouds destroyed any visibility, and he would have split-seconds to keep himself from hitting the tallest trees. Tactically, it would make him a harder target to follow, giving him an edge over some of the ferals with larger wingspans, though no small part of him enjoyed the added danger. He could control his craft through the trees and clouds; he couldn't control his adversaries.

Vincent had decided to take Zombie and the Duchess on a reconnaissance mission based on the data the Condemned were able to provide, leaving nine of the Reapers to provide close air support for the breach. Despite the heavy losses, the 101st had sustained in the fighting, the mission was still on, and finding the elf camp would be the first step in pulling out the refugees.

Vincent concentrated on luring out as many feral fliers as he could on his wild goose chase. His fighter's sensors were pushed to the limit, so he allowed his AMI to search for the signals given off by other AMI units in distress. The Condemned sent a burst packet of all the intel they had gleaned during their excursions, and Vincent's AMI filtered the transmissions. He didn't waste any attention on the groundpounders' data, however, and remained intent on his flying.

When a custom alert keyed off a moment later, it was all he could do to avoid vaping himself on a tree. Before launch, he had coded his AMI unit to filter through routine transmissions. Now, all the power the military-grade AI could muster focused to a single purpose: *Find Derek Rodrom.*

To hear it now—when he had hoped against hope that Derek still lived—was too much for Vincent to even comprehend. He sent a mental query to the AMI for further information, for once forgoing his preferred voice commands. As he continued to weave his ship through the forest canopy and roiling storm clouds, his mind filled in the details of the scientists and workers whose AMI units were listed as taken by the elves. The shock that hit him from the initial alarm was nothing when he saw the name in his minds eye.

<Sir, are you alright?> Zombie commed on a private channel. Vincent barely registered the fact that his shock had filtered across the bionet. He didn't have a thought to spare as he flew his ship and attempted to deal with this new data. His brother was alive—there was no doubt of that now—and he was somewhere in the jungle.

A lifetime of memories threatened to overwhelm him. After his father's death, losing Rodrom had almost taken Vincent out of the pilot seat. Only the small hope that he might still be alive had kept Vincent from breaking down completely, and that same strength kept his mother and stepfather from giving up too. Now there was a chance he might bring Rodrom home, and finally take something from the war besides death and destruction.

<Sir!> called Zombie. <Vincent! You're flooding the net! Are you hit?>

Zombie sent the question across the net along with his resolve and adrenaline-fueled calm. Vincent's turmoil mixed with Zombie's focus, and it became abundantly clear why the bionet connection was necessary. Before Vincent lost himself completely, he grasped on to Zombie's calm and pushed the memories and emotions back.

Another voice cracked across his mind with the slight distortion Vincent recognized as coming from beyond the portal. <Captain Barkhorn, your vitals indicate severe distress.> It was a corpsman. <Can you answer me?>

Vincent took a deep breath. He didn't need some paperpusher trying to pull him off the mission now. Gritting his teeth, he keyed the correct channel for voice communication; he wasn't going to use the bionet again unless it was absolutely necessarily.

"Medical, Reaper One. I must have a glitch in my programming. I am mission-capable, over."

There was a pause. <Captain, your vitals are well above normal operating limits. You are hereby ordered...> Vincent reached up and snapped three buttons on his console, and the transmission shorted out. Simultaneously, a flash of sparks illuminated at the nose of his fighter, where the communication equipment was housed.

"Well, shoot," Vincent muttered. "Looks like I've lost external communications." As he spoke, he saw one of Rover's claws grip the side of his fighter as the little mechanic moved to fix the damage. Vincent couldn't stop Rover from reestablishing long-range contact—it was his primary purpose, after all. But if he didn't hear the orders for a short time, he couldn't well disobey them, could he?

His short-range radio had been miraculously spared in the unfortunate overload, and he keyed a local channel. "Duchess, Zombie, Reaper One. I'm alright, just had a momentary shock. I've temporarily lost communication with higher. We need to expedite the mission." Vincent was careful not to say anything that could be used against either wingman, should things go south. The Duchess was the most likely replacement if he were relieved, and Vincent knew if it came down to a choice...

<I read you loud and clear,> the Duchess returned. When she spoke, Vincent realized it hadn't been her who had talked him down. She usually beat Zombie to the punch. When they touched down he would need to seriously evaluate how she was doing.

<What the hell was that?> Zombie sounded miffed. <Sir.>

Vincent's first reaction was to tell him what he'd told the medic—that it was just a fluke—but they both deserved a real answer. It was their fat in the fire.

"My brother was one of the captured scientists," Vincent said, preparing in his mind the next few maneuvers. He had to work fast before his coms were repaired.

<I thought you were an only child.> Zombie's confusion was stark in the bionet connection.

"He's my step brother, Major Derek Rodrom. And he's down there somewhere."

Chapter 48

Rodrom

"Bring me the human!" Lorelei snapped from within a tree shelter, startling Rodrom out of his focus. He looked up from the patient he was treating to see two guards approaching him. Rodrom bent back down to finish packing the shrapnel wound, finishing just in time to be growled at by the guards.

"You two must be my nurses. Hold pressure here, would you?" Rodrom didn't deem it necessary to look up, both to cement the illusion that he could not understand them, and because he was genuinely irritated to have been interrupted.

"Come with us, ironblood," the first trilled, and when Rodrom made no move, reached down to grab his arm. Before the guard made contact, Rodrom pushed himself up and stepped away. Simply gripping a staff had been enough to burn images into his mind, and every time he touched a new patient it was like cranking up the volume on a radio in his mind.

"Calm yourself, Fluffy. I'm coming," Rodrom said, allowing the guards to lead him to the tree where Lorelei worked.

Rodrom bent to slip under the root entrance, and was greeted by the now-familiar sight of elven medicine being practiced. Alien as the Verdantun might be, Rodrom could tell the healers were worried.

He looked to Lorelei, and felt a sharp pang of regret and anguish. He had never seen such cracks in the mask she used when interacting with him, and with her beautiful features marred by what was so clearly pain, Rodrom was certain he would do anything she asked of him.

"They can't fix him," Lorelei said softly in English. "He's dying, DerekRodrom, and weavers aren't enough."

Rodrom stepped up beside her without prompting. The other healers in the chamber were too focused on their chants to notice him. Sprawled out on a raised root table in front of them was a Verdantun in the throes of agony; Rodrom quickly realized, to his horror, that the elf was trapped between transformations.

Like a malfunctioning hologram, the Verdantun was in a constant state of flux. In one moment a high-cheeked, amber-skinned face appeared, then in the next it morphed into the muzzle of a snarling bear . Fingers became paws, fur became skin, muscles enlarged, shrank, expanded, and twisted. At the center, like the eye of a hurricane, was a patch of unshifted, unchanging skin. The Verdantun's right breast, beneath which his heart beat.

"He was struck with one of the metal shards. It pierced his weaveroot. He cannot take a true form," Lorelei explained.

Rodrom looked down at the shifting elf in confusion. "Can it be removed?" he asked.

"No, DerekRodrom, his weaveroot is as much a part of him as yours is a part of you. He may have beast blood in his veins, but to

251

remove it is to kill him."

"Not the weaveroot, the metal," he clarified, fully understanding for the first time that the alien tech growing inside him was not going anywhere.

"I... I know not," Lorelei stammered, her expression pained. "We do not cut, you know this. How could we remove anything?"

"You send these healers away and let me do my job," Rodrom said firmly, ignoring the dissonance in his mind that had been growing since he entered the chamber. Between the weavers, Lorelei, and the wounded soldier, it was almost too much: His weaveroot screamed in a symphony of pain and determination, drawn from the rhythms of those surrounding him.

"Yes," Lorelei whispered, shocking Rodrom more than the situation already had. She had never relented so easily before. Who was this soldier? Before he could ask, Lorelei raised her staff and her musical voice rang out clear: "Weavers, leave me, there are too many wounded this day. I will continue his healing. You are needed elsewhere."

As they always did, the Verdantun obeyed Lorelei's command without question or comment. They simply ceased their chant and moved from the tent without so much as a backwards glance. The thought that Lorelei was more than a simple camp healer was already planted in his mind; none of the others carried a weapon quite like hers, and they all snapped to attention like toy soldiers when she spoke.

"I will sing him into as deep a slumber as I can manage." Lorelei planted her staff and slid her hands up to the sides of the soldiers face. There was a change in his biorhythm as she did. "You must remove the metal from him. I know you have created tools from discarded weapons. Please."

Rodrom did not think to question her. He simply dropped to his knees beside the soldier and opened the hidden compartment in his bag, bringing forth the glass scalpels he had made from a stolen knife.

Lorelei saw the blade and nodded once, then sang a song so hauntingly beautiful it rocked Rodrom back on his heels for a moment. His training reminded him again and again that this wasn't his crisis, but to hear such raw emotion mixed with the power of the weaveroot... It was too much to ignore.

Lorelei stopped singing for a moment and stared at Rodrom. "Of course, you are so new to its songs. How could you concentrate?"

From one of the plants that grew along her arm, she pulled out what looked to be a large seed. Cupping her hands around it, she sang a strangely uplifting and quick set of notes. Vines pushed out from between her fingers, twisting up and around her arms. When they grew to almost her elbows, she stopped, and opened her palm to show that the seed had grown in size and shape. It was a rough four-pointed star, with vines twisting around each point and then out in two strands. In the center was an unshaped green gemstone. She handed it to Rodrom.

"Take this and place it around your neck. It will temporarily block out the life song of those around you. So you can concentrate."

Rodrom grasped the pendant and took hold of the two vines. He reached up to tie them around his neck, where they came alive under his touch and weaved into a circle, leaving the pendant hanging just low enough to hide beneath his shirt. He looked up and breathed a sigh of relief. He had not appreciated how much he enjoyed silence until the music ended.

As Lorelei looked on, Rodrom gritted his teeth. "Today, we work miracles," he said, and pressed his glass scalpel into the shifting alien's flesh.

Chapter 49

Johnston

Johnston stared at the monitor in disbelief. He was no stranger to what lay beyond the portals, but at least those things made a bizarre sort of sense. They had an order about them. Fire elementals defied the laws of nature, but they did what you expected fire to do. Burned things. Elves turned into monsters, shaped trees, and did other druidic things. Dragons, Ogres, and Goblins destroyed everything in their path.

He had never seen the kind of power that came out of the shuttle, and even his Psykin was beyond terrified.

At first it had seemed that the crew of the shuttle had thrown a girl to her death, and he had watched in a mixture of confusion and horror as she tumbled to the planet below. Then the sky split apart and the girl fractured into an untold number of lighting bolts, all directed at the shuttle.

From his bridge, he controlled the half-kilometer-long gunship and all her fighters. He should never have felt powerless, and yet, in that split-second, he could do nothing but watch as the girl split, arced, and

254

flashed towards the civilians. It seemed he had finally found the source of the problems that had plagued his ship.

But the shuttle was not destroyed by the lightning as he had expected. Instead, the girl reformed on the hull, clinging to the emergency railing, looking like nothing more than a civilian in horrible danger.

"What the bloody hell are we looking at?" Johnston demanded.

For once, he was met with blank stares. No one on the bridge so much as breathed.

"We must have something on record. Some rumor, some idea of what we are dealing with. She must be some kind of elemental that can control electricity." The more he spoke, the more he convinced himself that this must be the case. It was something he had seen before, could wrap his head around, and could blow out of the sky.

The girl shattered into light once again, hitting the forward edge of the wing and bouncing along like a rag doll. Then she was falling again.

Perhaps the creature would destroy itself?

It would never be that easy. As the thing tumbled off the wing and fell, the sparkling blue electricity died away, only to be replaced with the glow of flames. Billowing fire shot out of the girl — so bright that Johnston had to glance away from the screen — and then she was gone. A phoenix glowed in her place. Wings of flame twisted and wreathed around an impossibly bright center as the creature rolled out of its fall and shot back toward the shuttle.

Fleet intelligence listed enough about elemental magic to tell Johnston that what he was seeing was impossible. There had never been a record of a humanoid breaking apart to become energy. Arm themselves with it? Constantly. Create armor from it? Easily. But never

255

had a person become the element, and certainly not two different ones.

"Tactical, I want you to blow that monster out of the sky."

"Aye, sir."

When it rains it pours, Johnston thought. And he would rain down everything he had on whatever fresh new hell the enemy had created.

Chapter 50

The Exile

A wave of positive emotions crashed against Exile's Web as her platoon advanced on the enemy. With the tide of battle changing to favor the Terran forces, the regular infantry surged forward along with the Condemned, their resolve as explosive as the missiles that cleared their path. With the Condemned at the head, a spear of determined soldiers left the safety of their hardened buildings to assault the jungle beyond. From behind her, Exile felt as well as heard the clatter and rumble of engines as more tanks streamed in from the portal to reinforce the advance.

All of the men on the field were visible in her mind's tactical map, so Exile knew that even with the reinforcements, the Reapers in the air were paramount to the success of their extraction of the scientists. Despite their resolve and apparent skill in combat, even the Condemned had their limits, and they were still vastly outnumbered.

The intel the Condemned had gleaned from their advances into the jungle had estimated the camp to be due west from their position,

257

although they had not gotten a chance to see it. With the Reapers flying overhead, they would spot it before the ground forces went too far off course.

Exile opened herself fully to her Web as she kept pace beside Killswitch, this time broadening her view to the entire battle, and took stock of the advance.

Roughly three battalions of regular infantry were moving to forward fighting positions, leaving some five battalions' worth behind. Four thousand men had been injured or killed in defending the portal. That left Exile with fifteen specialists, twenty-five hundred regular infantry, and twenty-eight functioning tanks to assault an unknown greater number of elves. No easy feat, but she did not waste energy on contemplating failure. She simply couldn't accept that outcome.

As she ducked through a blast hole in the dome and into the alley beyond, she allowed the positions of the other troops to intermingle with her normal vision. As she did, the lights of individual consciousness sparked into view. Her platoon of specialists had experienced enough difficulty with their coms, and she did not believe the others would fare better, so she took matters into her own hand. Using her Web, she pushed a gentle suggestion into the minds of the tank commanders.

Their minds flared in her Web as the suggestion took hold, and before her own men moved more than two hundred meters down the rubble-strewn path, the tanks had kicked into high gear and pushed to the front of the charge. Someone on the far side of the portal had had enough sense to equip half the tanks with bulldozer attachments, and those fourteen tanks moved to the front, slamming into the overgrowth around the facility to begin clearing paths for the men behind.

As if on cue, as the tanks reached the tree line, three of the

Reapers broke free of the fighting above and strafed the jungle, each letting loose a string of bombs and peppering the trees with plasma fire. A series of muffled explosions erupted seconds after as the miniature bombs tore apart foliage and overgrowth, as well as any elves who had been caught in the line of fire. With the Reapers' help, the tanks' advance into the jungle went from next to impossible to merely difficult.

Exile reached out for Killswitch. *<We need to defend those tanks. Their cannons are our best defense against the bear analogs.>*

Killswitch grunted. "I realize that, ma'am, but even with the bombs and those dozers, it'll still be slow-going."

<Then we go slow. Rescuing the hostages is our top priority.>

Killswitch's only reply was a flash of irritation, then as their path took them close to the tanks, he said, "My men's AMI units don't have a lot of range, and with coms down, you're our best source of communication. Can't you link us together like some kind of telepath radio?"

<Not while this many soldiers are afield,> Exile said. Her Web was already pushed past its normal limits. Killswitch was wrong about the AMI units' range, but she didn't have time to explain that, or give him the technical knowledge to fix it.

"Last nymph I worked with could," Killswitch muttered. "Alright, well, you're in charge anyhow. Best start giving orders."

They reached the rearmost tank, and Killswitch crouched behind it. Without waiting for a reply from her, he leaned out past the treds and peered into the jungle beyond. He pulled himself back just as two spikes whistled past.

Pushing down her annoyance, Exile reached out to the rest of the platoon, all of whom where adopting positions similar to Killswitch.

<Protect the tanks. We need their firepower.> Exile reached the

minds of the entire platoon.

As she did, she sent another suggestion to the commanders of the foot soldiers, urging them into the jungle beyond. Many of them would die in the close quarters, but she pushed anyway, with the quiet hope that they would not all perish. And if they did, she would still climb over their corpses to ensure her mission was completed.

Part 5

Chapter 51

Ele

Fire poured from Ele being like a river, forming into wings that pushed her through the air. The shuttle was her target; she could see the people inside. Gone were the colors of the sky and ship. She saw only the glow of the engines — only that which was like her.

Her thoughts were sluggish. It was difficult to remember why she needed to destroy the bright spots. She knew she was angry, and they were the reason why. Her fire pushed her through the sky. When she got close enough it would immolate them.

She never got the chance. Though she had no real body, when the round slammed into the center of her blaze, it still felt like she'd hit a wall — a wall that had been launched from a cannon and had fallen from orbit. It hurt. A lot.

But the round did not kill her. She was no longer a girl, no longer human. She was the flame, and the pain only made her angrier. The round passed through her molten center, melting in the intense heat, and passed through to the other side as slag. She staggered in the air, her wings bent as though broken, even though they were born of flame. The anger pulled her back together, forced her to burn even hotter. Her thoughts slowed to mere words: *Destroy. Consume.*

Another round struck her, and though it was traveling just as swiftly as the previous one, this one barely made it through her. The heat was so intense that the round melted before it even reached her, and it was liquid by the time it hit her center.

The air around her ignited in the intense heat of her anger. She was growing ever larger, ever stronger. And the bright spots were moving, running.

Chase. Devour. Ele twisted in the air and pulsed the heat to propel her forward. It was fast, but she was faster, and the more she grew, the easier it would be to destroy.

The dots were heading towards something. Something she couldn't understand in her primal state. It wavered like the absence of heat, and at the same time it was warm. It did not make sense, and that made her madder still. She would destroy the thing. Destroy the dots, destroy everything. Consume it all.

She stopped noticing the rounds that flared and died before they could even pass through her.

Two of the dots she chased flared in size, growing hot enough to block out all other sights. Then they were gone, devoured by the strange thing below her.

No! They were hers to burn. A swell of heat and rage poured off her, and she dove for the thing that had taken her prey.

Flaming wings pulled back, Ele put on all speed, her rage screaming a comet's trail behind her. There was no sound or grand flare when she struck the portal. One second she was an inferno made real, screaming and roaring towards the ground, and then she was gone. An impossible serenity took her place.

Ele passed from Aberdeen into the battlefield beyond, and her eyes took in the thousand bright lights of heat that scrambled beneath and flew above. She would consume them all.

Chapter 52

Vincent

"Rover, I've got a loose stabilizer in the port engine, see if you can lock it down." Distracting the robot from its task would only delay the inevitable, but it was worth it to Vincent. Rover retracted the tool it had jammed into the fried communication array and skittered over to the engine, just out of Vincent's view.

In a moment of maniacal distress, Vincent considered trying to shake the robot loose. He quickly dismissed it; even with the drag of flying in atmosphere, Rover still had fantastically strong magnetic clamps on his claws. Not to mention the fact that Vincent might need him.

Vincent knew he was hoisting a sail without enough rope, and it was only a matter of time before it collapsed on him. He needed to find that elf camp—he needed it yesterday. Desperation tinged with just a hint of panic grasped him, and Vincent pushed hard on his sticks, shooting his fighter well into the view of the pursuing ferals.

<Sir!> Zombie commed immediately as Vincent pulled up and

away from his wingmen.

"I'm fine, Zombie. You and Duchess stay low. I've got to see if I can find this camp," Vincent said, breathing heavily, his body pressed back into the seat. His warning lights flashed as the ferals he had been avoiding in the cloud cover made a beeline for his newly revealed position.

"Set the scanners to max, visual and thermal," Vincent ordered. He wouldn't have time to look on his own once the ferals closed. Without the element of surprise or his wingmen, Vincent's movements would have to be perfect. As if to emphasize that point, his ship bucked and twisted to port under an unseen force before Vincent could react and stabilize.

An eagle with a wingspan half a football field in length was tearing at his wing. Each beat of the massive wings shook him and threatened to tear off his fighter's wing and send him on an express trip to the ground.

He twisted his fighter, first port, then starboard, into a barrel roll as he tried to shake his new passenger off. Its claws tore unpleasant holes in the fighter's wing as the g-forces ripped it away. Vincent tried not to pass out.

As he righted himself, he could see the eagle flying up beside him. The grotesque bird twisted gracefully in the air with wings spread full, and with a cry Vincent heard through his hull, snapped both wings together and buffeted the ship with a blast of magic-strengthened turbulence.

"Damn it, AMI, find that base before these monsters summon a hurricane." Vincent twisted his ship away again. He depressed both floor pedals to the ground, deploying his wing flaps, slowing his climb. Twisting to bring the eagle into his sights, he flipped up the safety on a missile. "Seek the heat," he muttered, and when his crosshairs loomed over the monster, he slammed the trigger.

Without waiting to see if he'd hit the thing, Vincent pushed down on the sticks to level off his dive and give him more maneuvering room. His ship bucked again, though this time Vincent saw a flash of movement, and craned his neck. A falcon analog was clinging upside down to his starboard wing. Before he had a chance to react, it flashed in blaze of plasma, and Vincent was loose again.

<*Woo!*> Zombie called.

"I thought I told you to stay in the tree line," Vincent returned, though there was no anger in his voice.

<*Didn't copy that transmission, sir, must have a faulty connection. Will rectify.*>

Vincent smiled. "Alright, keep them off me long enough to find this camp." It had been reckless of him to fly solo, and he'd probably be a smear in the forest now without them.

<*No need,*> Duchess said. <*It has been found.*>

Vincent looked up to the portion of his screen that was receiving the Duchess's data on a direct beam transmission. The camp was approximately twelve kilometers away to the north, but only four kilometers from the portal where the ground forces were fighting.

In a moment of embarrassment, which was tinged with profound disappointment at his own hubris, Vincent realized his sensors were down, and probably had been since he disabled his communications suite. AMI had been warning him in a text field at the bottom of his screen, but in his haste he had ignored it, assuming he knew what he had broken.

He had nearly killed himself for nothing.

The moment passed quickly. He had found Rodrom, and now he

only needed to lead the ground forces to his location.

"Let's go clear a path."

Chapter 53

The Exile

"**Condemned Actual**, this is Reaper One. How copy? Over," the com unit crackled on Killswitch's waist. He snatched it off his web gear and thumbed the trigger.

"I read you, Reaper One. Send it."

"Grid coordinates incoming; we'll cut you a path. Out." The com beeped as it received the incoming data. Killswitch hoisted the view port that dangled off the side, evidence of Locksmith's repair job.

The Exile concentrated and summoned her spectral arm, then tapped the coordinates from the com unit into her MPU. A small hologram floated over her wrist, giving her current position as a blue dot, and the objective as a red downward facing arrow.

"We're only three klicks out." Killswitch drew his finger across the hologram between the two points. "Not as tough as I thought it would be..."

Killswitch's words were lost in the bellow of the tank they crouched behind as it fired its main cannon. The vehicle rocked back and coughed up dirt and leaves as the energy of the blast shook the ground.

She felt tug as a sharp influx of emotions and the edges of her Web shuddered. The elves had spread out around her advance and were nipping at her flanks.

She reached out for her platoon members closest to the incursion. Cowboy on the right, Rehab and Blackout on the left. <*The elves are pushing our flanks. Keep them off those tanks.*> Killswitch snapped off three shots over Exile's shoulder. "I get that you're concentrating, but keep your damn head down."

Exile crouched lower. Despite his disrespect, Killswitch was right; she was allowing herself to be drawn into her Web. *Distraction brings death.*

She allowed her Web to sink further back into her subconscious and took a good look at her surroundings. The dense jungle made it difficult to see much further beyond the paths the tanks had created for themselves. The vehicles were making slow progress between the massive tree trunks, and the soldiers were hesitant to move too far from their protective cannons.

Fear and uncertainty pressed down on her despite her efforts to concentrate on her surroundings. The elves had pulled back their all-out attack to run small raids out of the jungle. A sudden movement, a yell, and shots fired were all they had seen of the enemy since they had pushed off from the base. Either the air support had done more damage than Exile thought, or the elves were planning a big push. She assumed the latter.

Exile looked into the forest beyond, at the shadows and blackness between the oversized leaves and foliage.

Without a doubt, the Elves were watching right back. The feeling was instinctual. With her concentration spread so thin as to encompass the entirety of the advancing forces, Exile didn't have the power to reach out and touch whatever might lie beyond the shadows. Dropping her attention from the soldiers would be detrimental, since she not be able to reach out to encompass them all again.

Exile stared into the darkness, allowing her mundane senses to spy any movement. A pair of too-familiar yellowed eyes opened and stared back.

Exile suppressed the urge to grasp her horn. How could it be there? It was flying above her, disguised as a pilot. But there could be no mistaking those unblinking yellow eyes. They seemed to draw in the surrounding light. Exile tore her gaze away, opening herself back up to the Web. Better to be distracted by commanding her forces than by the Shadow. She schooled her thoughts, lest she have too strong a reaction and alert it.

"This is your plan?" came a high-pitched voice from behind her. Exile twisted around, but saw nothing. "To crash through the jungle with all the subtlety of a storm? Why spend months infiltrating and summoning me if you planned to die in such a fashion?"

Exile did not have the strength to maintain her Web as well as seek out the Shadow's mind for a connection. She could only listen. Killswitch gestured to her to stay with him as he crouch-walked down behind one of the tanks. The sergeant gave no indication that he'd heard the disembodied voice.

The voice came again, but it changed again in pitch and candor. As a soft baritone, it said, "This much noise, all these men, you will never make it to the camps. No wonder you gave me so much power. Compassion is weakness. You cannot save these men from death. They are outnumbered, and outmatched. Send them forward with their metal coffins to distract your enemy. Take your team and infiltrate the compound while they fight their worthless battle out here."

Exile narrowed her eyes. The monster wasn't wrong — it would no doubt work better than a concentrated push into the camp where the elves would fight like demons. Looking around at the men moving between the trees, she felt a moment of remorse, but quickly stamped it down, reminding herself what was at stake.

"You feel compassion for these creatures? Who have viewed you as an outcast, only to use you for the abilities that set you above them?" The Shadow laughed.

Killswitch remained oblivious to the noise. She knew the Shadow was just acting out its nature. Sowing chaos even as it drew in power.

The humans did treat her people with indifference at best, and more often than not, with outward contempt. If not for her abilities in combat, she had no doubt she would be treated as less than a second-class citizen. But the humans were a necessary evil, just like the Shadow. Worse things lurked beyond the fringes of space, and no amount of scorn, exile, or pain would make her forget that.

The humans were expendable though, she needed to treat them as such. When the voice came again, she did not need further orders to convince her of her course of action. Already she was reaching out to the infantry leaders with her Web, subtly altering their course so they would take the fighting away from where her own men needed to go.

"You should... What's this?" The Shadow hesitated. "That power..." A lance of pain exploded in her mind. "You must get me that power. Plunge the dagger into it, release me!" It screamed with a ferocity she had never experienced, and the Exile collapsed, her Web tearing and leaving her blind.

To give the Shadow what it wanted was to court death, but the pain—the pain was too much.

She nodded, unable to do any more. Somehow it was enough. The agony ceased.

<Send the other team to these coordinates. Gather the men. We are splitting off from the main body,> Exile told Killswitch.

She had not prayed a single time since leaving the conclave, but she prayed now to every god she could think. Prayed that whatever the Shadow had sensed had the power to defend itself.

Chapter 54

Rodrom

The surgery was not going well.

A medic could simply tell, without the aid of monitors or machines, when someone was close to death. It was a sixth sense that slithered down the spine and settled in the gut, a primitive feeling that focused the mind and body to an external danger. When Rodrom joined the Joint Fleet, he had himself been a medic, and the instincts he had developed on the line served him well as a surgeon. He had that feeling now more than ever. He feared that no matter his skills or abilities, he would not be able to save Lorelei's beloved.

She had not said a word since beginning her song. She simply knelt beside the warrior's head and allowed her lilting voice to fill the room. It was obvious this warrior meant more to her than any of the other wounded. She had never wavered before, not even an inch, since Rodrom had come to the camp.

Despite his concentration and his fear of failure, Rodrom thought he felt another emotion's oily presence in his mind. For the span of a thought, he believed it might be jealously, though he quickly dismissed that notion. He was trapped behind enemy lines, with an alien weapon grafted to his spine, and a writhing shapeshifter beneath his fingers. Jealousy was the last emotion he should feel.

Performing open-heart surgery was difficult at the best of times, with a team of nurses and physician's assistants, or preferably his holographic table. To do so on a vine platform, with a glass scalpel he'd fashioned himself, and tools shaped from branches and twigs, on a patient who was changing shape and mass, was damn near impossible. But it didn't stop him from trying. He'd already found a way to temporarily stop some of the shapeshifting. Once he cut into the wound to see how deep the shrapnel went, he had discovered that by pressing his palm onto shifting skin, that it would stop the metamorphosis. Was it simply the pressure from the contact, or a facet of the weaveroot? He didn't pause to figure it out.

With that obstacle temporarily bypassed, Rodrom was able to make the necessary incision to see deeper into the wound. The warrior's ribs were in the way, of course, but he also had no way to open the chest from the center. He had no bone saw, or any other necessary tools, for that matter. The best he could hope for was to push two ribs away from each another and make a hole large enough to fit his custom forceps through.

Rodrom snarled in frustration and grabbed the nearest stick from a pile beside the patient. Snapping it to the length he needed, Rodrom abandoned all concerns about sterility and jammed the stick between the ribs. When it did not fit, he snarled again.

"Fit, damn you!" he cried, and to his shock, the stick twisted in his hand and pushed itself between the two ribs. It was crude, and looked flimsy, but it was holding. The weaveroot must have been responsible, though he had hoped the pendant Lorelei gave him would have suppressed it entirely. He assumed music was the key to activating its powers, but perhaps just vocal intent was enough.

He grasped the stick again. "Extend two inches," he said clearly, and the stick again moved beneath his fingers, though it grew the amount he wanted and then kept right on growing. "Stop!" he cried out, and was relieved when it did.

The space he'd created allowed him to see inside the elf's chest cavity, and into the shrapnel that pierced its heart. Rodrom was horrified to see that the weaveroot had wrapped around the heart, and that its roots reached out to every part of the chest. An almost bark-like sac surrounded the heart now, and there the shrapnel lay quivering.

How could he even attempt the surgery? The shame of failure twisted through Rodrom's gut. Looking at Lorelei only redoubled his regret. He had not only let down his patient.

Lorelei's voice cracked and wavered as Rodrom stared at her. He tore his eyes away. The recognition was clear, even on her alien features. She shook, and slowly took her hands from the warrior's head. She opened and closed her hands, staring down at them as if they held some answer. A small cry escaped her lips, then another. The sound was so heart-wrenching that Rodrom felt as though his own chest were full of shrapnel.

He sat back on his heels, and moved his hands down to rest them against his thighs. His hands had not wavered an inch during the operation. The moment he sat back, however, it was all he could do to hold them still. He turned them over and looked down numbly at his palms as they wavered and shook. It was not just his hands that had betrayed him, but his entire body. His shoulders shook too as the adrenaline wore off, leaving him empty. His breath grew ragged and forced, his eyes unfocused.

The grief that filled Lorelei's scream needed no translation. Her anguish was palpable as she clutched the head of her fallen warrior. Rodrom remained motionless, swept up in her torment, unable to look away, unable to keep his distance. Tears fell unabashedly from his eyes, carving canyons through the grime on his face.

Lorelei cut her scream short, and turned to Rodrom with bloodshot eyes. "I will not let him die." Her voice scarcely was above a whisper. "Even if I must sacrifice everything to save him."

Chapter 55

Vincent

Vincent tore through lightning-strewn storm cover as he raced back towards the portal. The ferals that pursued them had broken off, and only the unnatural black clouds remained. He was forced to rely on his sensors to avoid colliding with anything; the uneven canopy below boasted several trees that would make short work of him. His frantic search for the elf camp had taken him far enough away from his other pilots that they had lost communication in the storm, and the com relays the ground troops brought through weren't responding.

Sensor lock. Vincent looked down. What on earth could he have locked onto that far out? It would have to be an enormous heat signature. An anomaly.

"Shit, break off, break..." A burst of static followed. They were close enough for direct beam com.

"Status report," Vincent called, but he couldn't break through the hurricane of voices. His pilots had abandoned their AMI's and were screaming to one another.

"Break right, Tanker!"

"What the hell is that thing?"

"Elemental!"

"Dragon!"

Wherever they were had the worst of the cloud cover. Vincent tried to skim low beneath it, but the damned elves had brought it down beneath the trees. He jerked back on the stick and tapped the throttle forward, pulling into a climb that left him dizzy.

"Fledgling, get out of here. Steel, I have your six," Havoc called. That was wing four. What were they fighting?

Vincent kept climbing.

"My rounds do not hurting this thing. How do we fight it?" Forge was frantic, and he never lost his cool.

Vincent burst into the sunlight above the clouds, and twisted into a spiral to see what they were fighting. Only flashes made it through the cloud cover, even as high up as he was. He twisted over, the straps cutting into his shoulders, then angled down and shot for the brightest spots. Zombie and Duchess followed in his wake.

He lost visibility within seconds. The dark clouds suffocated his view port as he pushed towards the only thing he could spot in the black. His pilots were still yelling, frantically trying to call out targets and defend themselves.

"Tanker!" several voices shouted at once.

"Pull up! Pull up!"

Vincent shot towards the position Tanker showed on the map. His HUD flashed with new coordinates, mapping out the other pilot's descent. Invisible in the ink-black clouds, he dove straight down to certain death.

"Break, break, break," Vincent called, silencing the yells. "Tanker, what is your status? Can you rectify?" He poured on the speed, his fighter bucking against the turbulence outside. Rain splattered across the view port as he pushed himself faster and faster.

Silence from the falling pilot. Tanker made no move to maneuver, his ship faring no better than a rock against the pull of gravity. Then he smashed into the canopy, and his signal winked out. Abruptly, without even the fanfare of an explosion, he was gone.

Maybe he ejected, Vincent thought, but he knew the truth. The signal he was tracking wasn't the fighters — it was the AMI nestled firmly in the pilot's brain.

Vincent banked, harder than he needed to, forcing himself down into the chair, the blood rushing from his head. He started to black out; he was pulling six, maybe seven g's. He forced his suit to tighten and clear his head. He had failed his pilot. Should have been faster, shouldn't have left them behind.

His craft shuddered as the hand gripping the stick betrayed him. He was losing it. It was all too much. Finding Derek, losing Tanker, betraying orders. He had to pull it together. Couldn't lose anyone else.

A collision alert squealed, and Vincent twisted in his seat as a flash of red and yellow screamed by above him. The temperature inside his cabin shot up and sweat stung his eyes. The ablative armor on the top of his craft held up against the sudden heat, but the shift in atmosphere caused him to buck.

"Rover!" Vincent cried.

"Yes, sir," the bot's voice came through the com.

Vincent started. He had been sure the bot had been along the top of the craft and would have been caught in whatever shot him.

"I thought you... Never mind, make sure the engines are alright," he ordered.

What *was* that? He banked again, following the heat signature that had passed so close. The storm clouds broiled as they moved to fill the gap left by the intense heat, causing even the sensors to lose track.

"All pilots break off," he ordered. "Form a perimeter around the portal. We need to cover the ground forces' exfil. We have an unknown weapon up here. Watch yourselves."

The heat sensors picked up on the signature again. It was flying directly away from him in the storm, back towards where he had identified the camp.

"Zombie, Duchess," Vincent commed, "You're with me. We keep whatever this thing is away from the ground forces until they can get the prisoners and get out."

The storm clouds were thinner the further he chased the bogie. He looked up from the sensor to see if he could spot it in the dark. A bright spot was pushing back the storm ahead of him.

<*I think I see it,*> Zombie called.

"I do too. Flanking maneuvers."

<*Make sure you get a good look at it, I don't want to get the silhouette wrong when I claim this kill,*> Zombie said, though he lacked some of his usual enthusiasm. Push back the grief. Finish the mission. They had all been trained the same way.

"Yeah, roger that."

The heat the thing was generating was insane. It was putting out the kind of emission the *Inferno* did, and her engines were the size of baseball diamonds. Vincent strained to catch a glimpse of it, wanting to know what it was just as much as Zombie before he blasted it out of the sky.

When he finally got close enough to see it, though, he forgot all about shooting it down.

The thing was completely engulfed in yellow and blue flames. It was too bright too look at, but when his screen polarized and enhanced, Vincent saw what looked like woman. A woman with blazing angel wings.

She stopped without warning, flaring the wings out to catch the air. Vincent dialed back on the throttle and flared his airbrakes, and she twisted around to stare at him with pinpoints of blue flame. He was forced to bank away from her, not wanting to risk the heat, when Zombie called, "Reaper Three, foxtrot one."

Vincent wanted to scream, to tell him not to fire, but couldn't even begin to explain why. This was the enemy — why had he hesitated? The elves looked human enough, and he had fought the Separatists in their fighters. Why hadn't he fired?

Zombie's missiles soared straight at the massive heat signature, and the flare of their engines was lost in the miniature sun. She twisted her wings around her like a cocoon, her form blurring until only a ball of flame remained. When all four missiles struck her, they were immediately consumed.

The wings snapped open like solar flares, throwing off blasts of heat and light. A second set of smaller wings unfurled beneath, spreading out as if she were...

"It's absorbing the energy. Break off, break off!" Vincent called out. The forest below lit up with the punishing heat, and the flames spread in waves. If she grew any hotter the damage would be unstoppable.

Just like Bastogne...

The realization hit him like a plasma bolt.

Chapter 56

The Exile

Exile threw herself behind the nearest trunk as a foliage-bending roar thundered through the jungle.

"What the hell was that?" Cowboy called, holding a hand to his ear.

"A problem," Killswitch muttered, pulling a pair of binoculars from his kit. He pushed aside leaves and held up the goggles. The Exile moved up beside him. "It looks like we've found them."

He leaned over and passed the binoculars to Exile, who took them in her remaining hand. Hunkering down, she pushed them to her eyes. Beyond the forest edge Exile could see the telltale signs of clearing efforts, and though there were still several meters of jungle to traverse between them and the camp, Exile could make out shaped tree shelters and Verdantun moving about. This surprised her, as she had assumed they would at least encounter minor patrols protecting the camp. But it looked like pure chaos. *Enemy mistakes are allied opportunities*, she thought, then broadcast, <*They are distracted. Now is our time to strike.*>

284

Killswitch nodded, then keyed over the bionet, <*Alright, men, you heard the lieutenant. Assault through the objective, weapons hot, find the colonists, and get the hell out of dodge. Keep quiet as long as possible; it's going to be a tough fight out of there.*>

The Exile pushed the binoculars back at Killswitch and moved forward. Her rank alone would not convince those men to blindly follow her—they were far too experienced for that. She would need to lead by example, and that meant taking point.

Exile reached for her Shell, and the energy fell about her. She pulled it swiftly around herself, and her arm coalesced into existence in the time it took her to unholster her two laser pistols. She took hold of their grips with flesh and spectral fingers.

Holding the weapons at the low ready, she advanced through the dense foliage in a crouch. She felt a twinge of discomfort; with her Web down she could not be certain her platoon was following her, and she had learned not to trust anyone. She glanced over her shoulder where the holo-blur of Killswitch was glued to her heels, his movements mirroring her own.

The Exile continued her advance, her more mundane senses straining for any sign of the enemy. This close to the camp, the guards must be hidden somewhere, and the elves' ability to shapeshift proved to be effective camouflage. Her holocammies kept her hidden as well, though, and it would become a dance of who could spot the other first. Time was of the essence, but Exile moved slowly, and tried to keep from rustling the foliage as she passed. When any of the particularly large leaves crossed her path, she willed them to stay still with the same energy she had used to shape water in the space station.

When she reached the edge of the deep undergrowth, the sight of the camp beyond twisted her wariness into suspicion. There was no way they would make it into the camp proper without some kind of welcoming committee. Slowly, she moved onto a muddy path twisting between the trees, and an army in chaos came into view. The elves were in full retreat, leaving behind everything too big to carry. Many of the trees had been set alight, no doubt in hopes that the Joint Fleet forces would lose intel along with the burning remains.

They were all running here and there, most in their native forms, though there did not seem to be any pattern to the movements. Some of the forces ran towards her, others away, and often with soldiers racing past one another carrying the same objects, as if they had no idea that what they carried was being pulled away from where they were going.

The Verdantun were leaderless.

<This is our opportunity,> Exile pushed. <I'll create a distraction. Key your AMI units for the refugees. We extract them in the chaos.>

For once, Killswitch didn't argue or sneer. <Cowboy, set charges as we move. Keep on me>

The Exile pushed forward into the camp, pulsing her Shell into her legs to give her speed. She dashed from tree to tree, her holocammies turning hazy as the surroundings blurred by. She reattached the pistols to the magnetic clamps on her rig and pulled two grenades from her belt. She thumbed the trigger on the first and cocked back her arm, focusing her Shell around her tricep as she did. She snapped the arm forward, fast as a whip, feeling the sharp twinge as she cracked the capsules along the back of her arm and forearm. A cool rush followed before she completed the arc as the chemicals raced through her. The grenade whipped through the air, easily clearing her line of sight, and landed some hundred meters away in the camp.

She passed the second grenade from her spectral hand to her flesh one and repeated the process, but with less force this time, directing the grenade further to her left. Pulling her two pistols from her hips, she pressed forward, silently counting down. When she finished, two thunderclaps roared through the camp—two rocks thrown into the already agitated nest—and the chaos reached its zenith.

The Exile used the fear and confusion to her benefit. As Verdantun raced by, unfocused, Exile snapped off a shot with her handguns, sending two streaks of light into unexpected victims. The small underpowered hand cannons would not kill outright, nor would they disintegrate on contact, but their vibrant blue beams did cause significant pain.

Leaving cries of pain and confusion in her wake, Exile moved swiftly, keeping her path erratic, and firing at random so it seemed as though the attack was coming from all sides. *Tension causes panic, panic breaks control.*

Above, engines droned as the air support drew closer. The inky presence of the Shadow was also drawing in. It was up there, still in the guise of the dead Psykin, and biding its time.

Chapter 57

Rodrom

Lorelei grasped her staff with shaking fingers. As she whispered to herself, Rodrom tried to think of something to say. How had he handled such situations before?

He could not think of anything useful.

Her amber fingers grasped the pendant with the glowing white stone, and then twisted. Rodrom heard a crack, and the five-foot staff fell away, leaving Lorelei holding a dagger in her hand.

"What are you doing?" Rodrom asked slowly.

"I was entrusted with its care," she told him. "I was supposed to protect it."

"Protect what? Lorelei?" Rodrom moved slowly too, lest she startle. She was in shock, needed help.

"You would not understand, DerekRodrom, you never will."

"Lorelei, just put the knife away," he said in his best soothing voice. It sounded harsh to his ears.

"I'm sorry," she whispered, and raised the knife.

"No!" Rodrom shouted, lunging forward.

It was too late.

Lorelei plunged the silver blade into her chest. Light erupted from the gem on the pommel, and she screamed.

Rodrom caught her as she fell, her head falling in his lap as she pulled in ragged breaths. The light on the blade started blinking erratically, blinding him. Rodrom tried to pull her fingers away to assess the damage. Her grip was steel.

Despite Lorelei being in obvious pain, her eyes remained locked in a distant gaze, and as her voice cracked from screaming she stopped, drew breath, and said a single word. A word Rodrom's weaveroot didn't translate.

Then the light died, and he held his breath in the dark. Waiting for whatever spell she had cast to activate or whatever the hell it was called.

Nothing happened.

His heart throbbed in his temples; he could feel the lingering time in each beat. For the span of perhaps a minute, complete silence settled in the root chamber. With effort, he looked away from her, expecting to see a guard, another healer, anything. Some result of the obvious magic she had just performed, or the reason she had just condemned herself.

Forcing himself to breathe, Rodrom looked closer at the wound.

A tiny light blossomed from the hole in Lorelei's chest. It was barely visible at first, but soon grew so bright that Rodrom was forced to look away, and even as he lifted his hand to shield his eyes, he was blinded by its radiance. It changed in hue, from red, to green, to violet, and every color in between, twisting as it moved across Lorelei's skin.

Light rippled out from the wound to bathe her, and she changed.

The foliage and vines that made up her clothing withered away, and Lorelei lay naked in his arms.

Her hair turned stark white, like freshly fallen snow, so bright that it seemed to glow. Her amber flesh paled to a shade darker than the hair, and shimmered as she struggled to breathe. Her eyes changed last. Where before they were deep green, they were now a kaleidoscope of striated colors.

Her body shone with such luminosity that the other colors around the tent seemed to dim; shadows clawed into the corners and stretched across the dirt-packed floor, twisting from the light she cast.

It didn't take long for Rodrom to realize the shadows were not moving because of the lights — they were stretching towards it. He shook his head, trying to sort out what was happening.

Like snakes through grass, the shadows slithered across the ground and connected with Lorelei. She screamed again, but with raw animal horror rather than anguish. The shadows twisted up her skin, leaving midnight tracings across the glowing surface. Wherever they touched, the light was burned away, leaving impossibly deep black behind.

Rodrom reached up to grab the pendant she had created for him. A dissonance so chaotic, and yet so beautiful that he could not fathom its existence, pounded through his mind. He could not let go, and through the agony that afflicted him, he watched helplessly as the shadows continued to climb across Lorelei's skin in swirling tattoos.

Darkness raced its way up her arms, across the exposed portion of her chest, up her neck, and along the side of her jaw, arcing across her cheek and ending over one closed eye. The shadows seemed to stop there, and Lorelei heaved a heavy breath, snapping her eyes open to meet Rodrom's. One eye still shone with the hue of every imaginable color, while the other was the deep black of an endless well.

Lorelei reached up with her unshadowed arm and clutched Rodrom's wrist, pulling his hand from the pendant and ending the song's trance. Lorelei's voice came then, strained and weak. "Something is wrong," she choked out. "Please, move me to him."

Unable to think far enough to argue, Rodrom took hold of Lorelei's hands, and as gently as he was able, moved them to the side of the shifting warrior's head, leaning her body over his lap. She closed her eyes, almost gasping for breath, but she held her hands steady.

That same blinding light shone once more, but this time it came from the palms of her hands and enveloped the warrior beneath her. Immediately, the warrior's shifting slowed dramatically to become an almost rhythmic dance. The churning change became a slow and purposeful shift that rolled over his body from head to toe. While he never remained completely in one form or the other, it seemed whatever Lorelei was doing was working.

The light changed in intensity to a deep green, the color of healthy leaves, and Rodrom could see that within the cavity he had created, the shrapnel was being pushed out of the heart, which continued to beat all the while. With analytical detachment, he waited until the shrapnel was almost completely removed, then reached out tentatively to pull it from the cavity, taking care not to touch the beating heart. Lorelei moved her head closer to Rodrom's chest in silent thanks, and for a moment, Rodrom's detachment cracked, and his chest tightened and ached. Lorelei continued her magic, and Rodrom watched silently as the warrior's chest knitted itself closed, pushing out the branch Rodrom had used as a spreader.

The light changed again, taking on the blue-green tint of ocean water, and the shifting ceased entirely. A Verdantun male now lay on his back, with no evidence of injury. Lorelei breathed a last sigh, extinguishing the light and allowing her arms to fall, and collapsed completely into Rodrom's arms.

"The grand general is safe," she murmured.

Then the entrance to the tree exploded as something slammed into it from above.

Chapter 58

The Exile

A brilliant light appeared ahead of the Exile, a spotlight between the trees. She could feel the hunger and excitement of the Shadow as she turned towards the light. This was the energy it had wanted her to seek out. This would be her undoing. She ran towards it, pulsing her Shell into her thighs and abandoning all pretense of stealth.

The dagger at her hip started vibrating, and tendrils of Shadow twisted around her. The light ahead grew more vibrant, and the black fingers streaked past her, drawing in the light as they shot like bolts through the forest. As she drew closer, she heard screaming, a long, ragged note.

Even with her Shell pulsing to keep up her speed, and the energy snapping through her body, she still felt drained and beaten as the Shadow reached towards the scream.

She couldn't beat it, couldn't run fast enough to keep up with that power. Any power she held over their bond would be nothing once it reached the light.

The dagger was close to vibrating right out of its worn leather sheath, the hunger rolling off it with an intensity that churned Exile's stomach. She regretted ever using the blade.

Above the Shadow, a fighter drew closer, and the sound of the engine drowned out the scream.

She squinted into the storm clouds to spot the silver ship plowing down through the storm, rocketing towards the light, where the tendrils had gone.

The dagger tugged her forcefully, knocking her from her feet and sending her sprawling in the mud. The crisp energy of her Shell waned with her concentration, and she was forced to rip the weapon out of its sheath before it shook apart her bones.

What have I done? she thought.

Ahead, the fighter smashed into the ground in a cacophony of shrapnel and fire.

The black stone connecting her to the Shadow ceased vibrating. A crack in it leaked white light. Exile threw up her good arm to shield herself, and then the dagger shattered into countless obsidian shards.

The connection was severed.

She was freed.

Exile screamed.

Chapter 59

Vincent

It was Ele. It had to be. She was always right there when fires broke out. The surface of Bastogne, when she had screamed that it was chasing her. The fire on the ship—she had been at the center of that as well. The torn and burnt uniform she had worn when he rescued her was another puzzle piece. Block stencil lettering, jumpsuit. She had to be some kind of scientist. Or worse, an experiment.

Vincent had flown up against flame elementals in the past. Phoenixes, salamanders, even sprites. Nothing had looked like, or burned as hot, as the creature Ele had become.

How the hell was he supposed to vape something that could absorb his missiles, that he couldn't even approach? Even if he could, did he want to? Ele had never seemed like anything more than a confused and frightened woman trapped in a war. If it was her in there, why was she attacking?

Vincent thought to reach out to her, to stop her before she destroyed another world, but could not think of how. The best he could hope to do was broadcast on a wide brand of frequencies and hope that she could hear him.

"Rover, could we jury-rig something to give off heat in a specific pattern? Find a way to communicate with her?" Vincent asked. Something made of fire would be drawn towards heat, wouldn't it?

Details of a plan scrolled across one of his screens. He didn't concern himself with the specifics, he just needed to know it could be done. Something about shunting heat into ablative armor.

Rover moved onto the top of the craft, and began cracking open panels and pulling out wires. Vincent concentrated on following Ele along her blazing path.

The map on his leftmost screen showed the estimated positon of the elf camp. Ele was getting close to reaching them. He needed to get the colonists out of there before she torched the place.

He put on speed, soaring around and past Ele. She didn't seem to notice his ship. The camp was just ahead, close enough for his sensors to start picking up the AMIs of the trapped colonists.

Immediately, he identified a cluster of them in what appeared to be large pits. There were more transmissions from the treeline; the Condemned would be fast approaching. As his computer crunched the incoming data, another tone alerted him to his worst fear: Rodrom was not among the refugees.

Vincent made two more passes, ordering the computer to continue its assessment, and in that time, the Condemned had reached the pits and begun drawing the prisoners out. The guards had been killed at some point between runs.

"Condemned Actual, this is Reaper One. Have you found any additional survivors? Over," Vincent commed.

There was a pause. "Reaper One, Condemned Actual. One of the doctors was taken into the camp. Our lieutenant's in there, causing a distraction. Over."

Vincent barely listened. Without a thought, he turned his ship and roared back towards the camp.

He was distantly aware of an inner voice telling him he was breaking every rule in the book. A tight strafe on an enemy encampment in broad daylight without air superiority and unknown defenses? Tantamount to suicide. But Ele wasn't slowing down, and neither was the wildfire of her wake.

Vincent strafed low over the jungle as he lined up his run. He had no plan, only that he would fly as fast and as well as he could over the camp, avoiding whatever came at him until his computer picked up Rodrom and Vincent got him the hell out of dodge.

<*Duchess, what are you doing?*> Zombie called out.

Vincent turned his attention back to his wingmates. His pilot's vital sign readouts showed an anomaly in the Duchess's biorhythm, and she wasn't responding to any of the communications sent to her. Vincent twisted in his seat, trying to spot her in the cloud cover.

A violently bright light filled the area, lancing out from the ground below. In the flare of light, he caught sight of the Duchess. Her fighter was pointed straight towards the ground.

Vincent pulled up, trying to get closer, to see what had happened to cause her tailspin.

"Duchess! Duchess!" Vincent called, but she didn't respond.

She was picking up speed, shooting down towards the trees below like an artillery round. There was no way Vincent could get to her in time.

It was all too much. Ele, Duchess, Rodrom.

Something inside Vincent snapped, and he did the unthinkable.

Reaching up with both hands, he grabbed the two handles beside the transformation controls and twisted to break the seal. Jets of white fog pulsed from the air vents, and Vincent called out, "Machine meld activate, authorization tango three mike four."

He pulled down hard on the handles, then released them and went limp. Needles shot out from his seat to pierce the ports on either side of his spine, and he felt a stab of sharp pain followed by numbing warmth throughout his head and back.

Details flooded into his mind at an unbelievable pace as a blue liquid filled his cabin. His seat unfolded so he was lying on his back. Everywhere the liquid touched, his skin went numb, and as it reached his neck he could no longer tell where he ended and the ship began. He opened his mouth and tried to relax as it filled over his head, and he nearly blacked out from panic when it filled his lungs.

Then his whole body was numb, and he was no longer a pilot. He was the Chimera.

The fighter also changed as the cabin filled with fluid. The wings bent back away from the canopy and angled toward the tail, while panels opened and inset turbines were revealed. They spun up, providing lift as the engines dimmed. The tail split in two and reconfigured into legs, the engines glowing on the back of each ankle. The craft's belly also split, and the two halves twisted out to become arms, the Gatling cannon mounted on one, the laser cannon on the other. The nose collapsed and moved to complete occlude the cockpit, and the missile launchers rotated forward to form shoulders.

The panels locked into place, the wings rotated again, and the engines roared. Vincent shot towards the ground.

With all the information flooding his mind, time slowed. Vincent saw everything fall apart through his new eyes.

Black tentacles erupted from Duchess's craft to coat her ship. The darkness seemed to suck in all light, and it twisted and writhed like a hundred serpents.

Rodrom's AMI had been located; he was inside a tree directly below. The place from which the light had originated, and the place where the Shadow was heading.

Ele came charging through the storm cover overhead, her wings held tight to her body, the clouds boiling away in her wake.

The Shadow smashed into Rodrom's tree.

A psychic scream tore through Vincent's mind.

He hit the ground on armored feet, sweeping his weapons ahead of him, mud and debris churning beneath him as he slid to a stop just beyond the wreckage of Duchess's ship.

He had fourteen minutes.

Then he would die..

Chapter 60

Rodrom

Rodrom shook his head to clear away the ringing. He had been too close to too many explosions in the last two days. He could barely hear his own groan over the obnoxious whistling in both ears. He really needed a change of profession.

"Lorelei, are you..." he began. Then he saw the pool of pitch dark oozing into the chamber.

Rodrom tried to get up, feeling the tear in his lungs as his heart demanded more oxygen than his synthetic blood could carry. The best he could manage was to push himself up on one knee. *Yeah, Derek, go down on your knees. Isn't that the way we always pictured it.*

The shadow finished dripping into the chamber and formed into a two-foot circle right in front of him. It looked like motor oil, or maybe ink, only decidedly evil. Rodrom tried to engage his clinical mind, to take in the details and make a plan, but he was too rattled. He looked back towards Lorelei.

She was lying on her side, one snow-white arm draped over her face. The black tattoos that came with her wardrobe change were the same shade of sinister as the pool forming at the door.

Rodrom needed a weapon. What he would do with it, he didn't know. But whatever force was behind the explosion, and the Shadow, was something he needed to fight.

Still wheezing, Rodrom pushed himself over to where Lorelei had dropped the end of her staff. It wasn't much, but it was more than nothing. Maybe he could strap his homemade scalpels onto the end of it. A quick glance over his shoulder showed the Shadow still congealing on the floor. Maybe it would just stay there, and he could pull Lorelei and her...

In all the confusion and chaos, he had forgotten what she had told him just before she'd fallen unconscious. This warrior on the table wasn't her betrothed, or any such nonsense — he was some sort of leader. A general.

If he hadn't already been struggling to breathe, Rodrom would have laughed at himself, but he had precious little time to pull together a plan and get everyone out in one piece. Better to laugh later than not at all.

He pulled himself far enough around the table to see past Lorelei and the general, to where she had pulled out the dagger and done whatever insane magic had given her the makeover. Drops of her blue blood littered the floor, along with five feet of white painted wood. Rodrom had never bothered to pay all that much attention to the weapon before, but as he looked now, he saw that it was similar to the ones all the healers carried — a sort of twisting staff of branches woven so tightly they looked like a single piece.

The last time he had touched one of those staffs, he had felt like he'd been strapped into an electric chair. But he moved the last meter without even thinking and reached out to grab it.

The moment his fingers wrapped around the smooth wood, he felt a thousand little pinpricks in his hand, like he had just grabbed a live wire. Then a wave of energy and power radiated through his body. The pendant on his chest shuddered and hummed, but Rodrom heard none of the music he had come to associate with the elves' abilities.

No, there was no music, but there was plenty of power. It hummed in the weapon and flooded him with wave after wave. He had no idea how to use the thing, but he pointed it over towards the Shadow and tried.

While he was fumbling, the Shadow had started pulling itself together. Already, a head and neck emerged from the dark pool. If left unchecked, it obviously intended to form a humanoid shape. Rodrom stepped forward and pushed the staff ahead of him like a lance, hoping to engage whatever mechanism would unleash the power it so obviously contained. No such luck.

The Shadow grew a torso, and Rodrom tried more combinations of thrusts and shakes, running his hand down the length of the staff to check for a recessed trigger. Rodrom tried not to think of how ridiculous he looked, and was for once thankful that Vincent wasn't around to see him.

He found absolutely nothing useful, and nearly threw the weapon down in frustration.

"Just fire, damn you," he cried, and the energy poured from him into the wood. It grew warm in his hand. He stared at it. "Please don't explode."

Then he thrust the weapon forward again, and the energy rushed from him towards the Shadow. The air within the chamber kicked up like a tornado had just swept in. The heat beneath his fingers was enough to make him want to drop it, but he had no choice but to hold on. His hand seemed to be fused to the wood.

All his equipment was blown to the floor and the wind tore at his beard. The pool of Shadow churned but stayed in place.

"More attack, less storm," Rodrom shouted, hoping the weapon would respond.

Luckily, the elf magic was listening, and the twisting whirlwind died down. Then to Rodrom's extreme displeasure, the wind shifted and blew a violent gust that threw him to the back of the room. He landed with a dull thud against the root walls. As he slid to the ground, he saw that he had finally affected the Shadow — in the worst possible way. The wind had disrupted its attempt to form into something vaguely human, and instead had blown it over to the elf lying on the table.

Just as it had with Lorelei, the Shadow seemed to stain every part of the warrior it touched. Unlike Lorelei, it did not stop with a tattoo pattern. It covered everything.

Rodrom pushed himself up with the staff, still unable to release it from his hand, and hobbled over to the table where the Shadow was consuming his charge. He pulled one of the scalpels off the ground and tried to pry the darkness away with the crystalline blade.

It was like trying to cut through tar. Wherever Rodrom pressed the blade into the Shadow, it just pooled and twisted, and when he tried to pull away it clung like glue. He released the scalpel before the Shadow connected to his own skin. He wouldn't be of any help if he was consumed along with the warrior.

The dark slime pulled in the scalpel, along with all the other tools that had fallen around the warrior during the miniature storm. Like some sort of symbiotic copycat, it absorbed them and then churned out more. Before Rodrom's eyes, the warrior went from a bear-skinned humanoid to a void of light studded with blades. A mohawk of knives erupted from between the creature's eyes all the way over and behind his head, then down his back. Longer blades erupted from his wrists and descended down the backs of both ankles.

The thing had become a living nightmare.

"Lightning, you need to shoot lightning now," Rodrom screamed at the stick grafted to his hand. Then he raised it over his head with both hands and slammed it down on the head of the monster.

To Rodrom's relief, the weapon did not sink in and replicate like the scalpel, and the screaming seemed to do the trick—something violent and loud struck the tree above hard enough to shake it.

Rodrom realized his mistake just as the Shadow sat up, swung a bladed arm towards him, and raked scalpel-sharp scratches of darkness across his face.

He staggered back, the staff finally falling free of his hand, as hot blue blood gushed from his wounds. He wasn't blinded yet, so he had an excellent view of the Shadow as it stood up, grabbed Lorelei, and dragged her outside the tree and out of view.

The blood was pouring between Rodrom's fingers and he already felt lightheaded. He had nothing left in the way of supplies, but Lorelei was in trouble. He needed to get to her before he bled out.

He stumbled towards the exit.

Chapter 61

Vincent

Vincent charged between the trees, using his ankle-mounted jump jets and turbines to gain extra speed. In the machine meld he was the fighter, so he could "feel" every truck he slammed into on his armor, but there was no exhaustion, and no real pain. Only him, his armor, and the mission.

Vincent had only experienced the meld once, when he had been forced to in his training. All the test pilots of the Mark 1 had gone insane from the stress of the mental transition from man to fighter. So the gnomes went back to the drawing board, watched one too many science fiction movies, and came up with the Mark 2. If humans couldn't handle becoming a fighter, they'd have the fighter become a man. That led to the transformation circuits, nanotech seals, and the augmentations that made the Chimera the versatile fighter it was.

But it went from the ultimate weapon to a last-ditch resort when they realized no pilot could survive more than fourteen minutes. Vincent had no intention of seeing what the end of those fourteen minutes looked like. He would charge through to Rodrom, grab him, and then charge right out again. Let whatever shadow magic that had attacked Duchess and the flashover that Ele had become sort one another out. Vincent had more than enough of magic, and he wasn't about to pit his ridiculous science fiction battle suit against any of it.

Despite being over-the-top, the armor could move. There was none of the delay that came from recognizing an obstacle and twisting a stick or pressing a rudder to avoid it. A fallen tree was in his way — he jumped over it, simple as that. A gap too small to run straight through — he twisted and leapt, firing the thrusters so he passed sideways between two trees. He hit the ground in a tumble, and was back up on his armored feet in seconds.

He landed close enough to Rodrom's signal that it was a short run, and within a minute Vincent saw the wreckage of the Duchess's ship, and the hellish creature that was crawling out of it.

Vincent had seen a lot of strange and impossible things come out of the portals, but he stopped dead in his tracks now. The thing was the size of a man, only covered in blades, and had impossibly black skin. It was carrying a female elf colored all over in black and white, and it was absolutely terrifying.

It was the same kind of terror Vincent had felt when he thought a member of his team was in danger, or even the kind when he had watched his father die. This terror was so overwhelming, so uncontrollably strong, that his mind fractured under the strain of it. He tried to reach for his father's knife, to find some comfort in the familiar, but his hands were cannons. He was trapped inside the metal body of his fighter.

The only thing that saved him was the meld. It wasn't just Vincent controlling the craft. His AMI unit was just as involved, and as much as he hated to let the computer do his work, in that moment he was glad to have it step in, and let loose with everything the Chimera had.

Missiles streaked from his shoulders; their payloads were smaller in the atmosphere but no less deadly, and they blossomed into violent fireballs all around the monster. His Gatling cannon roared, spitting out thousands upon thousands of armor-piercing incendiary rounds, each of which could obliterate a main battle tank. His laser cannon blinded him with its ferocity as it ignited the air between them, producing an unending stream of light as it fired continuously.

The AMI held nothing back, acting upon Vincent's irrational fear and firing until the barrel of the Gatling cannon melted to slag, the missiles were emptied, and the laser cannon had fired through every frequency.

Smoke curled up from his arms and spent missile pods, and he shook against the fear. Nothing could be left of the monster, not after that.

The smoke was too thick for Vincent to see the body. A part of him wished he had been more in control. He was helpless now, with all his ammunition and weapons spent. If he had to, the best he could do was try and punch it. The gnomes had been vetoed when they'd suggested adding a sword.

All of Vincent's scanners focused onto the Shadow. In the back of his mind the clock still ticked. He only had... eleven minutes left. He needed to get Rodrom and get out. His AMI was still blinking in the tree behind where Vincent had leveled.

And what about Ele, who would demolish everything if she passed close enough?

His sensors couldn't pick up anything. The smoke was too thick.

It clustered around where his missiles had erupted, and wasn't dissipating, even in the wind.

Vincent took a few tentative steps forward, and set his feet against the ground. Kneeling slightly, he braced himself with his arms and rotated his wings so the turbines were facing ahead of him. He poured on the juice, blowing gusts strong enough to lift his suit over the smoke. He needed to see that the thing was dead, destroyed.

Still, the smoke didn't move.

The fear started to creep in again. Vincent poured more power into the turbines, digging long furrows in the dirt as he was pushed backwards. But no matter how much wind he generated, the smoke stayed in a strange lump, almost as if it were...

The thing uncurled.

It was shaped like a bear, with a large bulky body and squat legs, a low-hanging head, and no tail. That was where the normal stopped, and the impossible took over.

A man made seemingly of pure darkness had been the most horrifying sight he could imagine. That man had now grown several times in size, taken on the proportions of a violent beast, and was covered from head to toe in what looked like swords.

Had Vincent's lungs not been full of fluid, he would have laughed. The fear was too much, and he couldn't handle the strain. For once, he took a page out of Rodrom's book, and just laughed.

The thing turned towards him, opened its mouth, and let loose a roar so loud and violent that Vincent was thrown backwards. When his back collided with a tree, he slid down to the ground, and felt one of his wings snap from the blow.

Before the monster could take his life, however, the universe decided to add insult to injury, and Ele, in all her flaming glory, slammed into the ground in a cloud of ash and dirt. The Shadow turned on her, and let loose another roar. The wave of pressure pushed aside trees and managed to dim some of her flame, but only for a second before she became too bright to look directly at again.

His chance of escaping gone, and with ten minutes left on the clock, Vincent laughed silently in the goo of his cockpit.

Only you can prevent forest fires.

Chapter 62

The Exile

Exile lay in the mud, clutching the pieces of dagger in her hand. She had done it, had done the very thing her people had cast her out for. She thought she could control it, that she had been strong enough, worthy enough to wield such power.

She was wrong.

And now countless people would pay for her mistake. The Shadow was no mere elemental that would run wild until destroyed or contained. It was a calculating, devious mind wrapped in a force of nature.

How could she have been so naïve? Without the Shadow in her mind, the idea of trying to control it seemed like a child's thought, not one of a skilled assassin.

How long had it been powerful enough to corrupt her thoughts? To turn her away from the convent she'd spent her entire life serving and into a tool? She had played right into its hand. Given it everything it wanted. She might have very well ushered in the end her people so greatly feared.

They shouldn't have just taken her arm and cast her out; they should have killed her. Their own misguided refusal to step away from their religious teachings had allowed Exile to usher a demon into their realm. And now that demon would destroy it.

A thunderous noise ripped through the trees, pulling her out of her head and shaking the ground. Explosions followed on its heels, and Exile took to her feet.

She pulled her Shell over herself and forced her legs to carry her with all the speed she could manage. With each footfall, she felt another of the precious internal capsules break under the strain. Her reserves ran lower and lower. She would have no warning when she ran out. Only a vague notion, and then a sudden end. But she threw all thoughts of self-preservation away and sped towards the sight of the crash.

She pulled up short before she burst into view, and located the source of the noise. A single Chimera was standing a hundred meters back from the smoking wreck of the Shadow's fighter, its form changed into the shape of a man. This was the research she had learned of on the back of psykin she murdered.

Every weapon on the Chimera fired until nothing was left, but Exile could see that it had done no good. The Shadow had absorbed a new host, one that could shapeshift on its own, and between the elven magic and the Shadow's power, it would be unstoppable. The armored, bladed titan rose up and roared at the Chimera pilot, throwing it aside like a leaf on the wind.

Then Exile saw something. The monster had been crouching over a prone figure in the mud. An elf with pure white skin and tattooed with Shadow. All was not lost. The Shadow would never protect something it didn't need. There was no sympathy or compassion in that creature, only a lust for power. The elf must have been the power source the Shadow demanded; there was absolutely no other reason it would have gone out of its way to protect her.

Out of nowhere, a fire elemental landed at an angle between the Chimera pilot and Exile, and its sudden arrival drew the Shadow's attention. Exile saw her chance. When the Shadow moved to face the new threat, she would kill the elf, and destroy whatever power the Shadow was so intent on protecting. She pulled her weapon from her shoulder and braced it against her ethereal arm.

The Shadow charged the elemental.

Exile lined up her shot.

Then Derek Rodrom, the human she had come for, ran out from the wreckage and crouched over the elf.

Chapter 63

Rodrom

Lorelei was still breathing. That was the first thing Rodrom checked. Crouched in the mud over her limp glowing body, he barely registered the battle occurring just behind him, or the mech suit leaning against a tree. All his focus was on ensuring that Lorelei would survive, his own injuries and safety be damned.

"Come on, Lorelei, I need you to wake up now," he said as he shook her.

He pulled up one of her eyelids, the one covering the kaleidoscope eye. Her pupils were slow to constrict from the light. In a human that meant they were good and out, and he figured it was the same for her as well.

"How can you sleep with all this ridiculousness behind us!" he called.

Shouting didn't make her any less unconscious. *Good job, Doc*, he thought. *Next you should try a bucket of water.*

He needed to move her. The shadowy knife monster had seemed

intent on taking her, and he had no reason to think that would change just because he was dancing with what looked like a girl on fire.

Problem was, he was running low on blood, and his lungs were already painting their picket signs and refusing to work. Rodrom didn't think he had the strength to get her as far away as they needed to be.

<Get away from her!> a voice cried out in his head.

Oh, good, more problems.

Rodrom turned to a see a Psykin wearing a formfitting fleet uniform. He noticed a few things all at once. She was missing her right arm, or rather, had some sort of hologram in the shape of one. She was wounded, and bleeding from a dozen or more of the wounds. Most importantly, she was aiming two pistols at him.

"Whoa there," Rodrom called with his hands raised. "I am a doctor."

<A doctor is the last thing she needs. Now move.>

"Pretty sure I am more qualified to make that judgment," Rodrom quipped. "Maybe lower the weapon and we can talk."

<If you do not move, I will shoot you.>

Rodrom believed her. This Psykin seemed half out of her mind.

"Now wait just a—" Before Rodrom could finish his reply, a metal arm slammed into the Psykin and knocked her a hundred or so meters away.

He looked up at the mech and called, "Thanks, I think. Unless you also want to shoot me."

<Derek, it's me.> The voice in his head was too familiar to be real.

"Nope." Rodrom shook his head. "I am hallucinating."

<Seriously, I'm here to rescue you.>

Rodrom continued to shake his head back and forth. "You came to rescue me, alone, in a cheap robotech knockoff? As far as plans go,

Vince, this has to be one of your worst."

<It didn't exactly go as planned.>

The two monsters were still duking it out. Rodrom watched as the flaming woman flared out her wings, and the woods all around her caught fire. She seemed to draw strength from this, and leapt forward to punch and claw at the Shadow. Wherever her burning hands touched, the black mass turned to gas, but by the time she pulled back, the wound had already healed.

The Shadow swiped a compact car-sized paw with swords for claws into her wing. An explosion of sparks and super-heated air burst forth. The woman staggered back, lifted her arms, and blasted a column of flame as wide as an operating table into the center of the Shadow.

<We need to get out of here,> Vincent told him. <Sooner or later one of them is going to win.>

"What the hell are they?" Rodrom asked, glancing back at Lorelei.

<Shadow has me stumped, but the fiery one might be my fault.>

"Really, Vince? Even for you, a girl made of fire is a bit much."

<She isn't always like that,> Vincent growled as best he could over the mental connection. <Seriously, Rodrom, we have to move.>

"I will not leave Lorelei." He bent back down to check that she was still breathing.

<An elf? I'm not risking your life for the enemy. Doctor or not, we need to worry about you.>

"That is awfully sweet, Vince, but I am not leaving her. She saved my life, and I think the Shadow wants her alive."

Vincent lunged forward, and Rodrom scrambled over Lorelei to protect her. When rifle shots rang out and the sharp pang of them hit Vincent's armor, Rodrom realized this was foolish.

"How is she still alive?"

Chapter 64

Vincent

Vincent's enhanced senses warned him of the Psykin's intentions barely an instant before she started firing. He managed to get his armored side between her and Rodrom, and the blasts slammed into him. Without his own weapons to retaliate, he was helpless until she stopped shooting. Any movement on his part would open up Rodrom to attack.

She would have to reload, and when she did, Vincent would charge. Even without his wings, his jump jets could bridge the distance in a single jump. If hitting her didn't finish her, maybe landing on her with all the weight of his armor would.

<*What are you doing?*> he called through his AMI.

<*Stopping that monster.*>

The two titans were still battling it out diagonally across from them. The Shadow's claws burned down to the wrists as it stabbed blades into Ele's side and threw her into the air. Ele flared her wings and hovered, throwing down handfuls of fire bright as stars towards the

317

reforming darkness.

<How will killing either of them stop those two?> Vincent gestured with the arm he wasn't using to protect Rodrom.

<The elf is powering the Shadow!> the Psykin screamed, and fired more blue blasts uselessly into Vincent's armor. Some of the shots hit near his cockpit, but it was protected by metal panels. She was only wasting power.

<Derek, buddy, how sure are you about this elf?>

"Damn it, Vince, just stop her," Rodrom snapped. Vincent's rear-facing sensors showed Rodrom crouched over the fallen elf doing something, but what he couldn't see. If he wasn't making jokes, then he was dead serious. Vincent shut the sensors off; it was disorienting to look in both directions.

Eight minutes.

<Lieutenant,> Vincent called, spying her rank on her uniform. <You can't get through my armor, and we don't have time for this. Help us escape.>

<No! You are the one who doesn't understand. That elf must die.>

In opposition to her own words, the Psykin threw down her weapons. One of her arms, which Vincent had only just noticed was some kind of hologram, disappeared.

What in the void?

Her remaining hand shot to her horn, and just as Vincent was about to charge, she started twitching. Her skin bulged around the joints like her muscles were trying to tear their way out, and within seconds, the attractive female had become a grotesque monster.

<Is anyone not hiding a monster under their skin?> Vincent cried.

But even as he said it, he could tell something was wrong. He thought he was seeing a monster claw its way out of the lieutenant, but his mind was not only human, and his machine senses told him otherwise.

The monster she had become slashed her arm at him, and Vincent stumbled back. It looked so real, and he had just seen two other monsters destroy women he trusted. Could his machine mind be wrong? If he charged in and tried to attack the psykin the AMI unit was so convinced was still standing there, would he be sacrificing his own life as well as Rodrom's?

Seven minutes.

"Vince, we do not have time for this. The Shadow's pulling ahead."

Ele looked hurt—as hurt as a being composed entirely of fire could look. Her massive wings were gone, and only a woman-sized spark of flame remained. The forest around her was burnt to the ground and smoldering, and as the Shadow pressed in on her, no more flames leapt to her aid.

The massive bladed monster swung blow after blow down onto Ele, who had her arms thrown over her head as she projected a flaming shield between them. Vincent felt a sharp pang in his chest.

He was out of time, out of options, and gave into the senses that told him what he saw wasn't there. He had already broken every rule in his book when he activated the machine meld. To throw away what he could see to trust the AI... How could he? Then he looked back at Rodrom, and knew he had no choice.

He charged into the growing monster, reaching his hand down to grab onto the Psykin.

The illusion broke. It was all in his head. She had used some Psykin magic against him, and the AMI had seen right through it. She was finished, and Vincent had her at his mercy.

He couldn't kill her, though. Not like this, not when she was helpless in his hand. She was struggling against the metal claws wrapped around her, and Vincent could think of no way to contain her. Save one.

He cocked his hand back and threw her as far as he could. She had survived when he'd hit her the first time. He was sure she could survive this time. At least it would give him enough time to grab Rodrom and his new girlfriend and get out of there.

The relief was short-lived. A roar erupted from behind him, so loud it shook him inside the suit, and he saw Ele collapse under the power of the Shadow. Blue sparks lanced from her rapidly dimming flames, licking over the ground and the Shadow. Whatever was happening was doing nothing to it, however, and before his eyes, Ele was crushed swallowed by the abyss.

Thunder cracked, and the Shadow was forced back. The fire was gone, and in its place was a crackling ball of lightning.

What is she? Vincent wondered, right before she twisted and shot straight for him.

With his enhanced reflexes, he had just enough time to realize the blast was coming, and just enough time to stay right where he was. The energy caught him in the center of his armor, sparking and arching over him like a living thing. He expected pain, loss of consciousness, anything to tell him he had been damaged, but instead the power meter in his mind sky rocketed.

Six minutes.

Chapter 65

Rodrom

Rodrom looked up from Lorelei at the lightning strike. Vincent staggered, went down on one knee, and blue snakes tore over his armored plates and into his joints.

"Vincent, no!" Rodrom screamed, helpless to do anything but watch.

Smoke poured from Vincent's engines and the lights along his frame dimmed. Then everything flared as if the power had been flipped back on. Fire poured from the engines on his legs and launched Vincent like a bullet towards the Shadow. The bear reared up, but it was too slow to respond, and Vincent collided into the center of its chest and barreled it over.

Whatever Ele had done had given Vincent an unbelievable edge. He moved too fast to follow, and everywhere his machine fists struck, a blue halo of sparks erupted. Vincent tore off spines, threw aside counter attacks, and punched with the ferocity of a tank.

The bear struggled to counter him, while bits of Shadow wisped off like smoke from a dying campfire. Each time it threw its paw, Vincent dodged out of the way and countered with a lightning-infused strike.

"You really need to wake up for this, Lorelei. They do not make anime this good anymore." Rodrom gripped the pendant on his chest again, hoping that whatever magic was inside him could wake her up. It was like dunking his head into a tank of white noise. The battle between Vincent and the Shadow was throwing up too much interference, or whatever the magical equivalent of that was. Rodrom had run out of ideas. He just hoped Vincent didn't run out of juice before he took down Ursa.

But when he looked back, the Shadow no longer seemed like it was being demolished as it had moments before. The initial shock of Vincent's sudden power-up and attack had faded, and the beast was adjusting. Without the advantage of surprise, Vincent was overwhelmed by the absolute strength of his larger opponent, and the Shadow took full advantage of that by charging in and attempting to pin him down. Vincent was using his jump jets to stay just out of reach, and got a few good licks in, but he could only keep it up so long.

Another kick of the thrusters, another lunge, and Vincent cracked his lightning fists across the Shadow's maw. Before he could pull away, the face he'd struck collapsed, then reformed with Vincent's arm in its jaw.

Vincent's other arm cracked the Shadow across its head half a dozen times in half as many seconds, but the bear's grip was too strong. Vincent couldn't get away.

That didn't stop him from lifting his foot and firing his engines for all they were worth. The jet flame pushed him back while ripping through the Shadow, and Vincent was freed from the maw to fly backwards onto his back.

Unfortunately, he only took one of his arms with him. The mental anguish of losing the appendage—machine or not—poured through the open bionet connection between them.

The Shadow turned, roared in victory, and stalked towards his fallen prey.

Chapter 66

Vincent

Vincent was in utter agony. The machine meld made it feel as though his own arm had been burned and ripped from his body. The pain and shock were overwhelming, and he cursed the gnomes for ever creating the meld to begin with. He was lying on his back, his wings crushed, his arm gone, and only two minutes remaining on the clock.

He was finished, and he hadn't even fulfilled his mission. He refused to die bonded with a machine, even if it was the only thing that had kept him alive long enough to fight the monster approaching him. The Shadow was moving slowly now, as if it was enjoying the sight of him writhing on the ground. Well, he would meet it head on, and be killed on his feet.

Vincent keyed the command to start draining his cabin, feeling the gel that suspended him falling away. His perception warped and twisted between the sensors outside and the pilot within, and he become increasingly disoriented. He heard voices. Voices that sounded like the other pilots in his unit. When his view fractured and shifted between

324

outside and inside, he could have sworn he saw other Chimeras in their machine meld forms.

When Vincent finally sat upright in his cramped cockpit and started hacking up the disgusting fluid from his lungs, he found it had not been a hallucination. He pulled his emergency release, forcing the armored panels to recede and his cockpit to open, and climbed into the muggy, smoke-filled air outside. He gulped down several breaths, and watched as the other pilots of his squadron fell out of the sky in formation around him.

Each landed with a flare of jump jets and a bend at the knees, then stood up tall and unloaded their weapons into the Shadow. The beast had managed against Vincent's assault, but under the combined attack of nine others, it began to falter.

Vincent wasn't sure if he or Ele had weakened it more, but the rounds started piercing into the coherent body, and the lasers carved out large chunks of the Shadow's flesh. It was still reforming, fixing the damage that they inflicted, but it struggled to keep up.

Each shot took its toll, and between the nine Gatling cannons, missile launchers, and laser fire, it was losing mass.. It roared again, sending out the invisible waves of force that had knocked Vincent down in his ship, but it couldn't knock over nine Chimeras.

Vincent cheered his pilots on, telling them to send everything, to empty their magazines into the thing. Before his eyes, the Shadow twisted and shrank, becoming the man-shaped mass he had first seen. With inhuman speed, it launched itself into the forest, and out of the line of fire.

Several of his pilots made to pursue it, but Vincent ordered them back. He wouldn't risk them all, not against that thing, whatever it was. He had Rodrom, and Lorelei, to consider.

Chapter 67

The Exile

Exile once more lay in the mud. Her Shell had saved her from the fall, but she was not sure why she'd allowed it to. She had failed, completely and disastrously. The Shadow was freed, it had consumed a power she could scarcely understand, and the one chance she had to destroy it had been foiled by the very human she had come to the planet to save in the first place. It was all too much: too many coincidences, too many variables that had aligned to bring them all here.

For once, the Exile started to believe that maybe the teachings had been right, that there were incomprehensible beings who saw to pulling the strings of the universe. Or had the Shadow known what was here? The pieces fit. The other Psykin being drawn towards her had been possessed, which led to her discovery of Rodrom.

All of it had been the Shadow's doing. How? She didn't think its power was so far-reaching, but it was the only alternative to a malevolent god. She had been set up, manipulated from the beginning by something she couldn't hope to control or understand. So naïve. So very, very naïve.

Something was approaching her through the jungle, and she felt the familiar AMI of the Condemned. She didn't want to be rescued, didn't want to go back to the fleet and face her failure. Better she die in the jungle.

Killswitch pushed his way between two trees and into view, and upon seeing her, lifted his hand and gave a signal to the others, who remained hidden behind him.

"You look like hell," he told her.

<The mission was a failure.>

"The doctor was just picked up by air support. Along with an elf prisoner. How exactly did the mission fail?"

The Exile snapped her head up. *<What?>*

"The Reapers, they dropped down in the elf camp and fought off an unknown, picked up Rodrom, and some new kind of elf. We need to move, ma'am, if you're done making me repeat myself."

They fought off the Shadow? Impossible—nothing was strong enough to do that. Or did its link with the elf hinder it as much as strengthen it?

If they took her back aboard the ship, then she still had a chance. Project Rebirth would continue through Derek Rodrom, She could ensure it did, and with that power eradicate the Shadow and save her people. She could find the elf and destroy her. Absolve herself of her sins.

The Exile pushed herself to her feet.

The mission wasn't over.

Epilogue

Johnston

Captain Johnston stood in his ready room and looked over the recordings playing across the surface of his desk. Recordings from pilots, from the sensors mounted on the *Inferno*'s hull, and from the cameras embedded in the ground troops' holocammies.

The images disturbed him far more than usual when it came to dealing with the other side. They had been fighting elves and their ilk for so long that it was almost normal. Almost.

But that woman had transformed into lightning and fire... and the recordings salvaged from Barkhorn's flight recorder after his fight were unbelievable.

A massive Shadow monster impervious to munitions, an elf that wielded light, and the monster that he had brought on board and unleashed upon the planet below. Only the elf had been recovered.

The girl known only as Ele was unaccounted for. There was no trace of the electric state she had become within Barkhorn's systems. The Shadow was also at large, which was most troubling. Whatever force controlled such a creature would be a threat to the fleet, and they needed to find it.

Johnston felt responsible for the Chimera pilots who had died under his orders. Those pilots were a part of a much larger plan, one he had been hesitant to put into motion. With only ten remaining, he couldn't afford to lose any more.

The pieces had all come together. The pilots had used their machine melds, Derek Rodrom had been rescued, and the threat justified his decision.

Still, he hesitated before making the call. This was not just a military decision. He was putting the future of humanity on the line, on the chance that they could build a weapon and win this war.

He knew he had no other choice, that any other admiral would do the same in his position.

He would have preferred it be them.

Historians would remember his choice in that moment. For good or ill, he was etching his name into the books of the next generations. He pressed down on the com link, and waited for the voice to answer.

"Yes, Captain?"

"I hereby authorize all resources to be allocated for Project Rebirth. You'll have everything you need."

"Excellent, sir. You won't regret this."

Johnston cut the connection.

"God forgive me."

Thank you so much for reading.

Please leave a review on Amazon to help support independent publishing.

The Saga continues in 'Rebirth by Fire' coming spring 2015

This book couldn't have happened without the assistance of several people.

My editor Leah Wohl-Pollack of Invisible Ink Editing

Cover designer James T. Egan of Bookfly Design

My Beta readers Katrina Schroeder, Greg San Fan Andre, Jordan Niehoff, Aaron Durette, and of course my lovely fiancée Danielle Pfanstiehl who has had to hear about this story more than anyone should.

And anyone else who was kept awake by the constant clicking of my keyboard on overnight shifts.

About the Author

PATRICK WORKS AS A PARAMEDIC IN HARTFORD CONNECTICUT, AND MOONLIGHTS AS A MEDIC FOR THE CT NATIONAL GUARD. WHEN HE'S NOT FEARLESSLY COMBATING THE COMMON COLD OR EXAMINING FEET AFTER A ROAD MARCH HE SPENDS HIS TIME MAKING THINGS UP AND WRITING THEM DOWN. HE LIVES IN COVENTRY WITH HIS INCREDIBLY PATIENT FIANCÉE DANIELLE, HIS DOG LOKI, AND HIS TWO CATS BOY AND GIRL.

www.ingramcontent.com/pod-product-compliance
Lightning Source LLC
Chambersburg PA
CBHW051950240626
47153CB00005B/1705